Carol Lawlor

LOST SOULS

LOST SOULS

Carol Lawlor

A Novel

iUniverse, Inc.
New York   Bloomington

Lost Souls

Copyright © 2008 by Carol Lawlor

This is a work of fiction. All of the characters, names, incidents,
organizations, and dialogue in this novel are either the products of the author's
imagination or are used fictitiously.

iUniverse books may be ordered through booksellers or by contacting:

iUniverse
1663 Liberty Drive
Bloomington, IN 47403
www.iuniverse.com
1-800-Authors (1-800-288-4677)

ISBN: 978-0-595-51531-8 (pbk)
ISBN: 978-0-595-61936-8 (ebk)

Printed in the United States of America

11/20/08

Contents

Prologue: 1985

*F*rom the exterior, nothing had changed. Surrounded
by a high wrought-iron fence, the old stone walls
of the Montreal Psychiatric Institute were as imposing
as ever. The handsome grey stone mansion, built in an
Italianate villa style on the slopes of Mount Royal, was
originally the home of 19-century shipping tycoon Sir
Richard Ripley. With its large solid tower dominating
the entranceway and expansive view of the entire city,
the mansion reflected wealth and power.

Arriving at the security gate, Tanya Kowalski gave
her name and drove up the long circular driveway to the
parking lot behind the building. She hadn't been inside
the gates for over a decade, yet she still felt her heartbeat
quickening. After turning off the ignition, she did a last-
minute check in her car mirror. Her hazel eyes were
bloodshot after too many restless nights. She smoothed
back her chestnut hair, grabbed her briefcase off the back
seat and got out of the car.

It was almost four o'clock, and her 30th nursing
reunion at the Mount Stephen Club wasn't until six—
barely two hours in which to do what she knew she had
to do. The heavy oak door to the main entrance looked
forbidding, quietly suggesting to the world that there was
something important and secretive going on beyond it.
The hinges creaked as she pushed it open and inhaled
the familiar antiseptic hospital smell. On the pale green
walls were large landscape paintings and beige curtains

were drawn across the two lead-paned windows in the entranceway. It had the old haunted house look she remembered so well.

The heels of her pumps clicked on the tile floor as she walked down the long corridor to the inner doors leading to the front desk. She stopped, looking directly to the left of the desk at a large portrait with its brass plaque inscription, "Doctor Samuel B. Strachan, MD, FRCP, Head of Psychiatry, Montreal Psychiatric Institute, 1959 to 1970." His dark, piercing eyes seemed to be looking directly at her. He'd never forget.

****

January, 1962

The ward was quiet as Tanya began her late evening rounds. She checked her watch. Nine forty-five. Beyond the window, a storm was blowing across Mount Royal and coating the old leaded window panes with wet snow. Tanya glanced out the window near the nursing station to see the white world beyond. It had been snowing heavily since she'd arrived for her four o'clock shift. For the past few days, temperatures had been hovering around 25 below, making it one of the coldest and snowiest winters in more than a decade. And more snow was in the forecast. Shivering, she draped her sweater around her shoulders to ward off the chill.

Tanya looked younger than her 28 years, a tall, slender woman with gaunt cheeks that made her eyes seem even larger. Her aquiline nose was a little crooked from a childhood accident. She wore no makeup except for a touch of blush emphasizing her pale complexion and full lips. As one of the youngest evening head nurses at the institute, her charge was Ward Five, temporary home to fifteen manic depressives, schizophrenics and suicidals, five of whom were in the Sleep Room.

Picking up a flashlight from the cluttered nursing desk, she slipped a clipboard under her arm and walked down the long, dimly lit corridor. There were two single and four double rooms on opposite sides of the corridor. At the far end was the Sleep Room with its five single rooms, all windowless. All the walls were a pale grey-green, but those with windows had a hint of aquamarine on the ledges. Some of the bedside lights were still turned on for patients who were leafing through magazines or books.

The hardwood floor creaked under Tanya's sturdy white oxfords as she fiddled with the keys to the narcotics supply, making sure they were securely pinned to her white cotton uniform. She had tied up her long hair under her cap from which a couple of tendrils had escaped, falling around her ears. It was always this last round that made her feel anxious. For some reason, nightfall seemed to bring out the worst behaviour in the patients. She had already given most of them their bedtime medication and a Seconal to help them sleep.

Entering room 309, she heard a shuffling noise and quickly shone her flashlight on the wall to the right of the bed. She frowned at Scott Beauford, a young, handsome alcoholic from Georgia. "My God, Scott, what are you doing?"

He twisted and turned in his bed, trying to pull out his intravenous. He mumbled something about hell, most of it inaudible.

Tanya put both hands on Beauford's shoulders. "Scott, it's okay—I'm here. Just try to be calm." But the young man bucked and cursed, his powerful hands gripping her forearms and pushing her away. Tanya shouted for the orderly, and in seconds Stanley was there. Over six feet tall and muscular, he was an overwhelming presence.

"Let's put him in restraints, Stan. I'll call Dr. Strachan."

Within fifteen minutes, Dr. Strachan arrived, deep creases on his craggy face. He peered over his small-framed glasses at Scott, then lifted the patient's eyelids and checked his pulse. "Let's increase his medication and leave the restraints on him. Get me his chart."

"Yes, Dr. Strachan." Tanya carried out the orders immediately, noting the time was ten-thirty.

Half an hour later when she checked in on him, Scott was in a heavily sedated sleep with the leather restraints around his wrists tied securely to the bed frame. His breathing appeared so slow that she placed her fingers under the restraints to take his pulse. It was 68 beats per minute, within the normal range.

Tanya pushed the curtain back slightly to take a closer look at him. Although he was only 31, he looked older. Still attractive, though, with his dark, ruffled hair, high cheek bones and thin lips. Dressed in a grey flannel nightshirt, he had two heavy blankets over him, for he always complained of the cold. Tanya leaned over and pulled the top blanket up to his neck. He stirred, pulling at his restraints, and made a whimpering sound.

In the next bed Saul Rosenfeld, mouth wide open, was snoring, a little dribble coming out of the left side of his mouth. On his shaven head was a flannel cap, as he was prone to colds and bronchitis after many years of smoking. She wiped his mouth with a tissue and felt his forehead. His fever seemed to have subsided somewhat after the alcohol sponge bath and aspirin. His lined face revealed a long history of shell shock. The only way to control his outbursts was with heavy medication and electro-shock treatment.

Tanya felt a melancholy overcome her. When was she ever going to toughen up? But it really was heart-rending seeing them like little helpless children. *God forbid I should end up like this.* She shuddered. Yet she knew it could easily happen to anyone. When she thought about it, there really was only a fine line between sanity and insanity. All she had to do was look at her own family—beginning with her domineering father, whose parents had immigrated to western Canada around the turn of the century from a small village in Poland.

Walter Kowalski was a hard-working, hard-drinking foundry man who liked controlling his family. Within half an hour of the factory whistle, he'd be lounging on their green velour chesterfield in front of the television with a glass of whisky, making demands that had to be met instantly. "When's supper?" he would say. "I'm starving." Tanya was usually in the kitchen helping her mother. One evening her father yelled, "I'm meeting the guys at the Legion at six-thirty. Can we eat earlier?" Tanya dutifully brought his plate out to the living room and placed it on his television tray. Nodding, he continued to watch the evening news. What a chauvinist, she thought, knowing then that she'd *never* marry a man like him.

Her mother, a delicate woman, toiled away, bearing children and serving her man. Raising six children in a small white clapboard house on a modest income, she had little energy left for nurturing. Tanya's eldest brother, Frank, withdrew into his own world, but being the second child and eldest daughter, she was looked upon as her mother's confidante, and in a way, a substitute mother to her younger siblings.

It had been painful seeing her mother weep about her husband's fiery temper and drinking bouts. Tanya would never forget the fights and name-calling. "Where the Christ is my blue shirt? I told you I needed it today," her father would yell.

Cowering, her mother would answer, "Sorry, I didn't get around to ironing it."

"You stupid woman. How many times do I have to tell you?"

Tanya would hear a slap, followed by sobbing.

Then there were the fury days when her mother lashed out, unable to control her anger and frustration. She'd preach the importance of a good education and career, delivering her sermon over her ironing board. "It's the only way out of a one-way street," she'd say again and again. She knew only too well, having quit high school at sixteen to clean other people's houses for a few dollars, because back in the thirties, work was scarce.

Tanya felt the heavy burden of her mother's weeping and outbursts. By early adolescence, she had already undertaken the role of the dutiful daughter; the caregiver; the mother. She lived in fear that her mother was on the verge of a breakdown. She could easily have fallen over the precipice and ended up in a gloomy institution like this. Although she cared deeply for her, Tanya vowed she would never end up like her mother. "On my grave," she'd mutter under her breath.

The summer of 1951 was a godsend. Her father was transferred to Montreal, and the family grudgingly moved east from the rugged northwestern shoreline of Lake Superior. Tanya was ecstatic at escaping the confines of a dreary, small mill town. She was only 16 and, surely, life was about to begin. Two years later, she left her suburban home to live in the hospital nursing residence on Pine Avenue in the heart of Montreal. There was no stopping her now. Or so she'd thought.

****

Tanya had been on Ward Five for almost two years now. The institute, an affiliate of the McGill Medical Centre, was recognized as one of the leading psychiatric hospitals in the world. The patients were long-term cases: schizophrenics, manic-depressives, obsessive-compulsives, and addictive personalities. Their chances of being discharged before the end of six months of therapy were pretty remote. Some, like Saul Rosenberg, had been in and out of the ward for years.

Tanya was particularly fond of Saul, as he was one of the first patients she'd helped admit to the ward. While the resident psychiatrist took Saul's history of depression, Tanya listened empathetically, making sure the patient was comfortable with a pillow behind his back and a glass of water. Saul had a nervous habit of shaking his head from side to side, as if he was saying, "no ... no ... no," when he meant yes. He was as vulnerable and trusting as any child she'd ever met. Instinctively, Tanya wanted to nurture him, make him better so that he could function in the world.

Tanya recalled how naïve and idealistic she'd been when she first arrived on Ward Five in the autumn of 1960. It was exciting and overwhelming at the same time as she didn't know what to expect.

"Welcome to Ward Five," senior psychiatric nurse Reva Rothwell had greeted her.

"Thank you," Tanya had responded. "I've heard nothing but good reports about your psychiatric therapy."

"We work as a team here on Ward Five," Reva had told her proudly.

Reva was one of the best mentors Tanya had ever had. Tanya admired Reva's professionalism and devotion to the patients. The ward was like a small community where patients and staff met in the large common room to talk and socialize. Tucked into a corner at the far end of the room was a television encircled by a sofa and metal chairs. Adjoining the common room was the dining room which was a hub of activity for those well enough to have their meals there. Nearby, the arts-and-crafts room housed the arts therapy where bold paintings decorated the pale walls. Ward Five exuded the spirit of a cohesive team of doctors, nurses and trained assistants, like the Psychiatric Institute itself. Head of the institute was the eminent Dr. Strachan.

Everyone agreed that Dr. Strachan was brilliant and could also be charming. He addressed everyone personally and looked directly at whomever he was speaking to. A small, vain man, he exuded tremendous power. In fact, Tanya considered vanity to be his forte. His greying hair was always perfectly combed and the shirt under his lab coat impeccably pressed. His eyeglasses gleamed. A formidable man, he was revered around the hospital. Whenever he entered a ward, conversations stopped and the staff jumped to his every need. Like others, Tanya was in awe of him and honoured to be part of his team.

Dr. Strachan had been instrumental in introducing radical psychiatric therapy in cooperation with McGill University. Long-term patients who had been traumatized in life were given new medications and involved in a sleep therapy to bring them back to their childhoods. Some of this treatment required electric shock to erase all the devastating events that had occurred when they were young. Once the patient was returned to this infantile state, the nurse would become a substitute mother, caring for and loving her child.

Tanya was intrigued by the therapy. Her experience in 'mothering' not only her mother, but her siblings, aroused in her a deep desire to become a caregiver. At times, she felt almost saintly, like Florence Nightingale, the lady with her lamp.

****

Tanya cast a glance back at room 309, checking to make sure Scott was still sleeping. She pitied the poor man. Scott Beauford had been born in Georgia, the second son of a wealthy textile manufacturer. His mama, a southern belle, was always protecting him from his father's rants. Beauford senior railed at him for being such a sissy, frightened of everything. Why couldn't he be more like his older brother—more athletic, more manly? Scott had retreated, as no matter how hard he tried, he couldn't please his father.

The further he was distanced from his father, the stronger his relationship with his mother became. Tanya had read in his records that they would spend hours reading together on the veranda, sipping lemonade and eating coconut cookies. Eventually the maternal comfort led to

Scott's affair with his mother. He became so devastated, he turned to alcohol. Desperate for help and having heard of Dr. Strachan's psychiatric therapy, he drove all the way to Montreal. Fortunately, he was not drunk at the time.

Now look at him, Tanya thought. *He doesn't look capable of doing anything, let alone having sex with his mother.*

Tanya looked at her watch. Eleven o'clock. The night shift would be arriving any moment. She left the room and went back to the nurses' station. Pulling out Scott's chart, she entered the date, January 13, 1962, and wrote: "Patient sleeping; restraints secured; IV glucose and water dripping slowly with medication. Has not become restless or attempted to pull out IV."

"Good evening, Tanya, how are our patients tonight?" Clare, the night nurse, smiled as she came around the desk.

"I hope you're well rested," Tanya replied. "You have a long night ahead of you."

"Are you okay? You look pale."

"I'm fine. Are you ready for report?" Tanya pulled her chair up to the desk.

****

It was almost midnight when Tanya arrived at her walk-up apartment on Prince Arthur. She slowly climbed the spiral wrought-iron stairs. God, she was weary and feeling very vulnerable. Recently, simple things had been irritating her more than usual. As she opened the door, she saw the blue light of the television.

Dressed in his old, green OR garb, Larry had been dozing on the sofa. He shifted his lanky body into an upright position and ran his fingers through his sandy-blond hair. His dark-framed glasses had fallen slightly down his nose. Tanya knew that he was also exhausted after his long shifts at the hospital. The residency was even more demanding than the Psychiatric Institute. Lately, what with him working days and being on call during the night in the cardiac unit, they'd scarcely seen each other.

He took off his glasses and rubbed his eyes with the back of his hand. "How'd it go this evening? You look bushed."

Tanya felt a twinge of irritation at some talking head on the television belabouring the virtues of living in Arizona: "The warm, dry air is not only good for your joints …"

"Larry, do you mind if I turn this off?" she asked.

"Not at all. Just wanted to know how the funny farm was this evening." She knew he was trying to relax her. Lately she'd been so stressed out when she arrived home.

Her uniform was badly wrinkled with some rust-coloured stains around the middle—evidence of the struggle she and Stanley had had putting the restraints on Scott. The dark circles under her eyes were heightened by her pallor and thin face. Strands of her hair clung to her neck. Sitting down beside him, she leaned her head against the sofa and closed her eyes.

"If you want the truth, it was one big hell hole."

He reached over and stroked her hair. "What happened?"

By the time she told him about the Scott escapade, she felt such a malaise that she started crying. Larry put his arm around her shoulder. "I know how tough it must be, but you're lucky to be working for such a great psychiatrist. I've heard that Strachan's a genius."

"Yes, but I'm looking after these patients every day, and I'm wondering if I'm capable of mothering them, like he expects me to. I'm finding it so stressful. I'm absolutely exhausted."

"Well, then why don't you get out of there before it totally grinds you down? Ask for a transfer."

"Oh, come on—it's not that simple. I can't just leave when things get tough. My patients need me," Tanya said defiantly.

"Well, what do you propose to do?"

Tanya turned toward him and put her head on his shoulder. "Larry, I'm not really in the mood right now."

"For talking? Okay, let's go to bed. We can talk about it in the morning."

****

It was five o'clock on Friday evening when Tanya arrived in the spacious common room at the far end of Ward Five. She rearranged the chairs against the wall in a circle around the room as Stanley set up the record player on the sturdy oak table near the entranceway. Another rectangular table at the back of the room was overflowing with paper cups and plates, juice, coffee, homemade cookies and an assortment of squares. She leafed through the records and almost laughed out loud when she saw "Love Me Tender." *I don't think so*, she thought. *At least not tonight*.

"Stanley, what do you think? 'Moon River' or 'There's a Whole Lotta Shakin' Goin' On'?"

"Why not both? It'll liven up the place." He raised his bushy eyebrows.

As the patients shuffled into the room, chatting and laughing, Tanya could feel the excitement level rising. This was one of her favourite nights on the ward: the Friday evening social dance. The only thing she dreaded was dancing with Saul Rosenfeld. How many times had he swaggered across the room, grinning at her? It was like dancing with a robot, a 65-year-old one at that.

Christy Amherst rounded the corner. She was one of the first to arrive, glancing around the room as she entered. At 21, she was the youngest patient on the ward. Tanya could have mistaken her for a high school student although she was heavily made up with rouged cheeks, blood-red lipstick and matching nail polish. This evening she had on a red felt skirt with a black poodle design stitched on the right side and a flimsy white cardigan buttoned up at the back. She was sporting bobby socks and sensible black and white saddle shoes. At the last dance she'd stumbled around in a pair of racy red stiletto heels, flirting outrageously with the male patients and orderlies.

As the room filled up, Tanya felt more animated than she had in a long time. Lively music and dancing had this effect on her.

Whoops, here comes Saul. She told him she'd love to; it just happened to be "Moonlight Serenade." Over Saul's shoulder, Tanya saw Christy curtsy in front of Stanley and take his hand, leading him to the dance floor. Stanley was a sensual man, with broad shoulders from years of lifting patients and hospital furniture; thick black hair flopping over his left eye like Elvis Presley's and the bluest eyes Tanya had ever seen. She marvelled at how well he danced while watching that Christy didn't snuggle up to him. There were rules at the hospital restricting staff and patients from dancing too closely. Not that a ruler was used as at some of Tanya's high school dances, but nevertheless there had to be some decorum. She smiled, recalling the teacher who chaperoned establishing the six inches between two romantically inclined dancers.

Leading Saul, she inched her way toward them. Christy had her head on Stanley's chest and her eyes closed. Stanley's body stiffened, attempting to hold her at arm's length, but to no avail. Sexual attraction—Tanya had seen it happen on the ward before with disastrous results. Once, old Mr. Bentley was caught embracing a much younger female patient in the television lounge. When Stanley attempted to separate them, Mr. Bentley roared obscenities at him as his partner fled the room in tears. He was quickly transferred to another ward.

Tanya excused herself from Saul and whispered to Christy that she would like to speak to her. Christy looked at her with glassy eyes and pouted. "What the hell are you doing ruining my fun," Christy shouted. "You always act holier than thou."

Tanya put her hand on Christy's right shoulder. "Please, Christy, listen to me. You know that dancing too closely is not acceptable."

She shrugged and threw Tanya's hand off her shoulder. "Who says so? You're not my mother. Just fuck off!"

"Hey, come on, Christy. Calm down—Tanya's right," Stanley stood between the two of them.

"If that's the way you feel, you can both fuck off," Christy screamed and ran out of the room, barely missing a collision with Dr. Strachan who was leaning against the doorway, watching with a perplexing expression Tanya thought could be either glee or contempt.

"Tanya, could I speak to you in the office?" he asked curtly.

"Yes, doctor—I'll just let Stanley know I'll be gone for a while."

Dr. Strachan looked preoccupied and fidgety when Tanya arrived in the office. The bags under his eyes were pronounced, and his skin was a greyish tone. He made her feel nervous when he was this tense. There was something about his moods. When he was upbeat, the staff responded accordingly; when his mood was black, a dreariness hung over the ward.

"I'd like to know just what went on tonight," he said. "From what I observed, it was utter chaos." He looked directly into her eyes.

Tanya felt her cheeks flush. "Oh, it was nothing, really. Christy just got a little carried away. You know how she likes to play the role of the seductress. So, I cautioned her about dancing too closely with Stanley."

"Is this the first time it's happened?"

"There was only one other occasion, and she apologized for her behaviour. She just can't accept what she looks upon as criticism. She's far too fragile."

"Maybe these Friday social dances aren't such a good idea after all." The doctor pursed his thin lips.

"I can understand how you feel, Dr. Strachan. But ..." she hesitated. "The patients really look forward all week to this get-together."

"What are you trying to tell me? *I'm* the head of this institute."

"Yes, of course, sir. Sorry ... " Tanya faltered.

"Sorry—for what?" He sneered at her.

"For being impertinent. It won't happen again."

"Should hope not. How is Scott this evening?"

"He's still in restraints and resting quietly in the Sleep Room. His IV was changed just before I came on shift."

"Good. Let me know if he becomes restless again. And Christy—we'll have to keep a closer eye on her; make sure there are no further outbursts."

"Yes, doctor. I'll watch her closely."

What is going on? Tanya wondered. Dr. Strachan's words, while even and controlled, had a sternness to them that Tanya hadn't seen before. As she stood there watching Dr. Strachan, she noticed his jaw clench before he turned on his heel and stomped out of the office. Something wasn't right, but Tanya couldn't quite put her finger on it.

After Dr. Strachan left, Tanya pulled out Christy's chart from the metal file holder. Although she was only 21, she'd had a history of depression for almost half her life. She attempted to cover up by playing roles: the betrayed one; the martyr; the femme fatale. She was as clever and crafty as anyone Tanya had ever met. As Christy was the sixth of eight children in a Nova Scotia farming family, vying for attention in any way she could was her way of surviving. It was her wit and cunning, especially where men were concerned, that seemed to get her what she wanted.

What she'd wanted most of all was the attention her younger sister got for being so pretty and smart. In her attempts to please her father and eldest brother, she had suffered terrible abuse and incest. As she'd relayed in therapy, she was only twelve when her father first approached her in the red barn one evening as she was cleaning the last horse stall. He had come up behind her, gently stroked her hair, and whispered in her ear, "Show your daddy how much you love him." It was only because she wanted to please him, wanted his love.

Tanya put the chart in the rack, then checked the lock on the narcotics cupboard before heading down the long corridor. When she reached the common room, she noticed the chairs were back in order after the dance. As she looked around the corner, she heard laughter. Saul, Christy and old Mrs. Barnicke were sitting on the well-worn brown velveteen sofa watching a rerun of an Abbott and Costello movie. A nurse's aide slouched back in an armchair was keeping a watchful eye on them. The long table at the far end of the adjoining room was set for supper, as the trays would be arriving from the kitchen momentarily. It was six-thirty.

Tanya turned and walked along the ward, checking each room to make sure that the patients were resting comfortably, IVs were dripping, and bedside trays were placed over the beds for those who would be eating in their rooms. When she arrived at the far end, she entered the Sleep Room, smelling the strong disinfectant the orderly had recently used to mop up the floors. There were five patients in the single, small, windowless rooms, including Scott who had been transferred there from room 309.

Most of the patients in the rooms had IVs dripping slowly and were sleeping, except for a new patient, Sarah Conway, recently transferred from Ward Three with severe depression. She had only been in the Sleep Room for a day, and Dr. Strachan had asked that she be carefully observed for any signs of aggressive or suicidal behaviour. Orders were to notify him immediately if she became restless, as he had expressed grave concern about her welfare and wanted to make sure that she was on the correct medication.

Tanya checked Sarah's blood pressure and pulse and noted it in her chart. A little high at 134/74 and 86 respectively, but nothing abnormal. Wiping the perspiration off Sarah's winsome face, she adjusted her pillow.

Sarah stirred, but appeared to be resting fairly comfortably. Tanya flipped through her chart and noted that Sarah had recently given birth to a seven-pound, three-ounce baby girl. "Wait a minute," she mumbled to herself as she took a closer look at the chart. Immediately, she thought about her cousin who had suffered postpartum depression after the birth of her second child a couple of years ago. It had lasted a little over three months, but once the baby was sleeping throughout the night and she was more rested, the depression subsided. Could Sarah possibly be suffering from postpartum depression and, if so, why was she admitted to the Sleep Room? Wasn't that a bit extreme? She shivered thinking about it.

There was a moaning sound from across the room. Tanya entered Scott's room and could tell from the expression on his face that he was having another one of his nightmares. She went over to his bed and gently stroked his brow, trying to calm him.

She didn't want to call Dr. Strachan this evening, as she felt so tired. Lately she'd dreaded going into the institution. She'd have to deal with it. Maybe get back to her yoga lessons—balancing her yin and yang; breathing in positive energy, exhaling negative thoughts. Anything would be better than going on antidepressants. She'd tried that once with little luck. Initially, there was the mood elevation, a feeling of well-being, but the downside was the inevitable weeping afterwards when she stopped the medication. It was like her security blanket had been taken away.

She noticed Scott's bed was soaked with urine. The pungent smell permeated the room. She rang the bell for Stanley to ask him to change Scott's diaper and draw sheet. What he really needed was a good bed bath and back massage, as his skin was looking a little red around his buttocks. Tanya prided herself on making sure none of her patients suffered from bed sores. They already suffered enough pain. She'd often wondered what was worse, an aching body or a tormented soul, but when she looked at her patients, she knew it was the latter. Their psyches were as delicate and vulnerable as a newborn. The soul was like a mysterious cavern with the steady ebb and flow of all the love, hate, loss and grief over one's lifetime.

As she left the Sleep Room, Tanya heard shouts from the common room. Christy was screaming at poor old Saul and Mrs. Barnicke. It was a full-blown tantrum about changing the TV channel to the "I Love Lucy" show, Christy's favourite. Tanya and Stanley rushed to the scene. As they entered the room, Christy threw a book at Saul, hitting him squarely on his left cheek. Blood and spittle dribbled out of the corner of his mouth as he lay sprawled on the sofa. Mrs. Barnicke was weeping and wringing her paper napkin in her hands.

"Let me out of here," she cried.

Saul was stunned and whimpered like a child. "She hit me." He put his right hand to his bruised cheek and let out a shriek when he saw the blood on his fingers. The nurse's aide tried to calm Saul as Tanya and Stanley struggled to restrain Christy, who was fighting to push them aside. She clawed and kicked Stanley, aiming for his groin, but missed, hitting his left thigh.

Tanya's voice quivered. "Stanley, restrain her—I'll call Dr. Strachan." As much as she loathed to do so, she had no alternative.

When Dr. Strachan arrived, the expression on his face was a mixture of controlled anger and utter contempt. His eyes narrowed behind his glasses as his pursed lips issued his orders. The most terrifying part was his steely gaze directed at Tanya: *I told you so.*

A feeling of helplessness and fear overcame her like a tidal wave. She felt faint.

"Put some restraints on Christy and transfer her to the Sleep Room where we can keep a closer watch on her," he said calmly.

Stanley strapped Christy in a wheelchair, then wheeled her down to the far end of the corridor. Christy was screaming, "What the hell did I do?"

"It's for your own good, Christy. We want to make you well, so you can go home soon." Dr. Strachan put his hand on her left shoulder as he walked beside the wheelchair.

"I hate you. I hate you all," Christy shouted, shoving the doctor's hand away. "You'll rot in hell."

"Get me her chart. Let's get her started right away." Dr. Strachan stared at Tanya.

Like a sleepwalker, Tanya walked to the desk and pulled out Christy's chart. It was evident the restraints had intensified Christy's anger by bringing back memories of her earlier childhood abuse. And Dr. Strachan, who'd ordered the restraints to control her, played a major role. Just like when Christy's father approached her in the barn that first night. Christy was once again the helpless victim. The anger, the betrayal—it was all there. Almost like when Tanya's mother had told Tanya about her father's adultery.

****

It was early evening. Montreal, draped with a soft blanket of snow, was as charming and graceful as ever. Tanya held Larry's arm as they strolled along Sherbrooke Street. Dressed warmly in her long, black military coat and Russian hat, she felt the snowflakes falling on her face. She loved this time of year. Everything looked so festive with the glittering shops and art galleries putting their finest displays in their windows. The doorman at the elegant Ritz Carlton hotel nodded as they walked by.

"Larry, you know what I'd really like?"

"Don't tell me—you probably want a trip to Paris."

She threw her head back and laughed, swallowing some snowflakes. "That would be great, but I'd settle for a long weekend. Just some time off to spend with you."

"You know how difficult it is for me to get away. We've never been busier."

His standard answer. She'd have to work on him, nudge him a little to entice him away from the hospital. This wouldn't be an easy undertaking.

They turned left onto bustling Mountain Street and climbed the stairs to Le Crêpe Bretonne, one of the most popular cafés in the city. How long had it been since they'd had an evening out? Lately, it seemed that one of them was always working some ungodly shift.

She reached over and brushed some snowflakes off Larry's hair. The collar of his tanned leather jacket was pulled up around his turtleneck. She looked at him. He was handsome with his square jaw jutting out and snow clinging to his eyebrows. It was his quirky sense of humour that had initially attracted her. He could be so charming and witty when he wanted to be, and he was a great lover.

But there was another side to him—the cold, reserved Larry, especially around the hospital. For some reason he was trying to protect himself, make sure people saw him as a godlike figure. Why couldn't he just be himself rather than struggle to create an image of perfection?

She was well aware of how much she depended on him. He was the only person she could talk to about her growing concerns on Ward Five—how controlling Dr. Strachan was becoming. However, lately when she'd brought up the subject, he had brushed it away, implying that she was overreacting. He just didn't take it seriously, which infuriated her. She'd constantly listened to all his woes about the hospital, and all she needed was a little sympathy in return. But better to forget all of that this evening and revel in a long overdue evening out.

As they shook the snow from their boots, Louis the maitre d' looked up from the bookings and said, "Bonsoir, Dr. Byron, mademoiselle—good to see you again."

"Bonsoir, Louis. Great to see you have the fire lit tonight."

"I have a nice table for you in the corner by the window."

As they sat down, Tanya looked out the window at the glow of the street lamps. It was now snowing quite heavily. The candle on their table flickered, casting a shadow on Larry's rosy cheeks. The waiter approached with a basket of freshly baked bread, and they ordered a carafe of red wine and escargots in garlic butter. The escargots were the best in the city. Sipping her wine, Tanya felt the tension slowly ease away.

Larry leaned forward and put his hand on hers, squeezing it gently, "Tanya, you look great. I like it when you wear your hair up. It makes you look very sophisticated."

She smiled at him as she raised her glass in a toast, "Here's to us. No hospital, no Psychiatric Institute, just the two of us."

"Salut." Larry reached over and clinked Tanya's wineglass. "I didn't realize how much I needed this night out."

"We both did." Tanya's eyes held his. "Larry, what's happening to us? We used to have fun, do crazy things. Remember the night I crept into your residence after my shift?"

"How could I ever forget? It took most of the next day to recover from that midnight assault."

Tanya laughed. "Don't be silly. You loved every minute of it."

"Yes, but I was sound asleep. All of a sudden I felt hands caressing my body and … "

"And what? It didn't take you long to respond. Hopefully, you knew it was me in the dark, not some stranger."

"How could I ever mistake those moist lips and sweet warm breath on my neck?"

Tanya took a sip of wine and looked at him seriously. "I know things can't always remain the same in a relationship, but sometimes I worry. Are we going to end up like so many other couples going their separate ways?"

"Of course not. It's just that I've been so preoccupied with my work, I've barely had time to think about anything else."

"Well, thanks a lot," Tanya tried to sound light-hearted. "What about me?"

"Come on, Tanya. Let's not go the guilty route. It just adds stress to our lives."

"I guess we, of all people, should know better. There's nothing worse than stress. All we have to do is look at our patients."

"I thought we agreed," he said. "No shop talk."

She felt her cheeks flush with the red wine. "Well, what would you like to talk about?"

Larry cleared his throat. "There's something that's been bothering me."

"What's that?"

"We've been together almost two years, yet I know next to nothing about your family. Why don't you like to talk about them?"

She was feeling quite mellow now with the wine and the crackling of logs in the fire. Since she had moved to Montreal, she'd rarely talked about her family background. She didn't like to think about her working-class roots in a small northern Ontario industrial town. The huge smokestacks of the foundry belching grey clouds of smoke dominated the city. When the northerly winds blew off the mountain, she could smell the putrid odour from the pulp mill. The strong sulphur stench made her gag. All she wanted to do was leave it behind and move on, become another person. Her family had moved back to their hometown five years ago, and couldn't understand her; why she was so restless. Why couldn't she move back with them, settle down, meet some nice young man? All very simple, wasn't it? Whenever Larry asked about meeting them, she felt the tension in the back of her neck.

"They're different. I don't think you'd find them that interesting. I actually wanted to leave home from the time I was sixteen." She thought about her uncle, her mother's older brother, who had forever been stroking her shoulder, telling her what a lovely young woman she was becoming. His stale, smoky breath repelled her.

"You never told me that before."

"I find it difficult to talk about. I went into nursing so that I could get away from home. Moving into a residence at eighteen was the perfect solution. As for psychiatry, it seems to attract people who are a little mad."

He laughed. "Especially your Dr. Strachan."

Tanya felt the vice on her temples. "You know, even though we said we wouldn't talk about our work, I was thinking the same thing."

"Let's not spoil the evening. Sorry I mentioned his name."

"Yeah. Tonight is just you and me." Tanya thought of Larry as her anchor, the person she could count on.

And this evening she had him all to herself. Away from that damn hospital. She tried to change the subject. "You know Larry, I sometimes envy you. You seem to have a sense of yourself."

"What do you mean?"

"Such strong determination. You know what direction you're heading in."

"If you're saying I'm ambitious, you're right. You know I've wanted to be a doctor from the time I was five. When you grow up in a small, conservative place like Ridgetown in southwestern Ontario, a doctor—well, a doctor is someone we looked up to."

"Like the great healer?"

"Something like that. It may sound like a cliché, but I wanted to help others, and I also wanted the prestige. And as you know, there's always been a conflict between my father and me. I don't think he's ever forgiven me for not joining him in his insurance business."

"But at least you have things in common with your family."

"Not really. It may look like that, but there's always been sibling rivalry. My younger brother has never stopped competing with me in school, in sports, in friends. It's impossible for me to have a relationship with him."

"Is he still working with your father?"

"Yes. There's a real bond between them. Let's just say I'm happy to be here in Montreal, away from family pressures." He twirled the stem of his wineglass, spilling some wine on the white tablecloth.

"Well, I am too."

After her last difficult relationship with Mischa, a man ten years her senior, she had vowed she'd never make the same mistake. Tanya had met Mischa one weekend at a psychiatric conference at McGill and was enthralled with his intelligence and self-confidence. However, after their six-month love affair, she'd realized to her horror that he was very much like her father: a domineering, short-tempered Eastern European.

But Larry was different. He was someone she could relate to. And he respected her independence. The only thorn was his belief that doctors were superior, god-like figures gliding along the hospital wards in white lab coats, making their daily rounds. He faithfully supported all doctors, including Strachan. It was like an old boys' club from which she felt excluded. She shook her head to wipe away the doubts.

It was almost a year since Larry had moved most of his belongings into her apartment, and chaotic as their life was, it was good to have him around. Besides, she loved sleeping with him. He really did have a passionate side, sometimes nudging her in the middle of the night to make love.

Larry took a piece of bread and dipped it in the garlic butter. "You've got me thinking, Tanya. I know I haven't been the easiest guy to live with."

"There could be worse."

"What I'm saying is, I have the last weekend in February off. How would you like a trip to Quebec City? Can you get away?"

"I'd love to. I can switch weekends with Reva. She was hoping to get the 14th off."

"Great. There's a little *pension* inside the walls of the old city. It's not a lot of money and handy to everything. Let's see if it's available for the weekend."

Tanya leaned over and squeezed his hand. "You've got a deal."

Larry reached into the side pocket of his tweed jacket and pulled out a small blue velvet box. "I've got a better deal," he said, and slipped the marquis diamond ring on the third finger of her left hand. "What do you say, Tanya? Do you want to get married?"

She jumped up from her chair, knocking over her wineglass, threw her arms around his neck, and kissed him. "Oh, Larry, do I ever."

Applause rang out from the other patrons in the café.

"Claude," shouted the maitre d'. "*Une bouteille de champagne avec nos compliments.*"

When they left the restaurant an hour later, the snow was halfway up Tanya's knee-high leather boots. She playfully kicked the snow as they walked back to the apartment on Prince Arthur. Larry had his arm around her shoulder.

They both felt a little light-headed climbing the wrought-iron stairs. *Happiness in life was really simple*, Tanya thought. *Something as simple as being with some one you loved.*

"Would you like a nightcap?" Larry called out to Tanya who was changing into her lacy black peignoir.

"I'd love one," she poked her head mischievously around the corner. "We have some wonderful port left over from the party."

"Okay, let's take it into the living room. I'll light a fire before I slip into my robe."

They made love in front of the fire slowly and gently like the snow falling on the rooftop.

****

A few days later while they were sipping their coffee at breakfast, Larry looked up from his newspaper. "Is there something bothering you, Tanya?"

"Why?"

"Last night you tossed and turned, calling out something about Ward Five, but I couldn't make it out."

Tanya hesitated. She knew how much Larry didn't want her condemning Dr. Strachan's therapy. But she couldn't control herself. She had to talk.

"I've checked Scott Beauford's chart. He's way over the original prescribed dosage of sodium amytal and Largactil and becoming more catatonic every day." She then told him that Dr. Strachan had prescribed electro-shock therapy for Beauford after he had attempted to pull out his IV. He'd received between 30 and 60 electro-shocks in a short period of time. In between treatments, he'd been given 1,000 milligrams of Largactil to sedate him. With all the drugs in his system, he was now practically in a coma.

When Tanya started becoming suspicious, she went over all the charts thoroughly. What she discovered was devastating: patients in the Sleep Room were being heavily medicated with drugs such as sodium amytal, the so-called truth drug. They were then sent to a basement laboratory where they received electro-shock treatment to depattern them. In other words, they were being brainwashed. There were even taped recordings placed under their pillows while they slept, telling them over and over again how to behave.

"Dr. Strachan calls it the Sleep Room. I call it the Zombie Room. And to think, Sarah Conway, who is simply suffering from postpartum depression, is going through this too." Tanya shook her head.

"It sounds strange, but surely Strachan knows what he's doing," Larry commented.

Tanya spoke softly, "I'm not sure I believe that anymore. My instinct tells me that something dreadful is about to happen."

****

There was no doubt about it—the pressure was building. For the past two weeks, Tanya hadn't been able to get through her evening shifts without the antidepressants her family doctor had prescribed. When she arrived back at the apartment, she needed a drink to relax her before bed. If Larry was on call at the hospital, she'd pour herself another drink and turn up the volume on her record player. Night after night, she'd play the song from *My Fair Lady*, "I Could Have Danced All Night." It seemed to uplift her and soothe her soul, easing the torture of the ward. She'd open the window and light a cigarette, then inhale deeply. It made her feel dizzy, almost euphoric. Then she would rest her head on the back of the sofa, close her eyes and sing along with the music. *"I could have danced all night ..."*

****

Tanya knew that things were going from bad to worse when Christy was transferred to the Sleep Room. Even to an experienced nurse such as herself, to see Christy transformed from a spunky, defiant young woman to a helpless, meek child was shocking.

Dr. Strachan had insisted that Christy was out of control. All her childhood abuse was affecting her judgment and behaviour. It was absolutely necessary to restrain and medicate her, then try some electro-shock therapy to erase all the bad memories. Tanya remembered the first time Christy returned from the basement laboratory, strapped on a hospital stretcher, lying on her left side with a pillow behind her back and a plastic airway in her mouth to drain the saliva. Stanley helped transfer Christy to her bed in the Sleep Room. Tanya had kept a close watch, checking all vital signs throughout the evening as she was concerned about Christy's slow, laboured breathing.

Then there was Sarah Conway, whom Tanya continued to worry about. She was very upset about not seeing her baby. She kept weeping, repeating over and over that she wasn't a good mother; as how could she leave her own baby who needed her? Her guilt was incredible.

Dr. Strachan had told Sarah that it was important that she concentrate on getting better. If she would just try to relax and let him take care of her, he assured her that the new medication and treatment he was prescribing would help her get over her depression so she could return home to her baby in no time.

He was so convincing. Who would doubt the man? He had complete control of the staff and patients—the healer, the great god; saviour of all the poor unfortunates. He'd save their minds and souls; make them better persons able to survive in the real world. But instead, old Saul Rosenberg was diagnosed as a paranoid schizophrenic and shipped off to the Atwater Psychiatric Hospital for long-term care.

The pressure kept mounting. Then one grey November evening, Tanya was making rounds on Ward Five. Christy, whom she thought was under control, had only feigned constraint. She was so clever. When Tanya left the room, she seemed to be sleeping peacefully. However, as soon as Tanya was at the far end of the ward, she heard Christy's loud cry, "Get the hell out of my room!" By the time Tanya raced back to the scene, Christy had torn her room apart; throwing everything from her bedside table into the middle of the room. She was now running around screaming at Sarah Conway who was weeping uncontrollably.

"Christy, please," Tanya pleaded. However, it was no use—Dr. Strachan had to be called immediately. He quickly entered the room and shouted orders, "Restrain her. Quick, get her medication. We've got to put an end to this once and for all."

It was this evening on November 13, 1964, that Tanya lost faith in Dr. Strachan. After all his Sleep Room therapy, the patients were no better off. Just look at Scott, Christy and Sarah—they were worse than before their treatment. *What exactly is going on?* Tanya vowed that, no matter what, she would find out.

****

It was a chilly January evening with a brilliant full moon casting a golden glow through the nursing station window. Snowflakes were falling gently. Tanya stood up from her desk and walked down the corridor of Ward Five. When she reached the Sleep Room, she glanced at her watch. Nine forty-five. Less than two hours to go.

As she entered Scott Beauford's room at the far end, she noticed how slowly he was breathing. She put her hand on his forehead and felt the perspiration around his temples. His pulse was only 52 and irregular; blood pressure was low at 92/51. Tanya called out his name, but there was no response. He was in a coma.

Returning to the nursing station, she put in an emergency call to Dr. Strachan. He arrived twenty minutes later.

"What seems to be the problem?" he bristled as they walked toward the Sleep Room.

"Doctor, I'm worried—Scott's not responding at all."

"He's not supposed to be. He's in sleep therapy."

"But I'm concerned about his vital signs."

"Well, let's see."

As they entered the room, Dr. Strachan checked Scott's blood pressure. It was still low with an irregular pulse. He leaned over and pulled Scott's eyelids up to examine his pupils, which were quite dilated. Tanya wiped the sweat off Scott's forehead and neck and watched his chest rise and lower slowly with each breath.

"He'll be okay," Dr. Strachan said, as he wrote something on his chart.

"Are you sure?"

"Yes, I am sure." Dr. Strachan glared at her as he slowly formed each word. "Shall we go to the nursing station?"

"Yes, Doctor."

As they sat in the station going over the chart, Tanya felt uncomfortable, then nauseous. She took one of her deep yoga breaths to calm herself. Looking at the back of

Dr. Strachan as he leaned over writing in the chart, she had an urge to put her hands around his supercilious throat.

"I've decreased the Largactil slightly. He should be fine," he said.

"Dr. Strachan, I have to tell you how concerned I am about Scott and some of the other patients in the Sleep Room."

"What are you talking about?"

"Scott is in a coma. And Christy and Sarah are almost there. Isn't something wrong with this?"

"I beg your pardon. I've never had a colleague question my therapies, much less a nurse."

"I'm sorry—I'm only thinking about our patients."

"Look, it's simple: I write the orders, and you carry them out. If you don't like it, you can look for another job."

Tanya caught a glimpse of herself in the nursing station mirror. She looked terrible. The pallor of her skin, the dark circles under her bloodshot eyes and the small lines forming around her mouth revealed the months of stress and tension she'd borne.

Something snapped inside her. "That's precisely what I intend to do," she told him defiantly.

"Very well. And not a moment too soon." Dr. Strachan pushed back his chair abruptly, picked up his briefcase and walked briskly out of the ward, slamming the steel door behind him.

****

"You did what?" Larry shouted, as Tanya told him about the evening. "How the hell could you do such a thing?"

"I'm telling you, Larry—it was impossible for me to stay on that ward. Don't you see the toll it is taking on me?"

"Of course I can see. But I never thought you would quit, just walk away."

"I had no choice once I confronted Dr. Strachan."

"No you didn't. But you *shouldn't* have confronted him in the first place."

"And why not?"

"He's a world-renowned psychiatrist, well respected internationally."

"Larry, what does it take? I told you about the drugs, electro-shock and brainwashing that's going on." She attempted to calmly relate the events of the evening, the pressure mounting to the inevitable explosion. She felt she had no alternative but to quit. Now she was exhausted.

Larry had been staring at the fireplace as she spoke, but now he slowly turned his head toward her. He was visibly shaken. "You've been through one hell of a lot lately. I can see the strain in your face," he said, his voice cracking. "Do you have any idea of what you'd like to do now? Or do you just want some time off?"

"I've been giving it a lot of thought over the past few months. I've checked out some journalism courses at McGill and they've got a great roster of instructors. The one who particularly caught my interest was Max Callaghan who writes for *The Montreal Gazette*.

"You mean that muckraker who writes on health issues?"

"Larry, he's an investigative journalist. From the way he writes, I think he'll be a great teacher."

"I'm not convinced."

"What would it take to convince you?" she asked.

"Maybe our weekend away. I love you, but I don't know if I'll ever understand you. As a matter of fact, why don't we make this Quebec trip our honeymoon?"

"I told you before: you've got a deal." She raised her glass.

****

Winter, 1974

It was late afternoon when Tanya circled up the winding road to Auberge Saint-Pierre. She shifted her red Peugeot into low gear and slowly let out the clutch. The car lurched forward, then the engine let out a rumbling sound and stalled. "Damn it!" she said as she gripped the steering wheel. "Of all times, don't let me down now."

However, nothing, not even the car, could dampen her elated mood. The sky was a brilliant azure, and the sun cast sparkling diamonds on the tall snow banks. Fortunately, the roads had been plowed recently, partially baring the cobblestones and making the drive less arduous.

She started the engine again and gingerly edged the car into the gateway of the stone walls surrounding old Quebec City. Magnificent ice sculptures of polar bears, dragons and eagles on both sides of La Grande Allee towered over her. Bonhomme Carnaval, Quebec's winter carnival snowman, jauntily sported a red beret and matching sash as he smiled and waved. Tanya laughed and waved back.

It was ten years ago that she and Larry had been here for the winter carnival on their honeymoon. So much had happened since then. When Larry told her that his next cardiovascular conference was at the Chateau Frontenac in Quebec City, she didn't hesitate to accept his invitation to join him for a long weekend. They needed some time away.

"Why don't we stay at Auberge Saint-Pierre for old time's sake?" he'd suggested.

"Love to. I wonder if that rascal Jacques Pierre is still there. One thing for sure—he is no saint. He flirts outrageously with all the ladies."

"Then I'll have to keep an eye on him."

Larry and a few colleagues from the Montreal Medical Centre had left earlier in the week by train to present their new research on cardiac angioplasty. Doctors from across North America were gathering at the grand old hotel to present their latest discoveries in cardiac bypass surgery. Over the past month Tanya had seen very little of Larry, as he'd either been at the medical library working on his research papers or at the hospital. In a span of six-and-a-half years, he had become one of the top cardiac surgeons in Montreal.

Meanwhile, Tanya had found herself spending more and more time at McGill pursuing her studies in journalism. She loved the camaraderie of her fellow students, most of whom were younger than she, and the straight-talking, unassuming professors. Quite a contrast to the conservative doctors at the Montreal Medical Centre.

Tanya turned left and skilfully manoeuvred the car into a parking space in front of the Auberge Saint-Pierre. The 18th-century stone inn with a crimson door looked exactly as she remembered it. The four leaded-glass windows enhanced with black shutters looked out on a small cobblestone courtyard. It was a handsome building, done in the classic French-Canadian style of that century.

"*Bienvenue, madame*," Jacques Pierre greeted her. His dark hair was greying around the temples but his brown eyes twinkled impishly. The creases in his face were more prominent, giving him a roguish appearance. She guessed him to be approaching 50.

"*Bonsoir,* Jacques. *Je suis* Madame Byron.*"*

"*Ah, comment allez-vous?*"

"*Très bien.* It's great to be back. You know, it's been ten years, but everything looks the same."

"We like to keep our old charm. That's the way our visitors like it, no?" He put his hand under his chin and cocked his head to one side, revealing an affable gap-toothed grin. He looked like Mandrake the magician.

"Absolutely *charmant*," Tanya told him.

"Dr. Byron called to say that he would be here around six o'clock. His conference is running a little late. I've given you room nine overlooking the courtyard."

"Goodness. Isn't that the same room we had last time?"

"Dr. Byron wanted to surprise you." Jacques winked.

Tanya slowly climbed the stairs to the second floor and dropped her overnight bag on the bed. It was now four-thirty, just enough time to sink into a warm bath and relax before Larry arrived. How she'd been looking forward to this getaway. She glanced out the window at the snow falling on the ornate lamplights. It was good to be back. They'd had such a great time on their honeymoon walking arm in arm, dining at cozy cafés and making love well into the night. Maybe the memories would reignite the spark in their relationship. God knows they needed it. In preparation for the weekend, she'd gone to a sex shop on rue Ste-Catherines and purchased a book of erotica by Anais Nin and black garters and lingerie. These items were neatly tucked in one of the pockets of her suitcase.

Suddenly, Tanya felt a malaise creeping over her. She called a halt to this feeling and gave herself a little pep talk: *I'm not letting anything ruin this weekend. I've waited too long for it.*

After tonight, she and Larry would have the rest of the weekend to themselves. However, this evening, they were dining at the Café Aux Anciens-Canadiens with Sheldon Schmedeck, one of Larry's Montreal colleagues. Just before he'd left for Quebec City, Larry recounted how much Sheldon and his wife, Clarissa, were looking forward to meeting her.

"You know what Sheldon told me the other day?" Larry asked her.

"What?"

"About nine years ago, Clarissa's mother was undergoing treatment for depression by none other than your Dr. Strachan. Apparently, at first she seemed to be improving. But things changed dramatically. She went into a deeper depression, completely withdrawing from her family and the staff at the institute."

"Not another one." Tanya grimaced.

Larry looked at her suspiciously. "I hope this evening won't be ruined by their talking about Strachan and Clarissa's mother. If it comes up, let's make sure we change the subject."

That put an abrupt end to the conversation, but Tanya filed the information away for another time.

She ran the water, then slowly lowered herself into the warm bath, feeling the tension easing out of her body. Leaning back, she closed her eyes, letting the water perform its magic. She had at least half an hour of sheer indulgence. Then she smiled to herself as she thought of the last time they'd been at the hotel. Larry had surprised her with his prowess, making love sometimes twice a day. One afternoon when they were at the Quebec Museum of Modern Art, he'd come up behind her and whispered in her ear, "How about heading back to the Auberge for a little matinee?" And that was after they'd already made love in the morning. He was a different man once he was away from the hospital.

What she'd heard about Quebec City was true. A quaint city of romance, built upon the passion and spilt blood of *les français et les anglais*. The French and English fought it out on the Plains of Abraham, just outside the old walled city of Quebec. Yes, Quebec City, with its cozy cafés and cobblestone streets, dimly lit with lamplights, did something to its visitors. It engulfed them, brought out their romance and passion.

She heard a key in the lock. "Hi, anybody home?" Larry called out.

Tanya stepped out of the bath and slipped on the white terry cloth bathrobe hanging on the bathroom door. She had her long auburn hair pinned up behind her ears and her cheeks were flushed from the warmth of her bath.

"You look gorgeous," Larry told her as she entered the room.

"You're not bad, yourself, Dr. Byron." Tanya put her arms around his neck and gently kissed him. "I missed you."

"I missed you, too."

"How is the conference going?"

"You know what they're like —a lot of networking, but some great new research coming out in the field. We had quite a turnout. But first, I want to hear all about your trip. Would you like a drink?"

"Sounds great. How much time do we have before we meet the Schmedecks?"

He reached over and undid the sash of her robe and gently stroked her breasts. "It will be enough."

****

Tanya was still feeling the euphoria of their lovemaking as she and Larry entered the café. After stamping the snow off their boots, they handed their coats to the waiter. Sheldon Schmedeck waved to them from across the room. Tucked away in a corner by one of the snow-covered windows, Sheldon and Clarissa looked like lovers enjoying a little rendezvous. A fire in the huge stone fireplace on the far wall cast an orange glow across the dimly lit room.

As they approached the table, Larry said, "Hi, Sheldon—you look pretty cozy there. Are you sure you want us to join you? We could find something on the other side of the room and leave you two alone."

Tanya squeezed Larry's arm. "What is it about you and Quebec City?" she whispered in his ear.

Larry put his arm around Tanya's shoulder. "My wife, Tanya—Sheldon and Clarissa."

Clarissa reached over and held out to Tanya a hand that was cold as ice. "I've been looking forward to meeting you," Clarissa said.

Her look was so direct that Tanya found it unsettling. What was it about her eyes? They were so sad, almost haunted. Tanya noticed how her hands trembled slightly as she swept her thick black hair behind her ear. She was dressed in a scarlet gabardine suit, double-breasted with gold buttons. The blush on her cheeks and red lipstick matched her outfit.

"I've just ordered a bottle of Chateauneuf-du-Pape," Sheldon said. "Will you join us in a toast to a great week?" He was tall and gaunt with a crooked nose and wide grin. *Probably he was once one of those gangly teenagers whose feet are too big for their bodies*, Tanya mused. She liked him immediately.

She said, "Larry told me how exciting the conference was. Congratulations on your presentation. I hear it was a huge success—well accepted by the powers that be." Sheldon beamed like a child at her. She knew Larry and Sheldon's latest technology in angioplasty research had been hailed as a medical breakthrough. It was considerably less invasive than performing open-heart bypass surgery, and was fast becoming the preferred treatment for coronary heart disease where possible.

As the two men became engrossed in reviewing their conference presentation, Clarissa turned to Tanya and said directly, "Sheldon tells me that you worked at the Montreal Psychiatric Institute with Dr. Strachan."

Tanya nodded. "I was there for four years in the early sixties working with Dr. Strachan. Actually, it was 1964 when I left. Dr. Strachan was chief of psychiatry until 1970." She glanced at Larry. He was fully occupied with Sheldon, gesticulating as he explained something to him. Tanya took a sip of her wine and let her gaze rest upon Clarissa, who was nervously toying with her napkin.

"Were you on Ward Five with the Sleep Room?" Clarissa asked.

"Yes, I was the evening head nurse."

"Well, I guess we missed you by a year or so. Mom was there in the mid-sixties—the fall of 1965 to be exact."

Tanya could see where the conversation was heading. Larry was pulling on his right earlobe, a sign that he was becoming restless. Even though he was still engaged in a spirited dialogue with Sheldon, he kept turning toward her.

"Clarissa, why don't you and I meet for lunch next week when we're back in Montreal? I can see we have a lot to discuss," Tanya suggested.

Larry signalled the waiter. "Do you have another bottle of Chateauneuf-du-Pape?"

"Oui, monsieur."

"Oh, and while we're at it, is everyone ready to order?"

They were, and the dinner continued with no further discussion of the institute.

****

Tanya moaned as she looked at the bedside clock. Three o'clock in the morning. She glanced out their window overlooking the courtyard. Snow was swirling around the lampposts. Larry's steady breathing was the only sound in the room. Damn it, she couldn't sleep, no matter how hard she tried. Counting sheep didn't help. When she reached fifty, she gave up. Then she tried her yoga deep breathing for relaxation. Nothing was working. Thoughts were whirling around her mind like the snow outside.

It must have been Clarissa—those melancholy eyes—talking about her mother. It brought back all the old memories—Scott Beauford, Saul, Christy, Sarah. She missed their innocent childishness; their neediness. They had made her feel wanted. And guilty. How many times had she questioned herself? Why had she abandoned them? She tried to convince herself that it was the only thing she could have done. Her anxiety was getting worse; she couldn't sleep and she worried that her judgment wasn't as sharp as it should be. There was no alternative. She had to resign. What she had needed was a complete change, and returning to McGill seemed to be the answer. At least, temporarily.

She looked at Larry's profile by the sliver of light shining in the window. His hair was receding slightly making his forehead appear more pronounced. Over the years, he had gained a few pounds making his cheeks look fuller. His chin jutted forward like a smiling quarter moon. He looked so peaceful.

****

The following day, despite the lack of sleep, Tanya felt surprisingly energetic. She was looking forward to spending time alone with Larry so that they could talk. She always wanted to talk; to discuss their relationship. After touring some art galleries, they found a small restaurant tucked away in an alley where they assuredly would not encounter Larry's colleagues. As they sat sipping their red wine, their eyes met.

"So, tell me about yourself," Larry teased.

"My name is Tanya Kowalski and I *was* a psychiatric nurse. Presently, I'm embarking on a career in journalism. I've been going to school part-time while doing some freelance writing." Tanya laughed. "And what about you, sir?"

"I'm a humble hard-working physician who believes in caring for my patients to the best of my abilities."

"Very honourable, I must say."

"Yes, quite. Seriously, Tanya, you've become quite independent since you started pursuing this journalism of yours."

"It's something I have to do."

"Why?"

"I need to have something meaningful in my life besides you, and that's a career. You know what happened to my mother. She became such a subservient woman to my father because she didn't have a career. Like many women of her generation, she felt trapped."

"I can't ever see you being subservient … even if you didn't have a career."

"What are you getting at, Larry?"

"What's wrong with a traditional life? Having kids; volunteering at the hospital?"

"We've been over this before. I've seen too many unhappy women burdened with kids. Besides you know how much difficulty we've had trying to conceive."

"Yeah. I don't understand it."

Later that evening when Tanya retrieved the Anais Nin book and stepped out of her little black dress revealing her sexy lingerie, Larry lovingly stroked her shoulder. She excused herself for a moment and slipped into the bathroom. Opening her vanity case, she pulled out a round plastic container and popped a birth control pill in her mouth.

****

Tanya waved at Clarissa as she entered the Maritime bar at the Ritz Carlton. The oak-panelled room with its comfortable leather chairs was a great meeting place. She watched Clarissa coming across the room toward her looking as glamorous as the first time they had met. Her hair was pulled back in a tight chignon, emphasizing her high cheekbones, and her long raccoon coat with its upturned collar framed her face.

"Cold enough for you?" Tanya laughed, as Clarissa slipped out of her coat, placing it on the banquette beside them.

"I'll say. Must be about twenty below, and apparently more snow is on the way. Just what we need."

"I've ordered a carafe of red wine to get rid of the chill." Tanya noticed Clarissa's dark brown eyes still had that haunted look.

"Sounds good—I'd love some."

Tanya could feel the tension, as Clarissa shifted in her chair. She thought more small talk might put her at ease. "I'm glad you could make it today. How's everything going so far?"

"Very tiring. I've been trying to arrange an exhibition at my art gallery for the past two weeks. It's a lot of phone calls and running around."

"But that sounds interesting. What kind of exhibition are you having?"

"Contemporary Canadian artists. It's a broad range of painters—Arthur Schilling, Robert Genn, Jack Reid and some young new talent."

"I'm a real Schilling fan," Tanya told her. "When is the show?"

"The opening's in a couple of weeks. How about I send you an invitation?"

"Great—I'd love to come."

Tanya leaned back in her chair. Taking a sip of her wine, she looked directly at Clarissa. She could sense the moment was right. "And ... how is your mother?"

"Not very well. When I visited her last Friday, she didn't recognize me at all." Clarissa twirled the stem of her wineglass. Her hands always seemed to be in motion.

"When we last met, it was difficult to discuss anything with Larry and Sheldon celebrating their success at the conference. Would you like to tell me about her now?"

"It's painful, but I've got to talk about it—especially to someone like you who worked in the Sleep Room with Dr. Strachan." Clarissa hesitated, looking furtively around the room.

"Please go on." Tanya spoke gently.

"I still have nightmares. Mother has been seeing psychiatrists for as long as I can remember, but over the years, she was becoming more withdrawn and isolated. Then about nine years ago, in 1965, she was referred to Dr. Strachan. We were told that if anyone could cure her depression, it would be this world-renowned psychiatrist. She seemed to improve at first, but after six months of Dr. Strachan's medication, electro-shock treatments and reprogramming, she was like a vegetable." Her eyes filled with tears.

"I'm so sorry." Tanya had a sick feeling in her stomach. How many times had she seen this same thing happen?

Clarissa shook her head. "Here was a bright woman reduced to being fed and wearing diapers. She had such a vacant look in her eyes ... " Her voice trailed off.

"Where is she now?"

"Right after Dr. Strachan diagnosed her as a paranoid schizophrenic, he sent her off to the Atwater Psychiatric Hospital. He was so convincing, saying it was the best solution, that we signed the consent form. Now I'm wondering, why the hell would he do that? I've heard horror stories. It seems like such a hopeless institution, where once you're admitted, you don't leave. I've heard that they lock the door and throw away the key." Clarissa shuddered.

"I don't know if it's quite as bad as that. But, yes, it is a chronic-care mental institute where patients diagnosed as incurable are sent. However, I believe there's still hope for some of them."

"Tanya, I need help—I'm desperate to get my mother out of the Atwater."

"I *want* to help," Tanya told her. "Would it be possible to visit her at the hospital? I'm interested in seeing if there is anything that can be done for her."

"I usually visit her every Friday at four o'clock in the afternoon. I could make arrangements for you to come along."

Tanya opened her day journal and glanced at the following week. It was a busy one—meeting with Reva Rothwell on Wednesday and Max Callaghan on Friday.

"How about a week from Friday—March 17th?" Tanya suggested.

"Okay, I'll call the hospital. I know you've seen a lot in your years of psychiatry, but I'm warning you, be prepared."

****

Tanya glanced at her watch: three o'clock. Barely an hour left to sift through the research material before she had to leave. She was sitting at a long rectangular table at the McGill University Library with a stack of medical books spread out in front of her. Leaning over, she reached into her briefcase, took out her day journal and checked it once again: *Wednesday, March 8th, 4:30 p.m. Meeting with Reva Rothwell, Psychiatric Institute, 5th floor.*

This was one appointment she didn't want to miss. Reva was now head nurse on Ward Five. Since her resignation ten years ago, Tanya had seen Reva at miscellaneous psychiatric gatherings and social functions that Larry had no interest in attending even if he hadn't been too busy at the hospital. Lately she hadn't minded, as it freed her to pursue her journalism career.

She turned a few pages of the daily planner. *Friday, March 10th, 4 p.m. Meeting with Max Callaghan, McGill University.* Currently, she was researching a health project for him, and he wanted to hear more about Dr. Strachan's bizarre therapy at the Psychiatric Institute. He was so intrigued that he'd suggested an investigative piece on Strachan. Tanya felt a surge of adrenaline. She worked best when faced with a challenge, and, according to her calendar, there were plenty of those this week.

It was becoming increasingly difficult for her to concentrate, so she started packing up her papers. Maybe a cup of tea at the campus café and a leisurely walk up the hill to the Psychiatric Institute would help her relax. When she arrived at the café, she went directly to the washroom and applied a little lip gloss and bronze blush to her cheeks. She tucked her white blouse into her navy pantsuit and tied her hair back with a gold barrette. Then she checked the mirror one last time before putting her briefcase under her arm. *Et voila`*—a woman on a mission.

****

It was four-twenty when Tanya entered the elevator and pushed the button for the fifth floor. The heavy metal doors moaned as they closed behind her and the elevator stood still. She felt a moment's panic, like being in a prison with the walls closing in. Suddenly, there was a grinding sound and the floor slowly began ascending. She counted the numbers as they lit up over the door : one … two … three … four. It seemed an eternity until Tanya heard the *ting* announcing floor five and the doors laboriously parted.

Stepping off the elevator, she looked at the pale green walls leading up to the double windowless doors of Ward Five. She felt a tightness in her chest as she pushed open the doors and the familiar smell of ammonia and rubbing alcohol permeated her nostrils. It was a smell she could never forget.

The last time she'd been on Ward Five was a decade ago, shortly after that fateful evening of January 13, 1964, when she'd had her final confrontation with Dr. Strachan. It was the night he'd walked off the ward through these same doors.

Right now the nursing station was bustling with activity after the evening report. Tanya didn't recognize the evening nurse or attendants on duty. She identified herself and felt light-headed as she walked along the corridor. Reva's private office was set well back from the nursing station, promising the privacy Tanya had hoped for.

Reva's office door was ajar, so Tanya tapped on it and adjusted her briefcase under her left arm. Inside Reva was sitting at her orderly desk. She raised her head from the telephone receiver and smiled, signalling Tanya to enter.

Tanya was surprised at how much Reva had changed since she'd last seen her at the annual psychiatric nurses' meeting. Her masses of auburn hair were now cropped short and streaked with grey. Although she still had her warm smile and penetrating blue eyes, there was a weariness to her face, and she had little pouches under her eyes. Now in her mid-forties, she had never married. She and a woman named Lydia shared a flat near the institute, and Tanya was one of the few who knew they were more than just roommates. Lydia worked in public health, and Tanya had become quite fond of her.

Reva rose and offered Tanya a seat opposite her desk. "You don't know how delighted I am to see you back here. I'll close the door so we can speak in private."

"I was a little apprehensive after all these years, but now that I'm here, it seems as though I've never left."

"I wish you hadn't. As I told you, some of your old patients are back in therapy and asking about you."

"I'm not too surprised about Scott Beauford and Christy Amherst. Both had major issues.

Are they still getting lithium and electro-shock therapy?"

"No—when Dr. Beaudoin took over, she cut back on both. As a result, the patients are more alert. I think you'd find her therapy quite progressive."

"I'm relieved to hear that," Tanya told her. "What kind of changes has she made?"

"Her approach is more hands-on, mainly getting the patients involved in day-to-day activities. She encourages them to use the common room for meals and socializing. Thursday afternoons we have a social with tea and cards. And she's reinstated the Friday evening dances that Strachan cancelled. It makes the patients feel like they belong to a group."

"That *is* quite a change from Dr. Strachan."

Reva looked at her seriously. "I know how concerned you were with his therapy."

Tanya thought about her suspicions. What was it about Dr. Strachan? The nurses carried out his orders without question, and the patients and their relatives trusted the man implicitly.

"Of course, I was concerned," she said. "Weren't you when you saw how our patients were becoming comatose, unable to feed or dress themselves? We didn't call it the Sleep Room for nothing."

Reva was silent for a moment. "I had my suspicions too. After I saw what he did to Beauford, I knew it wasn't right. And there's something else I think you should know."

"What is that?"

Reva hesitated. "You know how Dr. Strachan had set up his psychiatric therapy in cooperation with McGill?"

"Yes."

"Well, since he left for the States, I've discovered where the funding for his experiments came from."

Tanya turned to her. "What do you mean?"

Reva stood up, walked over to the door and opened it, looking out right and left down the hallway. She then stepped inside, closed it and checked that it was securely locked.

"Apparently, the CIA funded his experiments on our patients. By giving them massive dosages of drugs and electro-shock treatments, he was brainwashing them. Remember the tape recordings under the patients' pillows? Once he reduced them to an infantile state, the recordings would reinforce whatever he wanted to program into them."

Tanya's body went rigid. "Oh, my God. The CIA. Are you sure?"

"Absolutely."

"I've had my suspicions about the man for a long time. But never in a million years would I have thought the CIA was involved."

"Well, it was. And to make matters even worse, he was giving them LSD."

"What? You mean lysergic acid diethylamide?" Tanya was shocked.

"The very one. You know what a psychoactive hallucinogenic it is."

"My god—that's a criminal offence."

Reva leaned across her desk and whispered. "Right. It's been tormenting me for a long time. That's why I was so relieved when you wanted to come in and talk."

Tanya shifted in her chair and cleared her throat. If there was anyone Tanya could trust, it was Reva. She was such a dedicated woman, loyal to her profession and wanting the best for her patients. She truly cared about them. Tanya took a deep breath and pulled her chair closer to the desk.

"What is it? You look positively ashen all of a sudden," Reva said.

"I don't know how to say it, so I might as well get right to the point. I've been discussing the possibility of writing an investigative piece about Strachan with Max Callaghan at *The Gazette*. And I'd like your help."

"What are you saying?"

"Would you be willing to work with us?"

Reva looked surprised. "But Tanya, do you fully understand what you are proposing? If you go public, the institute will have to react to protect its reputation."

"This is about Dr. Strachan and his therapy, not the institute," Tanya reminded her.

"Yes, but it's impossible to separate the two. Strachan's work was done in connection with this hospital."

"Technically it was. But, you just told me the funding came from the CIA. I think this is what the public has to know. It was Strachan and his mentors at the CIA. The institute was conned like everyone else—the patients, their families, the staff."

"I understand this, but I have to consider my reputation and position at the institute."

"I'm well aware of that. And I honestly believe we can protect you if you are willing to help us," Tanya said.

"My god. Let me think about this. Right now I'm overwhelmed. And Tanya, please remember—if we meet again, it can't be here."

****

Max Callaghan's office was at the north end of a long corridor leading to the English department. Like the Psychiatric Institute, the old limestone buildings of

McGill were imposing. But on a blustery, 25-below-zero afternoon, the wind whistled through the small glass-paned windows. It was one of the coldest winters on record.

Max hung up the phone and reached for a cigarette, his fifth in the past hour. He knew he had the rumpled appearance of a reporter working around the clock—two days growth of beard, clothes that looked like he'd slept in them, and a furrowed brow. His metal-framed glasses were perched halfway down his nose.

How many times had he promised himself that this would be the day he'd quit smoking, but something always came up. It was the stress of the job—always a deadline. And if that wasn't enough, he'd have the medical field up his ass if he made one minute error. What a demanding bunch. Always so secretive about their work, it was like pulling teeth trying to get information out of them.

He had only himself to blame. Hadn't his father wanted him to study law at McGill, just like him? As a matter of fact, for as long as he could remember, his father was always emphatic about what was best for him: the right schools, the right sports; the right social activities—the list went on. That was the toughest part, being the eldest son. The demands were incredible.

By the time he was twelve, he was sneaking a shot of rye whisky from his father's liquor cabinet. It made him feel good, and eased the pressure somewhat. He'd top the rye in the bottle with water so his father wouldn't notice any missing.

And when you thought about it, he hadn't turned out that badly. Sure, he'd had a little trouble with his grades in high school, but some of the courses and teachers were utterly stupid. But Max always knew he had to get away from his father. When he'd informed him of his interest in studying English and history, his father barked, "Why the hell would you do that? Why don't you study something practical?" Max forever had been trying to prove himself, but he knew he was a disappointment. It was a no-win situation—so Max went his own way.

If only his mother had lived, there might have been a modicum of hope of reconciliation with his father. However, as his younger brother, Daniel, was now a successful criminal lawyer, hope was receding rapidly. Max always knew that Daniel was the favourite, the one who could do no wrong.

Now, some two decades later, here he was ensconced at McGill and *The Gazette*, working twelve-hour days. It wasn't that he couldn't ease up a little. He was caught up in the tough journalism life that had cost him a couple of marriages and a near alcoholic addiction.

What he needed was a new challenge, and if things went okay, Tanya Kowalski and her experiences at the Psychiatric Institute might be the ticket. She was sharp and eager with youth on her side. It was four o'clock, and Tanya had arrived for her appointment right on the dot.

He watched her as she shifted in her chair, crossing her right leg over her left. She was dressed in black leather pants and a red silk blouse open at the neck. His office was chilly so he didn't blame her for keeping her military jacket draped over her shoulders.

"What is it you found out from Reva that you couldn't tell me over the phone?" he asked her.

Tanya stood up, shut the door and turned to look directly at him. "Take a wild guess where the funding for Dr. Strachan's Sleep Room therapy came from."

"You've got me. The FBI?" Max joked, lighting a cigarette.

"Not quite—try the CIA."

"What? You're not serious?

"Yes, I am," Tanya told him.

"Holy shit. This could make it one hell of a big international story."

"And that's not all." Tanya emphasized each word.

"Don't keep me in suspense, Tanya. Spit it out."

"Well I told you about all the drugs, the electro-shock and the brainwashing. But apparently Strachan was also giving them LSD."

"Good God—this is absolute dynamite. How did Reva ever find out?" Tanya watched him as he reached over and lit another cigarette.

"I'm not sure. She wouldn't discuss it in her office."

Max noticed Tanya hesitating, as she glanced at some notes. "What's your take? Think she can back it up with evidence?" Max adjusted his glasses.

"Well, she's my only hope. But she told me all the old records are locked up in the basement vault. So I'm not sure I'll be able to get as much proof as I'd like."

"Have you spoken to her since your visit to the institute?"

"Once briefly on the phone. We're meeting next week at her apartment. She wants to talk, but *not* at the institute."

"Step number one is to convince her that we'll do our utmost to protect her if she can provide us with any documents to support this. Of course, there are no guarantees." Max inhaled deeply.

"That may not be as easy as you think."

"You mentioned what a devoted nurse she is. Surely she's as anxious as you are to nail that bastard Strachan for what he did to her patients." A blue cloud of smoke swirled through the air.

"Yes, she is. But she's worried about the institute finding out about her involvement. Her reputation, her career, would be at stake."

"It may not be an easy sell, but see what you can do, particularly about the CIA/LSD aspect. What have you come up with so far?" he asked her.

"I've done a rough draft. I'd like to start out with some patients who spent time in Dr. Strachan's Sleep Room. Two in particular who have been in and out of the institute for the past decade: Scott Beauford and Christy Amherst. Both have gone through all the drugs, LSD, electro-shock treatment and reprogramming and are now patients again."

"Sounds good. Lean heavily on the LSD. It's mind-boggling—no pun intended. What about the woman whose mother was a patient of Strachan's?"

"You mean Clarissa Schmedeck? I had lunch with her last week. She's devastated. Her mother has been diagnosed as a paranoid schizophrenic and is now residing at the Atwater Psychiatric Hospital—Dr. Strachan's dumpster for patients he gets tired of."

"Do you think you'll be able to visit her; get an inside story?"

"Clarissa is anxious for me to see what our 'good doctor' has done to her." Tanya paused and went on.

"You know, Max, every time I hear about another patient destroyed by Strachan, it tears my heart out. I've got to do something. The son of a bitch has to be exposed."

Max looked at Tanya. "I like your grit. I know you'll do a good job on this piece. But is it worth it for you?"

"No doubts whatsoever. I'm willing to take my chances."

Max peered over his spectacles. "Good stuff. I'd like to find out how the hell Strachan and the CIA got together. Give me a call as soon as you've talked to Reva."

****

When Tanya arrived at Café Les Halles Friday evening, the waiter ushered her to a table at the far corner of the restaurant. Larry was staring out the window with his chin resting on his palm. He looked up as she approached and smiled wanly. Tanya leaned over and kissed him on his cheek.

"Sorry I'm late. I was at the library and lost track of the time."

It wasn't an outright lie. She *had* been at the library earlier in the day. But she wasn't eager to tell Larry about her meetings with Reva or, particularly, Max. She'd have to ease into it. Maybe after he'd had a drink or two.

"I just arrived five minutes ago myself," he said.

She followed his gaze back to the window. Young lovers and dapper men with beautiful women strolled by. They watched as a street urchin ran up to a middle-aged man and slyly extended his hand. When the man reached into his pocket and unfolded a dollar bill, the boy beamed. His front tooth was missing. Tanya laughed and turned back to Larry.

She reached over, placing her hand on his. "You seem preoccupied. Is anything bothering you?"

"Nothing out of the ordinary—I'm just exhausted."

He had dark circles under his eyes and the lines on his forehead were more pronounced. She was well aware of the pressure he was under at the hospital. Since the latest cutbacks, his cardiac team hadn't been able to hire the staff it needed, and the long hours were taking their toll. At least he'd told her that much. Larry was becoming more withdrawn. When he wasn't working, he'd fall asleep after dinner in his La-Z-Boy in front of the television.

"Want to talk about it?" If *he* didn't, she did. Try to fix it. Years of psychiatry had done that to her. She loathed unresolved issues. When she put her mind to something, she couldn't let go. Like her determination to study journalism at McGill after she had left the Psychiatric Institute. Larry jokingly referred to her as "a dog with a bone."

She recalled how he'd looked at her dubiously. "Are you sure you want to make that commitment?"

She had, even though it had taken years. Now she was sitting across the table from him, having completed her journalism degree and asking him if he wanted to talk. She was proud of her accomplishment. There was so much to do in life rather than volunteer at the hospital like so many other doctors' wives.

"What's there to talk about?" he said. "It's a case of work overload. Everyone on the ward is working to maximum capacity." He placed his hand over his mouth stifling a yawn.

"I don't want it to affect your health."

"Don't worry. I'll be okay."

"Are you sure?" Tanya's eyes met his.

"How about a Canadian Club on the rocks? I need a stiff drink to relax.".

"You go ahead. I think I'll just have a soda water with lemon. My stomach is a little upset. Must have been something I ate at lunch."

"Oh, I forgot to ask. How was your lunch with Clarissa?"

More evidence of his long working hours and their lack of communication. Her luncheon with Clarissa had been over a week ago.

"Disturbing. She's so preoccupied with her mother, it's affecting her work."

When Tanya told him about their agreement to visit the Atwater, his eyes widened and he took a gulp of his drink. "I don't get it. It's been ten years since you left the profession. Why would you want to get involved again?"

"Clarissa has brought back all the memories—the injustice of Strachan and his Sleep Room."

Larry let out a long sigh. "Tanya, I don't want to see you so stressed out again. Remember how you felt on Ward Five?"

"How could I forget?"

"Do you really think you should pursue this Clarissa/ Dr. Strachan matter?"

"Absolutely."

"But the man has moved on. I hear he's in Washington."

"You're right. Apparently, he's a psychiatric consultant to the CIA," Tanya said.

"Well, then, I'd say he's in the big leagues now, wouldn't you?"

"Sure, he is. All the more reason to pursue it. He's ruined a lot of lives." She was beginning to feel agitated. "Why do you become so tense when I mention Strachan? Don't you remember telling me that all those drugs could trigger a heart attack?"

"That was a long time ago. He's gone now. Things have changed."

"I'll say they have. Ever since you completed your residency, I've noticed a real change."

"Like what?"

"You've become more conservative," she told him.

"What do you mean?"

"You used to question everything in medical school. Now you seem to go along with the status quo."

"Come on, Tanya—you know it's the nature of the profession. Hospitals breed caution. Any changes have to be thoroughly analyzed. It could be a matter of life and death."

Tanya looked down at her hands. "Yes, a matter of life and death."

"And darling, I have another question."

"What?"

"Do you honestly feel you are qualified to question the methods of a world-renowned psychiatrist?"

She was quiet for a moment and stared at him. Larry seemed to believe that he'd risen to a higher status than her. It was the antiquated doctor–nurse hierarchy. He adamantly defended the profession, and the most hurtful part was that he included Dr. Strachan.

"Yes, I do." Tanya picked up the menu, pretending to read it.

"Is your stomach feeling better?"

"Not really. But I think I'll have that drink now."

****

As they were driving home along Côte-des-Neiges, Larry shifted gears and accelerated as the black Mercedes ascended Mount Royal. Tanya leaned back and inhaled the rich aroma of the tanned leather seats. Beethoven's *Moonlight Sonata* was playing on the car radio. She reached over and turned the volume down.

"Well, I guess while we're at it, I should tell you that I met with Reva Rothwell at the institute. She's now head nurse on Ward Five."

"Whatever for? You're not planning on going back to work there, are you?"

"No. But, as you know, we've kept in touch since I left. Apparently, some of my patients are back on the ward. Remember Scott Beauford, the one from Georgia?"

"The one who was 'involved' with his mother? How's he doing?"

"Not well. Over the past five years, he's been in and out of the hospital. Now that Strachan is gone, I'm hoping to do something for him."

"How would you do that?"

"I spoke to Max Callaghan the other day about a possible investigative piece on Strachan. He was quite intrigued."

"You're not serious?" Larry's mouth hung open as he looked over at her.

"Larry, you really are becoming more right-wing every day."

"Or you're becoming more left-leaning. Journalism tends to have that effect."

"Touché."

"I asked you, are you serious?"

"Yes, I am. Max was fascinated to hear about my work at the Psychiatric Institute and my concerns with Strachan and his Sleep Room therapy."

"You told him about your concerns? Why?"

"I'm trying to unravel what Strachan did to the patients. Why he prescribed all the drugs, the shock treatments … the reprogramming."

"Are you saying that you want to work with Callaghan—do an exposé? I admit he writes well on health issues, but I don't think he needs to question any of our cardiac techniques. His job is to report, not pass judgment. Why not let it lie? I'll tell you, Tanya, you could ruffle a lot of feathers if you pursue this. I don't trust journalists."

"Oh really? What about me?"

"You're different. Of course I trust you."

Tanya put her fingers to her temples, massaging gently to relieve the pressure. "You heard what Sheldon Schmedeck said about Clarissa's poor mother. The woman is almost catatonic. Her life is pretty well over."

"I'm sorry this has happened to them."

"But she's not the only one. Think about the others."

Larry gripped the steering wheel. "Have you thought about how this might reflect on me at the hospital?"

"I don't think you'd be implicated in this at all. It's me, not you, who'd be involved."

"I don't know about that. Besides, things could become very unpleasant for you if this goes public," Larry warned her.

"Why is that?"

"There are a lot of people who think the man is a saint. And the institute will have to defend itself. If this happens, they'll try to destroy your credibility."

"I don't think so," Tanya said.

"Think about it, will you?"

Tanya glanced over at him. "I've thought about it for some time. And I've decided I'll take my chances. I promise, I'll do everything in my power to make sure you aren't implicated."

"How can you be sure?" Larry asked cautiously.

"I'm going through with this, Larry. And I hope I can count on you." She felt a lump in her throat.

****

Reva Rothwell climbed the wrought-iron stairway to her flat on Durocher Street. It was a one-bedroom walkup in a row of old buildings near the Psychiatric Institute. She hadn't felt so edgy in a long time. It was almost seven o'clock in the evening, and Tanya would be arriving in half an hour. Reva fumbled with her keys, then unlocked the door and glanced around the room. What a mess. Magazines and newspapers piled high beside the fireplace and a thick coat of dust on the radiator covers. She gathered some newspapers, lit a fire and placed the remaining papers in the hall closet. Then she ran a flannel cloth over the furniture. Any time she raced around in a cleaning frenzy, she checked herself. Shades of her mother, a compulsive cleaner, owner of a spotless house, who had lived by the principle that "cleanliness is godliness."

Reva glanced in the mirror above the stove and ran her fingers through her grey-streaked hair. She winced at the crow's feet around her eyes, which were bloodshot after the late nights she'd been keeping. Her skin had a pallor to it that made her look older than her 46 years.

Reva had always known that she was different. No matter where she was, she felt alone. Being an only child didn't make it any easier. Her mother, an outgoing, frivolous woman, was constantly urging her to make friends, to be popular and pretty. "Why don't you phone Betty and invite her over for supper? She's such a nice, pretty girl," she'd say. But no matter how hard Reva tried, it didn't work. Instead she retreated into her books and mystical drawings of ghosts and goblins. As her father travelled across the continent trying to make a living selling gadgets, she grew up barely knowing him. Hers was a woman's world.

Reva didn't know exactly when it started, but some time in junior high, she began to feel a strong attraction to young women. She denied it for years until she met Lydia, a perky, take-charge university student who had formed a small women's rights organization. For the first time in her life, Reva felt comfortable being with another person.

Throughout her psychiatric training she had observed some bizarre behavioural patterns in people. It's what had drawn her to the profession. It was comforting to know she wasn't alone in her feelings of alienation. Certainly, she felt guilt, but she could finally admit to herself that she was a lesbian. She loved Lydia. To the outside world, she and Lydia were simply roommates, but to each other, they were lovers.

By the time the doorbell rang, Reva had composed herself. She was well aware of the reason for this meeting with Tanya and simply had to confront it directly.

****

As soon as Tanya was inside, Reva asked her, "Can I get you a drink? Coffee, tea … or would you like something a little stronger?"

"I'd love some vin rouge, if it's on offer. I could use something to get the blood flowing again. This weather is unrelenting. It's been almost two weeks now."

"Why don't you pull up a chair by the fire and wrap the afghan around you?"

Tanya stood in front of the fire, rubbing her hands together. The crimson walls in the small living room were adorned with several framed Inuit prints, including one above the fireplace. Two large candles flickered on either side of the mantelpiece. A navy blue sofa with a Mexican blanket draped over its back separated the living and dining areas. In front of the sofa was a pine blanket box cluttered with magazines and books.

"I love your apartment. It's so cozy," Tanya said as Reva returned with a pitcher of wine.

"That's a gentler way of saying how tiny it is," Reva laughed as she handed Tanya her wineglass. She sat down on the sofa beside Tanya and put her feet up on the blanket box.

"Is Lydia working this evening?"

"Yes, she's on evenings this week, but fortunately has the long weekend off. We're heading up to Saint Sauveur early Saturday. What are you and Larry up to?"

"Not much. He's been so busy at the hospital lately he just wants to take it easy. I'm afraid he's been pretty stressed out since we went to Quebec City," Tanya told her.

"How's he feeling about you pursuing the Strachan story?"

"That's a touchy subject. We talked it over last week. He knows that I'm going through with it, but is fussing about the consequences."

"Is he worried about you or himself?" Reva asked.

"Both, I suppose." Tanya took a sip of her drink. "Now that Max Callaghan is involved, Larry's worried about fallout that might affect his reputation at the hospital. And he's still finding it difficult to understand why I want to go out on a limb. He questions it going public. Says my credibility could be destroyed. Let's just say that I have to handle it delicately."

"Tanya, do you think you *are* doing the right thing?"

"Absolutely." She looked Reva directly in the eye. "But I need your help."

"Well, you know what I've said. My biggest concern is being found out as an accomplice. You have to understand, I could lose my job. My reputation is at risk."

"You know I'd never do anything to harm you or your reputation. I promise none of this will go beyond us. Journalists aren't compelled to reveal their sources. And as for Larry, he would never say anything."

"Even though he doesn't want you to go through with this?"

"Hopefully, he'll come around. But one thing is guaranteed: you can trust him. He'd never discredit you, let alone me. I know him too well."

"I just need your commitment to protect me from any exposure."

"Well, you have it."

"Tanya, you know I want to see that monster Strachan brought to justice. I'm afraid of what he's capable of, but I hate the man. We can't let him get away with this." She rested her head on the back of the sofa and stared at the fire.

"I agree."

"It's all the recollections. I can't get them out of my mind—the Sleep Room, the basement laboratory, the electro-shock treatments." Reva's voice quavered. "And the helpless patients crying out, the sodium amytal injections, the LSD and then the vacant look in their eyes. They became catatonic."

"I know," Tanya whispered.

"It's good to have you here. To talk about it to someone who understands—who has been through it too." Reva reached for the pitcher on the blanket box and refilled their wineglasses.

"But you're incredible! How on earth did you ever find out about the CIA?"

Reva was silent for a moment. Taking a deep breath, she appeared to regain her composure as she explained how Dr. Strachan had missed a folder when he was packing up his confidential files to take to his new job in Washington. Somehow this *Private and Confidential* file got mixed up with the other ones he'd instructed his secretary to take to the basement vault. As it turned out, his secretary left for a new job before carrying out the order. Strachan had no alternative but to turn the work over to Reva.

Tanya shivered. "What happened?"

"Well, it was either my curiosity or suspicions that got the better of me. I opened the file and there, in black and white, was his correspondence with the CIA—confirming the CIA funding for his experiments of drug-induced sleep therapy, LSD, brainwashing and reprogramming."

"Oh my god. What did you do with the file?"

"Hid it. Right in the middle of the other files in the basement vault. I thought it might come in handy one of these years. You never know." She smiled slyly.

"Just think—if that arrogant son-of-a-bitch Strachan had done his own dirty work, we would never have known." Tanya lifted her glass.

****

Tanya identified herself at the Ward C nursing station and walked down the long corridor of the Atwater Psychiatric Hospital. She'd been to the Atwater only once before. That was about ten years ago, when Dr. Strachan had transferred poor old Saul Rosenfeld who'd started hearing voices threatening to kill him.

"He's a paranoid schizophrenic. The Montreal Psychiatric Institute can do nothing further for him," Dr. Strachan had said as he wrote the transfer order.

The melancholy ward with its pale green walls, tired beige curtains and antiseptic smell brought back memories of the Sleep Room. What was it about psychiatric hospitals? On one hand they were intriguing, dealing with the delicate human psyche. On the other, they were dark forbidding places where people were sent to be locked away forever or moulded into something acceptable to society. Like Play-Doh. She remembered shaping and reshaping her farm animals on the play table in her room. Pulling and stretching the red pliable dough, she'd change a bulky donkey into a beautiful, chestnut racehorse with an aquiline nose, long, slender legs and flowing tail. With a twist and turn she could change almost anything. It was magical. Too bad people couldn't be changed as easily.

Clarissa had arranged to meet Tanya in the lounge on the south side of Ward C at four o'clock. Tanya checked her watch. *A few minutes to relax.* She heard a cackling sound as she entered the lounge. A bored orderly slouched in an armchair, looked up at her and nodded.

Two patients dressed in green hospital robes sat in front of the television, laughing and pointing. Tanya smiled. It was the "I Love Lucy" show, with Desi and Lucy squabbling over the price of a new dress Lucy had bought. She thought about Christy Amherst. It was her favourite show. Wouldn't she love to be watching?

There was barely time for Tanya to flip through *TIME* magazine before Clarissa rounded the corner. Her raccoon coat was draped over her shoulders and the crimson cloche on her head matched her lipstick and nail polish. *What a glamour puss, always looking so sleek.* Clarissa was such a contrast to the dreary patients and hospital.

"Sorry, I'm late. I got caught on the phone with one of the artists in the exhibition," she said, looking uncomfortably around the room.

"It's okay. Just got here myself."

"I called the hospital to prepare Mom for our visit. They're so short staffed, I hope they were able to get her up in a chair." Clarissa pursed her lips.

As they entered the large open ward, the familiar smell of rubbing alcohol and antiseptic hung in the air. Tanya heard the whimpers, shouts and curses from the patients. Grey curtains drawn alongside each bed divided the ward and provided some privacy. Patients strapped into their chairs stared at them vacantly.

"Mommy, mommy, please take me home," an elderly woman cried out.

"Go to hell," shouted a white-bearded man from his bed. A nurse walking arm-in-arm with an old shuffling man turned and acknowledged them as they strolled through the ward.

Clarissa's mother was in a separate room with three other patients at the far end of the ward. Clarissa knocked on the door and turned right. Lying on the bed, Tanya saw a tiny, silver-haired woman propped up on two pillows with the head of the bed elevated. The pallor of her deeply lined face made her look like she had been carved out of ivory. She was dressed in a pale blue bed jacket over her hospital nightgown. The metal railings on either side of her bed were pulled up to keep her from falling out. Even with all her years of psychiatric nursing, Tanya was shocked at the frailty and ghostlike appearance of Clarissa's mother.

"Damn them," Clarissa muttered. "Couldn't even get her in a chair for our visit." She leaned over the railing, kissed her mother's cheek and turned back to Tanya. "Wet and salty—she's been crying again," she whispered.

"Poor woman."

"Mom, I'd like you to meet a friend. Tanya, this is my mother, Mrs. Smythe."

Tanya reached over and gently touched Mrs. Smythe's frail hand. "I've been looking forward to meeting you. How are you?"

Mrs. Smythe looked vacantly at Tanya. Her grey eyes had the same sadness as Clarissa's. Her lips quivered as she tried to speak.

Tanya stroked her forehead. "Is there anything I can get you? I think Clarissa has told you that I'm a nurse. I'd like to help you get better."

Mrs. Smythe's eyes widened and filled with tears.

"I worked with Dr. Strachan on Ward Five."

"No … not Dr … Strachan," Mrs. Smythe cried.

Standing on the other side of the bed, Clarissa reached over and touched her mother's hand. "It's okay, Mom— Dr. Strachan isn't here. He's moved to the States."

Mrs. Smythe closed her eyes and squeezed both Clarissa's and Tanya's fingers.

"Would you like to sit in your chair? We can help you get out of bed," Tanya said.

"I like to walk. Need slippers," Mrs. Smythe said. She then lifted her hand and pointed to a glass of juice with a bent straw on her bedside. Her lips were parched.

"Would you like a drink, Mom?"

"Thirsty …"

Clarissa wiped her eyes with her handkerchief and held the straw to her mother's lips. "Okay, let's get your slippers and dressing gown so we can walk to the lounge. Would you like that, Mom?"

"Yes … I like to walk."

As she helped Clarissa's mother out of bed, Tanya noticed how thin her legs were. Her knees buckled slightly as she tried to stand. Clarissa and Tanya took their places on either side of her, putting their arms through hers to steady her.

"You're doing really well, Mrs. Smythe," Tanya told her.

"I like to walk."

Clarissa smiled and dabbed at her eyes with a handkerchief. "I know you do, Mom. You are a good walker, always have been. You'll be dancing in no time."

My god. What the hell have they done to this woman? No doubt at one time she'd been a beautiful, vibrant person. Probably like Clarissa.

Arm in arm, the three of them walked slowly through the open ward.

****

Tanya could see how shaken Clarissa was by their visit to Atwater and offered her a lift home. Her perfectly made-up face was slightly flawed with tiny smudges of mascara under her bloodshot eyes.

"Thanks, but I have to get back to the gallery," Clarissa responded absentmindedly. "But if you're going along Sherbrooke, maybe you could drop me off … on second thought, why don't you come in for awhile, if you have time? I'd like to talk."

Snow was lightly falling as Tanya shifted into third gear and manoeuvred her Peugeot up Atwater Avenue, dogging in and out of the rush hour traffic. Clarissa was slouched in silence in the passenger seat, and Tanya's inner sense told her to let her be. She reached over and turned up the volume on the radio. Peggy Lee was singing "Cry Me a River." Tanya tapped the wheel in time to the music. *Haven't most of us cried a river over someone or other*, she mused. Twenty minutes later, Tanya turned right onto Sherbrooke and parked in an alley about a block from the art gallery.

As she entered the handsome limestone building, Tanya glanced at the bold Ojibwa painting on the right wall. A native woman cloaked in a scarlet, blue and violet robe stared out at her with penetrating, black eyes. The cascading colours flowed into the background of the canvas creating a rippling effect. It was dynamic.

Tanya took a closer look. "Is that an Arthur Schilling?"

Clarissa collected herself. "Yes. I think it's one of his best. He painted it in the mid-sixties, just before he turned to the bottle."

"What talent. How old was he when he died?"

"Only 44. But he'd been abusing his body for quite a while. I suppose he was trying to get rid of his demons … like most of us."

Tanya scanned the eclectic mix of contemporary paintings around the gallery. In the centre of the lofty open space, sculptures of falcons, peacocks and nightingales perched proudly on ivory marble pedestals. Green ferns surrounded the carvings, towering over the miniature rock garden with a waterfall.

"What a great exhibition, Clarissa. It's like stepping into a forest."

"Thanks. It's been an exhausting two months. Hope you can make the opening next Thursday."

"Wouldn't miss it."

Clarrisa's office at the north end of the gallery was as smartly decorated as she was. A mahogany desk with a brass lamp was set against the crimson wall. Over the desk was an Algonquin Park landscape by Group of Seven painter Tom Thomson. Neatly stacked papers on the desk were placed on either side of three gold-framed photographs. Two Quebec pine rocking chairs with quilted cushions faced the desk on either side of the door.

"Have a seat," Clarissa motioned toward one of the chairs. "What can I get you?" She opened the doors of a pine hutch revealing a minibar and small refrigerator.

"That's quite a stock you have," Tanya laughed. "I'd love a glass of white wine."

Clarissa's hands trembled as she poured the wine. She was an enigma. An attractive, chic urban woman who at this moment looked like she would crumble. She had turned into a fragile bird like her mother. Clarissa pulled up the other pine rocking chair to face Tanya.

"Here's to Mother." She raised her glass and took a sip. "What did you think?"

"I think she's a wounded woman who desperately wants to get better. You heard how she repeatedly told us, 'I want to walk.'"

"Mom was not only a great walker, she loved to dance. She was a beauty in her time."

"That's not hard to see. Tell me about her psychiatric history." But then Tanya hesitated. Was she sounding too much like a psychiatric nurse, asking too many questions and impatient for the answers?

"What I gathered from family stories is that my mother was an extremely sensitive child. She loved to perform, setting up stages in the garage for her plays and dances. She'd charge a nickel admission for anyone willing to pay."

"Sounds like a budding artistic entrepreneur."

Clarissa laughed. "Well, her older brother and sisters thought she was crazy. My grandmother thought she was great, but my grandpa had little time for her. He was preoccupied with making a decent living for the family.

Any spare time he had, he'd spend at the Blue Bonnets racetrack betting on the horses."

"Would he ever take her along?"

"No. He'd always go with his cronies. Some of them spent half their lifetimes at the track."

Tanya could see it unfolding. A creative child, ignored by her father, frustrated and unable to express herself to her family—a formula for depression.

"Whenever my grandmother tried to support her, she was overruled by my grandfather. And being so different from her four siblings made Mom feel more isolated. Even though her mother tried to draw her out in sports and mixing with other children, it was hopeless. She wasn't interested."

A photograph on the desk caught Tanya's attention. "Is that your mother?"

"Yes. Before she had her first breakdown."

"You look alike, especially the eyes." Tanya held the photo in her hands and examined the high cheekbones, the dark hair pulled back and the sad eyes. Mrs. Smythe appeared to be in her mid-thirties and had the lean body of a dancer. But when she asked Clarissa about it, she said no.

"She took some modern ballet courses, but never followed through. Instead her father sent her to the Mother House secretarial school where she could learn something 'useful.'"

Clarissa sneered and reached for the bottle of wine.

"She must have been so frustrated."

"That's putting it mildly. Shortly after graduating from the secretarial school, she met my father. Dad was infatuated with her. He was a self-confident, outgoing young intern, studying to become a plastic surgeon. I think she saw him as a substitute for her father. He seemed so attentive and loving. She didn't know he just wanted a possession."

"Just what she needed when she was trying to assert herself," Tanya commented.

"Right. To make a long story short, my dad was a great person, but not the right one for her. She needed someone who would bring her out, not control her. In a lot of ways, he was like her father: good provider, but controlling."

"I can see it happening," Tanya said. "I've had so many intelligent women of her generation as psychiatric patients, trying to break out and find something worthwhile."

"Mom was 48 when she first suffered depression and anxiety attacks and started seeing a psychiatrist. She'd been on antidepressants for years. I was fifteen and all I remember was how much I missed her at school when all the other mothers attended concerts and plays. I had the lead role in *My Fair Lady* one year, but Mom couldn't make it. She was too sick."

"You must have made a dazzling fair lady." Tanya could visualize a youthful Clarissa delighting the audience with Eliza Doolittle's "I Could Have Danced All Night."

"I don't know if I'd go that far." Clarissa laughed, then opened her silver cigarette case and offered Tanya one.

"Thank you." When Tanya leaned forward to accept a light, she noticed Clarissa's hand shaking as she flicked the lighter. "Are you okay?"

"I'll be fine. It's always the same after I've been to see her at the Atwater."

"What about the Montreal Psychiatric Institute? When did you say your mother was there?"

"Nineteen sixty-five. She was 63 years old and had been slipping deeper into depression. Dad had passed away unexpectedly of a heart attack two years earlier. She cried constantly. Fortunately, my aunt who'd never married was staying with her, but after a while it got to be too much."

"I guess we just missed each other. I left Ward Five the spring of '64. Where were you at the time?" Tanya asked.

Clarissa stood up and walked to the window overlooking the courtyard. She slowly unlatched the handle and pushed it open, letting the smoke in the room dissipate. Taking another drag on her cigarette, she turned around to face Tanya.

"In residence at Skidmore College in Saratoga Springs, New York, studying fine arts. It was tough being away, but I phoned and visited as often as possible."

Tanya watched Clarissa gracefully cross the room and waited until she was seated at her desk once again.

"Was she under Dr. Strachan's care from the beginning?"

"Yes, he was supposedly the great saviour. After all, he was world renowned in psychiatry."

"You're right. At the institute, he was treated like a god."

"Mom was so vulnerable. I think Dr. Strachan looked upon her as a challenge. First he increased her medication, and when that didn't seem to be working, he started electro-shock treatments, sometimes twice a day."

"So, it wasn't long after her admission that Dr. Strachan thought she was a good candidate for his sleep therapy?"

"Right." Clarissa clenched her jaw. "Within a month I barely recognized her. She slept most of the day; had to be fed and changed and whimpered like a baby. How could any one do that to a human being?"

Tanya's penetrating gaze met Clarissa's. "We've got to find out."

****

Driving away from the gallery, Tanya knew what she was going to do. She turned off Sherbrooke heading toward Westmount mountain. As she shifted into second gear, her Peugeot groaned as it began the ascent. She turned on the radio—Vivaldi's *Gloria*—the perfect music to accompany her drive home. It was so relaxing.

Tanya lit a cigarette and turned up the volume. She had promised herself once again that she would quit, but any time she felt stressed, she would reach into the glove compartment where she'd hidden her Du Mauriers. The first drag gave her a buzz, which seemed to calm her.

The visit to the Atwater Psychiatric Hospital had shaken her more than she wanted to admit. Perhaps after being away from psychiatry for all those years, she'd forgotten how tortured the patients were. But how could she forget? It was seeing Clarissa's mother with her haunted look, so desperate to walk. And afterwards, at Clarissa's gallery, the sadness of a daughter's love for her sick mother. It was such an uphill battle—the battle of the mind.

Night was falling as Tanya circled up her driveway. The large Tudor house was in darkness except for a light in the main hallway. Once again Larry must be working late at the hospital. *Damn it—he can't even get off early on Friday.* Ever since he and Sheldon had presented their research at the Quebec conference, they'd been inundated with requests from colleagues around the world. He was forever promising that things would settle down once they hired more staff. But it wasn't happening quickly enough.

Tanya unlocked the door and turned off the security system. A weariness engulfed her as she slid out of her pumps and poured herself a gin and tonic. Then she started sorting through the day's mail. One envelope caught her attention: it was addressed to her and marked personal and confidential. She recognized the handwriting:

Dear Tanya:

After much thought and consideration, I have decided to pursue what you and I have been discussing. I've tried to search for the answers to so many unanswered questions regarding happenings at the Institute. Now that our learned physician has moved south of the border, I feel it is in the best interest of my patients to find out the truth. What was really going on during his reign should be uncovered. There have been too many poor lost souls. Please call me at my apartment early next week during the evening so we can discuss another meeting. I would like to

*be brought up-to-date on your meetings with Clarissa
and her mother.*

*Sincerely,
Reva*

After reading the letter, Tanya rested her head on
the back of the sofa and closed her eyes. It had been an
exhausting day. She was more determined than ever to
pursue the Dr. Strachan exposé with Max Callaghan. The
turning point was the Atwater Psychiatric Hospital. All one
had to do was look at Clarissa's mother, Mrs. Smythe. A
prime example of what Strachan had done to his patients.
Even though Sally Smythe had been depressed before
her admission to the Montreal Psychiatric Institute, she
could still function in society. After Dr. Strachan's sleep
treatment, she was incapable of participating in day-to-
day life. And what about old Saul? To be admitted to the
chronic care Atwater hospital as a schizophrenic was
like a life sentence. What Strachan had done was almost
criminal.

Tanya heard the front door open. "Anyone home?"
Larry called out.

"In the living room." Putting her feet up on the pine
coffee table in front of the loveseat, she thought how great
the Arthur Schilling painting in Clarissa's gallery would
look over the fireplace. The time had come to replace the
tired-looking Jack Reid print. What the room needed was
more colour, and the Ojibwa woman's scarlet robe would
look outstanding against the ivory wall. Might even add
some zest to their lives.

Larry approached with two gin and tonics in his hands. "Here's to an evening off," he smiled, handing Tanya her drink. "Oh, I see you've already helped yourself."

"Cheers." Tanya clinked glasses as he nestled on the sofa beside her.

"Sorry, I'm late—I've been trying to get away since five."

"As long as I know you're trying." Tanya sipped her drink. She was beginning to feel mellow. It was good having him home, especially after she'd had a stressful day. He looked great. His curly hair, greying at the temples, made him appear distinguished. He was wearing a blue button-down shirt open at the neck, and her favourite sports jacket—a tawny tweed with leather patches on the elbows.

"How did your day go?" Tanya asked.

"Busy. Some colleagues were in from Boston." Larry rattled on enthusiastically about meetings, rounds with Sheldon Schmedeck and the latest cardiac equipment, but Tanya only half-listened. Lately, she'd become less interested in his work. Maybe it was jealousy. He was spending more and more time at the hospital. Even though she was pursuing her journalism career, it felt lonely to come home to an empty house every evening.

Perhaps she should have reconsidered her decision to put off having children and not kept taking the pill. Then there was the abortion she'd had years ago. She could never tell Larry about it as he just didn't understand that she wanted to establish her career before having his child. Now what she needed was something to fill the gap. Perhaps this was the real reason she was so fiercely pursuing Dr. Strachan.

She glanced around the room. What was the point of having this beautiful house if it wasn't lived in? She knew other doctors' wives who had gone through the same thing. Some had even ended up as patients at the Psychiatric Institute. Was her fate to be the same? God only knows she'd fought it hard enough. She'd noticed she was drinking more than she ever had. Maybe it wasn't that bad, one drink here, one there, but nevertheless, she was starting to think about it.

Larry reached over and touched her hand. "Is something wrong? You're so distant."

"I'm wondering about our relationship. It looks like we're heading in opposite directions." Tanya turned to him.

"I know it's been pretty hectic the last few months. But I honestly think it'll ease off in the next little while."

How many times had she heard those words? "I hope so. It would be great to spend more evenings together. It gets lonely eating alone." She took a sip of her drink.

"We're looking into hiring more staff in the new year. That should ease the workload."

"Larry, it's not just the damn workload. It's *us* I'm talking about. I want more time together. Time when we're talking about us, not the damn hospital."

"Whoa, calm down. Okay, let's talk about us."

Tanya sensed the barriers around Larry whenever she broached the subject of their relationship. It was his defence. What he wanted was the perfect image—the successful doctor, loving wife, beautiful home—and to ignore any untoward feelings. That Tanya could be remotely discontent was unthinkable to him.

"How about a weekend away so we can relax and talk things out?" he suggested.

"Sounds good to me. When?"

"As soon as these guys from Boston leave and things get back to normal."

"What's normal, Larry?"

He ran his fingers through his hair, a long-time nervous habit, then abruptly changed the subject. "How was your visit to the Atwater?"

"Pretty unsettling. Strachan has committed Mrs. Smythe to a life in that dreadful institution. It's depressing."

"Do you think there's hope for her getting out?"

"That's what I'm counting on. Even though she has that wild look in her eyes, she's determined to walk. She keeps repeating how she wants to walk. No doubt away from Atwater."

"Hope she'll be able to do it," Larry said.

"Clarissa was pretty shaken, so I went to her gallery afterwards."

"I heard how tough it is on her. Sheldon's been telling me what she's going through. How her mother's terrified of Strachan returning."

Tanya looked at Larry, the sceptical Larry. He'd been so opposed to discussing Strachan's therapy. Perhaps now that Strachan had moved south, there was some hope. As Reva was now showing her support, Tanya knew that the investigative piece with Max Callaghan was becoming a reality. But she'd have to proceed delicately with Larry. He was concerned with professional courtesy at the Montreal Medical Centre. As a doctor, he felt strongly that one doctor doesn't discredit another. It was like a club, and as a member, he had reached the pinnacle of his cardiovascular specialty.

"What are you saying, Larry?" Tanya reached for her glass.

Larry hesitated and spoke slowly. "Ever since our trip to Quebec City, I've been thinking. You know we have a close association with the Psychiatric Institute. I don't want things to backfire."

"I know how difficult it must be for you."

Larry took a sip of his gin and tonic. "It is. Especially working closely with Sheldon, whom I like and respect. It's tough seeing him so concerned about Clarissa and her mother."

"I know. Clarissa's told me how supportive he's being."

"While we're at it, tell me what's happening with Reva and the Institute," Larry said.

"I've just received a letter from her saying that she wants to be part of the investigation. The prosecution, so to speak."

Larry set down his drink and threw his hands up. "Oh, for Christ's sake. Is she going to be the whistle-blower?"

"Yes, thank God. And by the way, I've invited her as well as Clarissa and Sheldon for dinner next Saturday evening."

"You're not serious?" His eyes widened.

"I am. I thought it would be interesting to get them together. See what they have to say." Tanya inhaled slowly, trying to calm herself.

"We'll see. What about that reporter at the Gazette … that Max Callaghan?"

"I'm meeting with him next week. I'm sure he'll be pleased with what's transpired over the last little while."

"Just be careful with him. He seems a little jaded. I think he'd go to any length to get a story."

"I'm sure he would. But we need a Doberman like Callaghan to unravel this."

"Why don't we get back to talking about us?" Larry said.

"Okay. You mean our weekend away?"

"Your cheeks are flushed. It's good to see you so animated." Larry laughed.

Tanya reached over and tousled his hair. "What about supper? Are you hungry?"

"Why don't we just order a pizza?"

Tanya put her arms around Larry and kissed him. "I have a better idea. Why don't we make love? The pizza can wait."

****

Tanya glanced admiringly over the pine harvest table and adjusted the crystal wineglasses. She had carefully chosen the Café de Paris place mats with crimson napkins and a bouquet of red roses with two large candles on either side, as she wanted to set a genial mood for the evening. There was no denying it: she couldn't remember fussing more over a dinner party.

In the living room, Larry was arranging some logs on the fire. The fireplace cast a flickering reflection on the opposite wall beside the snow-covered leaded windows. It was another snowy Montreal evening, the kind that Tanya loved. On nights like this, she felt like she was wrapped in a blanket, sheltered from the outside world.

"What music do you want?" Larry asked.

"Something lively. How about Chopin's *Piano Concerto No. 1*?"

Larry leafed through the pile of record albums.

Larry, thanks for going along with this dinner party," Tanya said, entering the living room through the open French doors.

"How about giving me a hand? I can't seem to find the album."

Tanya reached over and put her hands on Larry's shoulders. He turned to look at her. She was wearing her black cocktail dress and the sexy black pumps she'd bought in Quebec City. Her hair was crimped and held in place with a barrette behind each ear. She'd added a touch of blush and lip gloss, making her lips look sensuous. Larry leaned forward and kissed her. "Here's to a good evening."

Reva was the first to arrive. She'd taken a taxi from her apartment on Durocher Street and was stamping the snow off her boots when Larry opened the door. Her grey hair was cut short, emphasizing her broad forehead and tired eyes. Perched on her nose were small metal-framed glasses. She wore a long khaki coat over a navy pant suit and white turtleneck.

Tanya noticed Reva fidgeting with her woollen gloves. Perhaps she felt nervous around Larry, wondering what to expect. After all, she knew how he'd initially been opposed to the exposé.

But Tanya was hoping that this evening with Reva and the Schmedecks would encourage Larry's support. And what a great resource he would be. Once Reva retrieved the files from the basement vault, he could help in interpreting their contents.

Reva pushed her glasses up on her nose and cleared her throat. "What a lovely home."

"Thank you. Here, give me your coat. I'll hang it here." Larry opened the closet.

The doorbell chimed again. Clarissa, looking glamorous in her raccoon coat and hat, and Sheldon, dressed in a camel hair coat, were ushered into the vestibule.

"Why don't we all go into the living room?" Tanya suggested.

"What a great evening for a dinner party," Sheldon commented as they rounded the corner into the living room. "Think I'll warm my hands by the fire."

"What'll you have? I've made a pitcher of martinis, but if there's anything else you might want ..." Larry offered.

"I'd love a martini." Clarissa brushed her hand over her hair to make sure it was still in place after removing her hat.

"Make that two ... three ... all around," Sheldon said as he counted heads.

As they toasted each other, Tanya looked around the room. What a feat to get everyone together. Back in Quebec City, the situation had seemed hopeless. But things had fitted into place like a mosaic. No doubt it was the strong bond between Larry and Sheldon—their camaraderie; their old boys' club. She was under no illusion that she would play the trump card, as that one was held by Sheldon. Even though Larry loved her and wanted to help, he still resisted, reluctant to make a commitment. It was meeting with Clarissa and Sheldon, particularly Sheldon, that might alter Larry's attitude.

She smiled as she watched Larry charm Reva. She'd never seen Reva so buoyant as when she laughed at one of his silly jokes. Clarissa joined in, much calmer than when they'd last met at the Atwater Hospital. Surprisingly, she was not wearing red this evening except for her lipstick and nail polish. She had on a pair of black leather pants and a silk, creamy-coloured shirt open at the neck. She'd tied a black scarf around her neck and tossed it playfully over her left shoulder. As usual, she looked gorgeous.

Listening attentively to Larry, Sheldon stood beside Clarissa. As Sheldon adjusted his dark-framed glasses and took a sip of his martini, his arm brushed against Clarissa's. He had a boyish-looking face and a twinkle in his eyes. *What a pair*, Tanya smiled to herself: Sheldon, the soft-spoken caregiver and the flamboyant Clarissa. They were about the same height, as Clarissa was wearing strappy high heels. When Larry had told her that there was a rumour around the hospital that Clarissa and Sheldon were swingers, Tanya had been astounded. Clarissa, maybe, but certainly not Sheldon. She chuckled thinking about it.

Tanya excused herself to check on their housekeeper, Martha, who was helping in the kitchen. After a few minutes, she returned to the living room. "Dinner will be on the table in five. Come and take your seats."

****

Tanya had laboured over the seating arrangements. It was like a puzzle, trying to get it right with five people. How much easier it would have been if she and Larry had sat at opposite ends of the table with their guests in between. She had considered asking Max Callaghan, but thought better of it. Larry was still hesitant about trusting a reporter, particularly an investigative one who wrote about the medical field. She'd have to ease him into it. Max was a little gruff, but not a bad guy.

As it turned out, Reva sat to the right of Larry who was at the head of the table. Clarissa was on his left. Tanya, who was next to Clarissa, sat opposite Sheldon. Everyone was in a jovial mood after the martinis.

Larry served the wine and raised his glass. "A toast to Tanya for bringing us all together this evening."

"To Tanya!" Glasses were raised around the table. Tanya felt her cheeks flush.

"It's great to have you all here together," she said. "It's not easy with everyone leading such busy lives."

She glanced at Larry, and their eyes met. *What a change*, Tanya thought. He was more spirited than she'd seen him in a long time. His tense edge had dissipated, and he was more like the old Larry she'd known, the medical intern she'd fallen for—a little bit reckless, questioning everything and bright as hell. *No doubt about it, he's going to have an impact on the world*. She smiled at him, and he winked back.

Sheldon cleared his throat and turned to Tanya. "Clarissa and I want to say how much we appreciate your visiting Mrs. Smythe at Atwater. We went to see her the other day and she actually gave us a small smile and said hello. You've definitely had some effect on her."

"I'm convinced she wants to leave the hospital. She wants her freedom, no matter how tough it'll be," Tanya said.

"It's been over five years now, but until recently she was showing little sign of improvement. Actually, over the last few months, she'd been more withdrawn than ever," Clarissa told them.

"It must be so difficult seeing your mother like that, Clarissa," Reva said.

"It's devastating. But what about you? How do you find the energy to deal with the patients and their families?"

"Some nights I'm so exhausted all I can do is have a warm bath and fall into bed."

Larry turned to face Reva. "But don't you feel guilty administering so much medication to the point that some of your patients are catatonic?"

Tanya felt her body stiffen. *What was Larry up to?*

Reva took a gulp of her wine. "I'm merely following orders. Fortunately not Dr. Strachan's any more, but nevertheless, doctor's orders. Things have changed on the ward since Dr. Beaudoin took over. But still, quite often, I feel a tightening in my stomach when I see the patients whimpering or helpless. The residue of Strachan's experiments."

"What I'm trying to get my head around is why you want to go out on a limb to get Strachan. Aren't you afraid of losing your job?" Larry persisted.

"Tanya has assured me I won't be exposed. So now that I've made my decision, I guess I'll have to take my chances." However, Reva's voice was quavery.

"Assurance, yes, but there are no guarantees this thing won't backfire, blow up in all our faces," Larry warned her.

This was the closest Tanya had ever come to wanting to murder someone. For God's sake, what the hell was Larry trying to do by playing the devil's advocate? After all her labours, convincing Reva, getting everyone together—just when she thought the whole thing was a fait accompli, Larry was trying to unravel it. But perhaps he was simply trying to find out if Reva was totally committed and wouldn't crumple once things became difficult.

Entering the dining room with a tureen of steaming lobster bisque, Martha placed it on the sideboard. "Just leave it there, Martha. If you want to get on with the main course, I can ladle it out," Tanya said. "Larry, could you help me pass the soup around, please?" She rose from her chair, giving him a chilling look.

"I'd be delighted," Larry acquiesced, looking a little sheepish.

The only sound for the next few minutes was the scraping of the ladle in the soup tureen. Reva twisted her napkin in her lap and Clarissa stared down at her soup bowl as Tanya and Larry politely served everyone.

Sheldon cleared his throat. "I think we have to work on this as a team. I mean, we've come together for a common purpose—to expose Strachan to the world. Look what he's done to his patients. Come on, Larry, you took the medical oath: basically that means we have to do all we possibly can do for the health of the patient. A doctor is responsible for doing his very best, for being *noble*. That's what the French refer to as noblesse oblige—privilege entails responsibility."

"So then why on earth did Strachan do what he did? Why would he break his oath and hurt his patients?" Reva said.

"That's what we intend to find out," Sheldon responded.

"I can only add this, from my very personal experience," Clarissa said, slowly putting down her spoon. "I want my mother back. I want her led out of that psychiatric maze."

All eyes were upon her. Sheldon reached over and put his hand on Clarissa's.

"I do too. She deserves better than what she's been getting. The bottom line is that both Clarissa and I support Tanya and Reva. What do you say to that, Larry?"

"Hey, come on, give a guy a break. Especially in his own home. Destroying the reputation of a man in Strachan's position is a pretty serious thing. You have to be damn sure you know what you're doing."

"I think if you look around the table, you can see total commitment," Sheldon said.

"How about a truce?" Reva said as she raised her glass.

Raising his glass, Larry looked at them silently.

****

Although Tanya was tempted to phone Max first thing Monday morning, she waited patiently until their Wednesday afternoon meeting to relate her successful weekend. It gave her time to digest the dinner party and tell Max succinctly what had transpired. After all her years of psychiatric nursing and living with Larry, she had mastered two key traits in her life: discipline and control.

But lately, she'd felt the urge to break out, do something wild.

"You're not going to believe this, Max." Tanya said as she rounded the corner into his office at McGill.

Max looked up through a film of smoke. He was hunched over his desk, which was overflowing with his usual newspapers, magazines and ashtrays. He motioned to Tanya. "Come on in. Pull up a chair."

"I've got some great news."

"Enthusiasm—that's what I like." He put out his cigarette and reached for another one. "Why don't you shut the door so we're not disturbed."

He was even more rumpled than the last time she'd seen him. Tanya resisted the urge to reach over and smooth back the shock of hair falling over his right eye. There was a quirky magnetism about him. Or maybe what she found so appealing was how different he was from Larry.

Max was a bit of a renegade, a lefty as they'd say back home. Tanya never knew what he was thinking. His hazel eyes revealed nothing. And when he scrutinized her, she found it unsettling. It was like he was dissecting her thoughts.

"Coffee, cigarette?" he offered, smiling. "I want to hear every detail, no matter how minute."

Tanya shifted in her chair as she inhaled. "Never in my wildest dreams did I think they'd come on board. It's like making a stew. Throw all the ingredients in a pot and hope for the best. Well, this one turned out to be a triumph."

"Even Reva?" Max leaned back in his chair and watched her carefully. She knew the Strachan story could be one of the biggest ever at *The Gazette*.

"Yes. Even Reva," she said.

Tanya opened her briefcase and pulled out some notes she had jotted down after the weekend. She told Max about the tension at the dinner party, which gradually subsided, perhaps with the aid of the martinis and two bottles of red wine. She would have tried anything to get on with her agenda. Nodding intermittently, Max encouraged her to go on. She sipped the cup of strong coffee and smoked a couple of cigarettes as she described her coup.

"Sheldon Schmedeck—he's the one to keep an eye on. If there's anyone who'd convince Reva to remain loyal, it's him," Tanya said.

"What about Larry? Could he convince him as well?"

"That's a problem. We'll have to leave it for the time being."

"Okay, so tell me about Sheldon."

"First of all, he's devoted to Clarissa. And secondly, he has this honourable, noble trait about him. He's a justice seeker; a do-gooder, as some might say." Tanya thought better of telling Max of the swinger rumour. Best to keep it on a professional basis.

"We certainly need someone like him."

"I think the vital thing is his personal involvement, his having witnessed the degradation of Clarissa's mother."

"He's not concerned about his reputation at the hospital?" Max said.

"If he is, he's not saying anything … at least not to me." When Tanya thought about it, she observed that most people had some sort of an agenda—Sheldon, Clarissa and Reva seeking justice; Larry wanting to maintain the status quo; and Max pursuing the great story. And what about her? She, too, wanted justice. But if she were honest with herself, what she needed was something to fill the void in her life. Throughout her years in psychiatry, she had seen a common thread in people: the need to be recognized, accepted and loved. And each individual attempted his or her way of meeting this need, some better than others. The evidence was in the debris left behind of those who had failed. Tanya had been witness to it over and over again.

She wondered how Christy Amherst was getting along. Reva had told her that Christy had recently been readmitted to the Psychiatric Institute. And Scott Beauford had finally been discharged and was heading back to the States, somewhere around Washington, far away from Georgia and the bad memories. She didn't know what he was up to, but she was sure he still had plenty of anger. Hopefully, if he stuck to his daily medication, he'd stay in control. Whatever happened, it was impossible to watch over them forever.

Max inhaled deeply. "What about the files? When do you think we can get hold of them?"

"I think Reva is a little overwhelmed."

"What about you, Tanya?" Max looked at her over his glasses.

"Like I told you, I'm committed."

"I'm glad to hear that because without you and Reva, there's no story. I'm counting on you to keep everyone on side."

"I'm doing my best."

"I know you are. I'm just being overly cautious. A couple of years ago I had a bad experience when my main source reneged on coming forth to discuss Carlo Pasquali, the Montreal gangster. The story died. I don't want this to happen to our exposé of Strachan."

"It won't. I want to write this story as much as you do, and nail that bastard Strachan."

With each passing day, Tanya was more determined to pursue the disclosure of Strachan's discreditable psychiatric experiments. She was now aware that this determination dated back to her early childhood whenever she saw injustice. She loathed it when one person took advantage of another. This desire for justice emanated from her mother and father, and was something that had followed her throughout her life.

"That's reassuring." Max shuffled through some notes on his desk. "Now what about Reva and the files?"

"I'd like you to talk to her; restore her confidence."

"I'll do my best. Any suggestions?"

"How about the three of us meet next week at her apartment? I think she'd feel more comfortable there."

"Fine with me."

"Okay. I'll call her tonight."

He glanced at his watch. "Hey, the hand's over the five o'clock marker. Can I buy you a drink at the Berkeley? It's a bar around the corner."

****

Reva closed the shutters on her living room windows. She was perspiring and could feel her heart pounding. *What have I gotten myself into?*, she asked herself. As if her life wasn't challenging enough. She'd been so edgy lately that she'd found herself snapping at Lydia. Thank goodness, Lydia was out of town now at a nurses' convention in Toronto and had called to say she wouldn't be back until the weekend. That meant one less thing to worry about. Lydia had been asking a lot of questions, no doubt out of concern, but it disturbed Reva. Everyone looked suspicious. Were people looking at her and whispering? Had anyone seen her in the basement vault going through the files?

She lifted the phone receiver to check that it was in good working order. The dial tone hummed in her ear. She checked the lock on the door—working. Absent-mindedly, she looked under the sofa cushion—no tape recorder. She thought of how she really had to get a grip on herself or she'd lose it completely. Lately, she noticed the crow's feet around her eyes, deep creases around her mouth and white streaks through her hair. Her eyes seemed to be permanently bloodshot. She hadn't slept well for the past week.

All she could do was console herself, once again. She had made the commitment to pursue the Strachan exposé. Seeking justice was the honourable thing to do. And that's exactly what she was doing. She wouldn't stop now.

She thought about poor Christy Amherst, who was going through a rough period with her crying outbursts. One minute she was in a rage, throwing things across the room; the next, she was weeping uncontrollably. Reva was finding it increasingly difficult to administer Christy's large dosages of antidepressants and tranquilizers. Fortunately, Christy was no longer receiving electro-shock treatments. That horrible, dingy room in the basement had been quiet for some time now, but the ghosts still hovered about. Reva shuddered as she remembered the twitching patients, frothing at the mouth. *Lord, give me strength to carry through with this, if only for Christy's sake. Not to mention Scott Beauford, Saul Rosenfeld, Sarah Conway* … the list went on. She knew she wouldn't have any peace until this thing was resolved.

It was almost eight o'clock. Tanya and Max would be arriving any minute. *Big decision—what to serve them?* Reva knew how much Max liked his drinks, but maybe it was best to serve tea or coffee so that things didn't get out of control. On the other hand, her nerves were so frayed that a drink didn't sound like such a bad idea. She decanted a bottle of red wine and placed the pitcher on the pine box in the living room.

The medical files on Christy and Scott were locked in her escritoire in front of the living room window. She'd see how things were going before unlocking the desk. It was just one more safety precaution. *Don't want to rush into anything that can't be undone.* Reva had carefully gone over the files to make sure nothing had changed. There it was in writing, all of Dr. Strachan's orders and his correspondence with the CIA. Her hands shook as she read each word over again, making sure she hadn't misinterpreted anything. It was all there, waiting to be revealed.

She raced around the apartment, giving the furniture a last-minute dusting. When the doorbell rang, she took a couple of deep breaths and smoothed down her hair. Tanya and Max arrived together at eight o'clock sharp. After a brief introduction and shuffling of feet, Reva offered them a seat. It wasn't unusual that the conservation was somewhat stilted, as everyone knew the reason for the meeting, and was trying to act calm. The tension in the room was palpable. Understanding now why she had placed the wine on the table, Reva reached over for the pitcher and filled the glasses.

"To our quest," Max raised his glass. "Do you mind if I smoke?"

Three cigarettes were lit, as Reva opened a small window in the dining area. She was beginning to relax a little. She looked at Max as he held his cigarette between his index finger and thumb. He was left-handed, like her father. Her mother had always said that was a sign of intelligence. What silly nonsense. Could she trust this Max? Most people in the medical profession were suspicious of journalists. Said they'd go to any extent to get a story. But this was different. They needed someone like Max. Yet she'd heard that he could be ruthless in his pursuits.

Max's small talk was putting Reva at ease. She glanced over at Tanya. There was something different about her, but she couldn't quite figure out what. Tanya was dressed in faded blue jeans, open-necked white blouse and tweed jacket. Her hair was pinned up with some tendrils around her ears. And she was smoking, something Reva had thought she'd given up years ago. Maybe it was the anxiety of going through with this.

"Before either of you ask, the answer is yes—I do have the files." Reva could tell she had stunned both of them by being so forward.

"Did you have any difficulty getting them out of the vault?" Tanya asked.

"No. I did it on the weekend when there was only a skeleton staff. But, I just need one more reassurance."

"What's that?"

"That this thing won't backfire. That I can't be found out." She looked from Tanya to Max as she refilled their glasses.

"You have my total commitment," Tanya told her.

"And mine. You know that journalists don't have to reveal their sources … and that's exactly the way I intend to handle this." Max's eyes met Reva's.

"But I still worry," she said.

"You don't have to. We'll do everything possible to protect you."

"Should I get that in writing?" Reva asked.

"I don't think that's necessary," Tanya assured her.

"Very well." Reva rose slowly and walked toward the escritoire.

****

Tanya left Reva's apartment light-headed after a couple of glasses of wine and the lively conversation. Revitalized by having support and armed with their agenda, she returned home and enthusiastically related the events of the evening to Larry.

"I've been thinking about it, Tanya," he said, avoiding looking at her. "I just can't go through with this. I have to think of the hospital and my reputation."

"What about Sheldon?" she asked. "He's 100 per cent behind Clarissa, and he's not worried about his reputation, is he?"

"That's Sheldon's business. He's personally involved. It's his mother-in-law, after all."

"Well, what about your personal involvement with me? Doesn't that count for something?" Tanya said angrily.

"Look, I told you from the beginning, I was reluctant to get involved. But you just wouldn't let go, would you? Well the answer is a definitive *no*."

"What about Clarissa? What about the patients? Don't you give a damn about justice?"

"I told you before, I don't think we're in any position to judge Strachan's psychiatric therapy." Larry was becoming more pompous and Tanya hated it. She was up against the shield that surrounded him when he didn't want to deal with something. No matter what she said, he wouldn't budge. What he was doing was backing out. Just like her family—backtracking and leaving her disappointed.

She could have taken it if Larry hadn't been displaying such affection toward her lately. Obviously, she had misinterpreted it as his approval of what she was preparing to do. What the hell was wrong with him? He'd been waffling since their weekend in Quebec City. No doubt, he'd only been trying to please her, maintain the status quo. It was clear he was afraid of there being repercussions at the hospital if he supported her exposé.

Tanya could feel herself losing control as an adrenaline rush overwhelmed her. All her life she'd always felt the pressure to please everyone, say the right thing. But this had obviously gone over her limit. She reached over and grabbed the vase of flowers on the windowsill and threw it at him, barely missing his right shoulder. The crystal shattered on the tiles in front of the fireplace, with water and broken-stemmed red roses scattering about on the carpet.

She was horrified. She'd lost control, something that had never happened to her before.

Larry looked at her in disbelief, turned abruptly and walked out of the room. She heard him shout, "You can go to hell!" The front door slammed behind him.

Later, no matter how hard she tried to reconcile her thoughts, she recognized that something had died in their relationship. Now it could never be the same. She felt exhausted as she sobbed to herself, vowing to carry on with her plans. Ever since that evening, there had been a strained politeness between them. Two strangers living under the same roof. Tanya knew she had to make a decision.

****

Spring 1975 – Summer 1977

THE EXPOSÉ

Inhale deeply, all the positive life-energy forces; exhale slowly, all the negative thoughts, Tanya repeated to herself as she immersed herself in the tepid water of the indoor swimming pool at the Montreal Athletic Club. Ever since she'd met with Reva and Max, she'd been consumed by negative thoughts. It wasn't the meeting itself that had gone amiss. On the contrary, everything had gone surprisingly well, with Reva and Max working together better than she had ever hoped to see. They seemed to have a mutual respect in which they sensed the nonconformist in each other. Once Reva was assured anonymity, she was quite forthcoming with her reports and files. There was an eagerness about her that Tanya had never noticed before. After all her years of emotional repression on Ward Five, Reva appeared almost euphoric about releasing the information.

The water soothed Tanya's body and soul as she took bold strokes from one end of the pool to the other. She'd always found water calming. Water was feminine, like the love and nurturing of a mother. Perhaps it derived from a person's time in the womb, curled in a fetal position, floating in the amniotic fluid and safe from the outside world.

Back and forth she swam, kicking and splashing, releasing her fury. Fortunately, there was no one else in the pool to disturb her thoughts. Larry had betrayed her. If she couldn't rely on him to keep his word, who was there? The hurt had turned into anger. She recalled why she had left her home at an early age. Simply to get away and, along the way, make a better life for herself. Her mind was made up. That's exactly what she was going to do and no one, not even Larry, could get in her way. She had made her resolution.

****

"What happened to you? You look terrible." Max ushered Tanya into his office at *The Gazette*.

He scanned her pale face. Her hair was dishevelled and dark circles underlined her eyes. A splash of scarlet lipstick accentuated her paleness. His eyes travelled down to the coffee stain on the cuff of her left sleeve and the rips in her jeans.

Tanya knew he'd never seen her in such disarray. "I haven't been sleeping well, lately. I guess the pressure's getting to me." Tanya was tempted to tell him about Larry, but thought the better of it. Best to leave it on a professional level, although lately she'd noticed that things were changing between them. Some sort of karma going on.

Max lit a cigarette. "Don't worry. Just try to relax. It'll all work out."

"I hope so." Tanya pulled the light oak chair up to his desk.

"You'll see—we're going to bring this thing to trial."

"That simple, huh? Where do you propose we start?" Tanya said.

"I've been going over the files. And what I've seen is absolute dynamite. It's all there: the drugs, the CIA, the Sleep Room and the biggest prize of all, LSD. And to think, those bastards from the CIA funded the whole wretched mess." He took another drag of his cigarette.

"Reva did a wonderful job, didn't she?"

"I have nothing but admiration for the woman. And I mean it when I say I'll do everything in my power to protect her." Max opened a thick beige file. Skimming the pages, he read aloud, "Scott Beauford, age 31; diagnosis schizophrenic; long history of depression, alcoholism, sexual abuse relating to his involvement with his mother."

"That's a great place to start, don't you think?" Tanya said.

"Couldn't be better." Max looked like he was experiencing a surge of adrenaline as he flipped through the chart. Page after page. Drugs for depression, anxiety attacks, electro-shock treatments, LSD, tape recorders under the pillows … brainwashing … CIA. Sweat trickled down his neck. Tanya was staring at him when he looked up.

She cleared her throat. "It's pretty thorough, isn't it?"

"Bloody fantastic."

"So, what's next?"

"Let's see. We can't interview Christy Amherst, as she's still in the Psychiatric Institute. But there's nothing to stop us from contacting Scott, is there?" Max asked.

"Not that I can see."

"Well then, I say it's time to take a trip. Where did Reva say Scott was living now? Washington DC?"

"The last she heard, yes. He has a sister there."

"How about checking it out? Hopefully, he'll want to talk."

"I'm sure he'll have plenty to say," Tanya agreed.

"You think he'll be pretty forthcoming?"

"I think so. According to Reva, he still has a lot of anger."

"That's a good sign. It means he wants to tell his story," Max noted.

"Right. As long as he's on his daily medication, he'll be fairly lucid."

"Can you double check to make sure he's in Washington and then I can make my flight arrangements?"

"Certainly." Tanya hesitated. "But, you know Max, I think I should go too."

Max's eyes widened as he examined her. "Well, I *could* use some help."

"Will *The Gazette* be picking up some of the tab?"

"Yes. I'll tell Charlie, the day editor, that it's important we both go to Washington."

"Okay. I'll look into arrangements first thing in the morning."

"Great. But for now, what would you say about a little libation?"

"I wouldn't say no." Tanya laughed as she gathered her papers.

****

The flight was scheduled for ten o'clock Monday morning. It was barely seven but Tanya had already been awake for two hours organizing her notes and packing. She looked out the bedroom window at the sun rising above the eastern horizon. The buds on the old copper beech tree were bursting, and the golden forsythia shrubs were springing to life. What a feeling of renewal after the long, snowy winter.

So much had happened over the past few months. Larry was seldom home, but it was bothering her less as time went on. When they'd last talked on the phone, Larry had said he would move into the hospital residence. Although Tanya felt somewhat let down, she knew it was inevitable. Last week their meeting with a marriage counsellor had been cancelled as some emergency had come up at the hospital. And when she'd told him about the possibility of going to Washington, he expressed little interest. She knew she'd have to deal with it sooner or later. But right now she was focussed on the trip. Max would be around to pick her up within the hour.

Opening her closet, she carefully chose her wardrobe for the flight—a long black pencil skirt slit up the centre to her knees, a high-necked, lemon-coloured blouse and her houndstooth sports jacket. Smart casual. Quite a change from the last time she'd seen Max when he'd been shocked by her appearance. It would be interesting to see his reaction. Lately, she noticed how responsive he was to the smallest details, particularly about the psychiatric files. His inquisitiveness attracted her. For a fleeting moment, she wondered what he'd be like in bed. Probably quite passionate if he felt so strongly about most things. But enough of that. Better concentrate on how she would deal with the trip and reuniting with Scott Beauford.

She couldn't remember how long it had been since she'd last seen Scott, and wondered if he'd changed. She'd always been fond of him. He was such an intelligent and overly sensitive young man that it wasn't surprising he'd turned to alcohol.

She finished dressing and slipped into her black pumps. As the doorbell rang, she pushed back the curtain on the upstairs bedroom window and called out, "Morning, Max. Gorgeous day, isn't it?"

Max looked up and saluted with a mischievous grin. "Did you phone for a taxi, lady?"

"I'll be right down." She grabbed her suitcase off the bed.

****

Tanya gazed out the window as the airplane began its descent into Washington National Airport. The winding Potomac River cut through the verdant fields highlighted with pale pink and white cherry blossoms. In the distance, she recognized the Washington Monument and the Jefferson Memorial. The bronze statue of Jefferson stood proudly on the Tidal Basin. She closed her eyes and could almost smell the delightful fragrances of spring. How long had it been since she'd felt so good? Maybe it was just getting away from the tension at home. Ever since that horrible evening with Larry, there was a controlled politeness around the house that was becoming increasingly unbearable.

Max leaned forward and pointed out the Arlington National Cemetery, America's largest military burial ground. John F. Kennedy, hero of civil rights, had been buried there after his assassination in 1963.

"I remember it like yesterday. I was working on the Montreal underworld story when the news broke. Where were you?"

"In a phone booth at the Psychiatric Institute, talking to a friend. A colleague came into the nurses' lounge shouting the news."

"I think the whole world was in shock," Max said.

"You're right. It was Kennedy mania. They were like American royalty."

"He did a hell of a lot in his two-and-a-half-year presidency," Max said.

"What I admired most was his starting the war on poverty."

"And don't forget him standing up to that bully Khrushchev and intercepting the nuclear weapons going to Cuba."

Tanya nodded. "Not only daring and brilliant, but charming. I thought JFK and Jacqueline were the most glamorous couple. It was the Camelot image. Remember the photos of them smiling and waving from their open convertible?"

"Yeah. They seemed invulnerable." Max adjusted his seat belt.

"Just like we are, right?" Tanya said.

Max chortled. A group of middle-aged tourists at the rear of the plane applauded the throttling engines and the abrupt thud of the wheels on the runway. As usual they were told via the intercom to remain seated until the aircraft came to a full stop.

Tanya could feel the tension in the back of her neck building as she thought of the business at hand.

****

Tanya and Max checked into their rooms at the Georgetown Inn mid-afternoon. They had agreed to meet in the downstairs bar around five-fifteen. The first thing Tanya did was place a call to Scott Beauford who was staying with his sister near Georgetown University.

No answer, so she'd try a little later. She unfastened her briefcase and took out her notes. Everything seemed to be in order, but she wanted to go over Scott's chart one last time before their meeting.

She massaged the back of her neck. It was now five o'clock. This time when she carefully dialled the number again, a woman who identified herself as the housekeeper, informed her that she and Max were expected at the house at six for cocktails. It was only a short taxi ride from the Inn.

When Tanya walked into the lounge, Max was already sitting at the bar. He had actually combed his hair and put on a natty sports jacket. She swept the smoke away with her hand as she sat on the barstool beside him.

"You look a little unsettled. Can I buy you something to help you calm down?" he asked.

"White wine, please. Our meeting's set for six. I'm feeling quite apprehensive." Tanya reached for a cigarette.

"I'm sure everything will be fine."

"Easy for you to say. I guess you've been through so many stressful times in your career that it just rolls off your back."

"Are you implying that I'm an old hack?" He laughed, taking a sip of his rye.

"On the contrary—I'd say you're more of a seasoned journalist who knows the score," Tanya teased.

"Hey, come on, I'm 48 years old. Does that make me over the hill?"

"I'll have to think about that." Tanya took a closer look at him. With his combed hair, clean-shaved face and natty jacket, he was quite attractive.

He turned his head toward her and their eyes met.

"You're looking good, Tanya."

She felt herself blush and felt positively foolish. For a moment, she didn't know what to say.

"Want another?" he asked.

She looked at her watch. "I think we'd better get going. It's quarter to six."

"*Allons y.*" Max signed the bar tab.

****

Georgetown hadn't changed much in the three years since Tanya's last visit. The taxi took them through the historic district past the embassies and the handsome pre-revolutionary homes. They pulled up to a courtly two-storey, red brick town house surrounded with birch trees that was set well back from the road. A neat border of crimson tulips lined the walkway to the front door.

Before Tanya could ring the bell, the door opened. Scott stood towering over her with his boyish grin, arms dangling by his side. He was still handsome although his shock of dark, curly hair was now flecked with grey. Fine lines surrounded his mouth. His brown eyes, intense as ever, still had a sadness about them. She noticed how they glazed over as he looked at her from all the years of medication and psychiatric therapy. He was dressed in a blue button-down shirt and khakis and had a pale yellow sweater draped over his shoulders. With the outfit he wore an old pair of deck shoes with no socks, apparently remnants of his life in the south.

"Hi, Tanya. G-g-great to see you," he stammered.

"Thanks, Scott. It's good to see you again too," she said, taking his left hand in her right.

"I'd … I'd like you to meet my sister, Gloria." He spoke softly, lowering his eyes.

Behind him stood a strong-featured blonde woman of about five-foot-seven draped in a jade and gold sari. She had her hair pinned back in a French roll, emphasizing her broad forehead and high cheekbones. Her face was powdered, giving her an opaque complexion, and her eyes, outlined with dark eyeliner, revealed the same sadness as her brother's. Tanya looked closer to see the similarities between the two: broad foreheads, sad eyes and upturned chins.

After introductions, Gloria invited everyone into the drawing room. On the sideboard were two pitchers— Gloria pointed out that one held lemonade while the other was filled with mint julep laced with bourbon. Max headed toward the latter.

"So, you're with *The Montreal Gazette?*" Gloria's gaze and fixed smile rested upon Max.

He took a gulp of his drink. "Almost ten years this month."

"Well, I think it's a fairly respectable newspaper. I read your coverage of the Pasquali case when I was in Montreal. You certainly are thorough."

"Thanks. I try to be. And as objective as possible," Max said.

"Isn't that what it's supposed to be about?" she asked.

"Well, of course, but it's not always that easy."

"No, I guess not. It must take a lot of digging. And of course, cooperation on the part of the players." Gloria put her cigarette holder in her mouth, eyeing him.

Max was beginning to wonder what this woman was about. She was obviously playing the mother role, trying to protect her younger, vulnerable brother. What an edge she had. Like fingernails on a blackboard.

"Gloria, it's okay. He's a friend of Tanya's—I think we can trust him," Scott said.

Tanya glanced from Gloria to Scott. "You're right, Scott. You can trust him. He is a *professional*."

"Well, if you feel comfortable, Scott, we can continue with this," Gloria said.

Scott indicated he was fine.

Tanya turned to him. "Tell me what you've been up to since leaving Montreal."

"Not much. A little of this, a little of that … and, oh, some work at the university."

"He's been helping me organize my next semester's curriculum," Gloria interjected. She then described her curriculum vitae as a tenured associate professor of philosophy in the classics department. According to her, they made a good team as Scott was an indispensable assistant, typing up documents and keeping track of her students' records.

Tanya and Max exchanged glances indicating they both found Gloria to be a self-important, controlling woman. Tanya felt sorry for Scott being in such a fragile situation.

"I'm fully aware of why you are here." Gloria looked directly at Tanya and then at Max. "I've had time to mull this over. And as much as I fear repercussions, it's something that has to be done. Scott has suffered too much."

Scott sipped his lemonade and nodded in agreement from the opposite side of the room.

"I couldn't have gone through with this if Mother were still alive. Now that she's gone, there's nothing to stop me," he said.

Tanya turned to Scott on the sofa. "I know how painful this must be for you ... reliving all the horrors."

"It makes me angry. I thought after Dr. Strachan's treatment, I'd be going back to law school. He was supposed to be the best psychiatrist. But I had to drop out cause I couldn't concentrate enough," Scott said. "What did they do to me? I don't remember."

"That's what Max and I are here to tell you about."

As Tanya related Dr. Strachan's radical therapy of electro-shock, LSD and brainwashing, she could see the horror growing on Scott and Gloria's faces.

"Are you serious? Why didn't you stop it?" Gloria asked angrily.

"Yeah, Tanya—why didn't you try to stop Dr. Strachan from doing those horrible things to me?" Scott cried out.

"I didn't know at first. I only found out later," Tanya said quietly. "That was the reason I couldn't work for the man any longer. I had to leave after I saw what he was doing to you and the other patients."

"The man is a monster," Gloria shouted. "No wonder ..."

"Why did he do this to me? I want to know why," Scott demanded.

Tanya shook her head. "The only way we can get any answers is to go after him. Bring him to justice."

"Yes, go after him. *Go after him*," Scott repeated.

"That's what we intend to do. I know what you've been through. That man did things no one should have done."

"Well, you've got my support," Gloria said, gritting her teeth.

"Thank you. What about you, Scott," Max said.

"I'm so … so upset." Scott put his head in his hands.

"I don't blame you one bit," Tanya said gently.

"I'd like to …" Scott's voice trailed off.

"Like to what?" Tanya asked. When he didn't answer, she continued, "Do we have your support, Scott?"

Scott sipped his lemonade and stared at them. "Yeah … it's time for revenge."

****

Christy Amherst usually looked forward to her day passes. Anything to get away from the dreary psychiatric institution. The pungent antiseptic smell and old patients shuffling along the dimly lit corridors depressed her. But this particular Sunday was different. She was having second thoughts. Had she made the right decision when she'd agreed to the meeting at *The Gazette*? She hadn't seen Tanya Kowalski for quite some time and this guy, Vince or something, a journalist, was going to be there and wanted to talk to her.

Hmm, wonder if he's young and good looking. She had deliberately dressed in her black leather miniskirt and scarlet sweater buttoned up the back. After fluffing up her hair, she dabbed a little rouge on her cheeks and added some red lipstick. *Not bad, not bad at all.* She snapped her makeup compact shut. *You never know who you'll meet.*

If nothing else, it would be an opportunity to vent her anger at that traitor Dr. Strachan. He'd left her in such a state that she'd been readmitted after barely a year out. Now they were telling her there was a strong possibility she could be discharged as early as the end of June. So there was some hope. But she'd been feeling edgy and having trouble sleeping for weeks. What if she couldn't cope on her own? She was riddled with self-doubts.

The arrangements for the meeting had been made by Reva Rothwell. Tanya was picking Christy up in the hospital lobby at eleven o'clock and taking her to meet this journalist. Now it was five to. A nurse's aide had escorted Christy down in the elevator to the waiting room on the main floor. Standing guard was a young male attendant who looked intently at them as they entered the room. Christy settled on one of the green vinyl chairs in the windowless room and fidgeted with the clasp on her purse. Opposite her sat an elderly woman hunched over with her hands in a position of prayer. Unintelligible words flowed out of her quivering lips.

Beside Christy's chair was a grey Arborite end table with a stack of brochures. She reached over and picked one up. *Depression: How to understand and treat the illness*. Leafing through the pamphlet, she read, "Depression isn't just 'the blues.' It's a common mental illness that can change a person's thoughts, feelings, body and behaviour. Without proper treatment, depression can last for months, years or even a lifetime." A lifetime.

Well, hadn't she sought treatment? And where had it gotten her? She was still a patient at the institute and, quite frankly, didn't feel that much better after all her therapy.

****

As she shifted in her chair, Tanya entered the waiting room. She smiled, looking at Christy's flamboyant outfit. Christy cocked her head and grinned.

"Hi, Christy. Sorry I'm late. There was an accident on Pine Avenue, so I had to take another route. How are things?"

"Better once I get out of this joint." She stood up and adjusted her skirt.

"Well, look at you. Where'd you get those snazzy red shoes?"

"Back home in Nova Scotia." Christy beamed.

Tanya took Christy's arm. "The car's out in front."

"Great. Let's go—I can't wait to get out of here."

Tanya slipped into the driver's seat and put the key in the ignition. She glanced over at Christy who was slumped in the passenger's seat, staring out the window.

"Is something wrong?"

"What's this guy Vince like? I mean, is he someone I can trust?"

"You mean Max? He's a good journalist who wants to help us. We'd like to get to the bottom of what Dr. Strachan did to you and the other patients."

"What exactly did he do to us?"

"That's what Max and I want to talk to you about."

"Can you tell me now?"

"I think it's best if we discuss it in Max's office. All our files are there."

"So, at least tell me what you're planning on doing to Dr. Strachan."

"We're going after him to find out why he did what he did."

"But he's such a big shot. How can you do that?" Christy asked.

"It'll take a lot of work. But I think we can do it."

"What?"

"Seek some kind of justice," Tanya said.

"Are you serious? You think you can?" Christy's eyes widened.

"I do. Trust me."

"We'll see." Christy leaned her head back against the seat and turned to stare out the window as they slowly drove away from the grey stone mansion.

****

Max couldn't have played the role of confidant better. Within fifteen minutes of their meeting, Christy was relaxed and flirting coyly. It was obvious she loved the attention. He took a drag of his cigarette and looked at her over his glasses, asking questions, and prodding gently so that she felt comfortable in talking freely. His expertise at drawing people out had served him well. It was like fine-tuning. Most people, he'd found, loved to talk about themselves. And Christy was no exception.

But Max knew he had to keep some distance or there could be problems. He'd seen young, troubled women like Christy before, particularly when he was working on the Montreal underworld story. One of Carlo Pasquali's tarty ex-girlfriends had winked and smiled at him suggestively. He'd handled that one delicately by shifting his eyes down to some notes, scratching his beard and asking about her ill mother. Guaranteed to take her mind off sex. Without offending her, he had gently detached himself. Max lived by the credo that it was best to be on the cautious side, especially when women were involved. In his 48 years, he'd at least learned a few things.

Tanya sat quietly at the far end of the office, listening to Christy and Max's exchange. Clearing his throat from time to time, Max asked questions as he scribbled notes.

Christy was animated. "I mean ... Dr. Strachan promised me I'd get better. He said if I cooperated with him, did everything he wanted me to do, I'd be fine."

"And did you do everything he asked you to?" Max asked.

"Yeah, like most of the time. But sometimes when I'd get angry, he'd put those awful straps around my wrists." She rubbed her left wrist.

"What happened then?"

"I'd get even angrier," Christy pouted. "And then ... he put me in that horrible room where they kept giving me drugs. I even peed the bed. I felt so rotten."

"Christy, we now know what some of those drugs were. And they weren't at all helpful to you." Max watched her carefully.

"I knew it, damn it. Cause I wasn't feeling any better. I was feeling crazier and crazier. They thought I didn't know what was going on. But I did!" Christy shouted.

"Tell me what was going on," Max asked.

"It was like brainwashing. Like he was trying to make me into something else. He had a tape recorder under my pillow telling me over and over how to act if I wanted to be loved." Christy burst into tears.

"You're right, Christy. That's exactly what Dr. Strachan was doing to you. He was brainwashing you." Max reached for a cigarette. "Now I have to tell you something else."

"What's that?"

"In addition to the other drugs, he gave you LSD."

"Oh my God!" Christy put her hands over her face. "Is that the drug that makes you hallucinate? Is that why I saw all those red spiders and heard all those voices shouting in my head?"

"Yes—it is." Tanya walked over and rested her hand on Christy's shoulder.

Christy gripped the arms of her chair and stared silently.

"What are you thinking, Christy?" Tanya asked.

"I'm thinking, how the hell could he do that to me?"

"I don't know," Tanya said.

"He's a monster. He has to pay for this. When are we gonna get the guy?" She looked at Tanya for support.

"As I told you earlier, Max and I want to write about your time at the Psychiatric Institute."

"Yeah, I know that."

"Well, next month there's a big psychiatric conference in Montreal and Dr. Strachan will be here. He's one of the guest speakers. We thought it would be great to have the story published on the opening day of the conference. What do you think of that?"

"That's awesome … but it's kind of scary too."

"Don't worry. We'll always be here to support you," Max assured her.

Tanya pulled up her chair to face Christy and held her hands. She gently told Christy about their meeting with Scott Beauford and how he felt the same as she did. He wanted revenge—and rightfully so. They had all trusted Dr. Strachan, thought he was an honourable man. Even put their lives in his hands. And he had turned out to be amoral. The god of psychiatry had to be criminally charged.

****

After driving Christy back to the Psychiatric Institute, Tanya returned to *The Gazette* office. "Max, I don't know if we're doing the right thing. What if this backfires?" She paced around the room smoking a cigarette.

"What are you so worried about? You seemed to be okay before last week's meeting."

"That was before the great interrogation. I'm asking. Can this thing implode?"

"Not likely. But I guess anything's possible," Max admitted.

The series of meetings with the publisher, Frederick Morton and *The Gazette* lawyers had been stressful. For weeks, they had gone over all the documents thoroughly and cross-examined Tanya and Max. It was one question after another. Did they have all the facts? Were the documents authentic? How did Reva retrieve them? The lawyers stressed how crucial Reva was to building a solid case. Both Max and Tanya had reassured them that the evidence was there, and that Reva was totally committed to the exposé, but her identity must be protected. Only then did all parties feel confident to proceed.

"Okay, Max. I have to admit that I'm still concerned about protecting Reva."

"All I can say is that we'll do all we're capable of doing."

"And what about the patients? What if someone backs out of testifying?" Tanya asked.

"We'll have to deal with that if and when it happens."

"I appreciate your patience. I know you've been through some tough investigations before. But it's a first for me."

"Look, we're in this together. You gotta have faith."

****

Samuel B. Strachan stepped out of the shower and slipped on a white terry cloth bathrobe. Then he heard a knock on the door. "Breakfast, sir." A smiling porter wheeled in a cart with a silver tray draped with a white linen tablecloth.

"Thank you. Over there," Strachan pointed to the window.

He glanced at his watch. He'd have just enough time to eat breakfast and scan *The Montreal Gazette* before heading off to McGill. Everything was in order. Last evening, he'd read over his papers for his presentation to the International Psychiatric Conference. Perfect, as usual. He looked forward to the pleasant 15-minute walk from the Ritz, which he always enjoyed after a meal. Good for the digestion.

He lifted the silver lid on the plate and smelled the freshly baked croissants, peach preserves and fruit arranged as if it were flowers. The Ritz always had the best freshly brewed Colombian coffee, of which he allowed himself two cups, no more, every morning. He inhaled the strong aroma and took a sip of his coffee as he reached for the newspaper.

"What the Christ?" he cried out, as he looked at the front page. The bold headlines leapt out at him: CIA

Infiltrated Montreal Psychiatric Institute; LSD Used on Patients.

"What the hell is going on?" he muttered to himself, clutching the paper. He felt sweat forming on his forehead and his hands trembled. As he read, he attempted to absorb the words. How on earth could anyone know about this? He'd been reassured time and again by the CIA that everyone there was sworn to secrecy. Could there possibly be a whistle-blower in the CIA? No. It had to be an inside job, someone from the Psychiatric Institute. But who could possibly have knowledge of it? He tried to visualize all the people involved in the institution: the doctors, the nurses, the patients. Who the Christ could it be?

He mopped his brow with his napkin and checked the byline, a double: Tanya Kowalski and Max Callaghan. *Kowalski.* Hadn't he heard that name before? It certainly wasn't Scottish. He flipped over *The Gazette* pages to the end of the article. *Montreal journalist Tanya Kowalski worked as a nurse at the Psychiatric Institute from 1960 to 1964 when Dr. Samuel B. Strachan was head of the Institute.*

For God's sake, wasn't she that evening head nurse on Ward Five some ten years ago, the one who started asking him questions about the Sleep Room? He thought he had pacified her at the time, put her in her place. How dare a nurse question his therapy? And just what was she doing after all those years? He'd put all that behind him and moved on. It was now history in which he'd been well rewarded for his research and experiments on the patients. He'd seen them brought back to infancy with the electro-shock treatments and sleep therapy. He'd seen them weep at the sight of him, seeking his love and approval. Most of them would do whatever he asked. They trusted him, believed in him.

It was the CIA who'd suggested using LSD to see how the patients would react. The agency said it would be helpful in understanding soldiers at war. Understanding the enemy. And after all, hadn't he done it in the name of psychiatry? He'd be on the cutting edge of a new psychiatric therapy. Patients could be moulded into thinking the way that he thought they should. He knew what was best for them. He was their saviour.

There was a dull ache in his chest, and his heartbeat was racing, as he read the lines again: *Doctor Samuel B. Strachan, chief of psychiatry at the Montreal Psychiatric Institute knowingly administered LSD to his patients in a project funded by the CIA.* This was a bombshell. How could this be? Hadn't he covered his tracks? He'd had all those personal and confidential files with him when he left. His head was exploding. *Wait a minute. Maybe I didn't check all of them. God damn it. Could I have left something behind?* After all his years of clear, calculated thinking, this seemed impossible.

Think. I've got to think fast. I've spent too many years working toward this. Nothing is going to stand in my way. As the CIA's chief psychiatrist, he had doors open to him around the world. He couldn't bear the consequences of this story unravelling, revealing his experiments and involvement. He'd be ruined. Denial was the only answer.

The phone rang twice. Hesitantly, he picked up the receiver.

"What the hell's going on?" Marcus Maloney, the CIA chief bellowed into the phone. "It's all over the goddamn place. They're talking about our experiments in Canada. How could this be? I need an explanation *now*."

****

Max had set up a desk and phone for Tanya in a cubbyhole at the far end of his *Gazette* office. The makeshift partition between their desks provided a modicum of privacy so they could talk on their phones without being disturbed. Ever since the story broke, the phones hadn't stopped ringing. Shocked ex-patients, relatives, staff—anyone who had anything to do with the Psychiatric Institute had called. Tanya had just put down the receiver and reached for a cigarette when the phone rang again.

"Tanya Kowalski speaking."

"Tanya, it's Sarah Conway," a lively voice reverberated over the line. "This is absolutely incredible. Who would've thought it would come to this?"

Tanya felt a surge of excitement. Of all the patients she'd wanted to hear from, Sarah had been forefront in her mind. Here was a woman admitted to Ward Five, diagnosed as a severe depressive, when all she'd been suffering from was postpartum depression. Simply because her hormones were out of kilter after the birth of her daughter, she'd been put through Dr. Strachan's drug and shock therapy and ended up in the Sleep Room.

"Where are you? Are you all right?" Tanya asked.

"Still living in the Town of Mount Royal. But the important thing is that I think I'm getting there. I mean, it's been a long haul, but my husband Paul has been so supportive. I guess he knew there was light at the end of the tunnel. This time I've been out of the Institute for almost two years. So that's pretty good."

Tanya thought back, remembering Sarah at the Psychiatric Institute. She had constantly cried out for her baby, consumed with guilt about abandoning her.

"What have you been up to? How's your daughter?"

"Not a child any more. Calley will be twelve next month. Unfortunately, she's carrying around this stupid guilt. She thinks she was the cause of my depression. You know … the big *if.* If I wasn't born, you wouldn't have had to go through what you did …"

Damn it, thought Tanya. It was not only Sarah who had suffered from Dr. Strachan's therapy. It had a boxcar effect, first consuming Sarah, then her husband and now her daughter. Tanya dreaded to think of what could happen to the daughter who was ridden with guilt. She said to Sarah, "That's too bad. If you'd like me to talk to her, I'd be happy to."

"Maybe it would help having a professional talk to her. You know what it's like between a mother and daughter. Especially one who's heading into her teens."

"I do. Why don't you ask her if she'd like to come and see me?"

"Let me think it over, Tanya."

"I've thought about you over the years, Sarah. Do you have any other children?"

Sarah hesitated. "No, my years at the Institute were so … well, they were so traumatic that we decided not to have any more. I think it would've been a big mistake."

"I understand."

"But what about your story about Dr. Strachan? Is there anything I can do to help?"

"Absolutely," Tanya told her. "Would you be willing to testify in court?"

"I would. But I'm not sure if I'm strong enough to stand up to the man."

"I'm sure you are. We'll be there to support you."

"I'll do my best. So how are you going to handle it?"

"We think Strachan should be criminally charged. But it won't be easy. We'll need all the evidence we can get. Why don't you come into the office so we can discuss it?"

****

Samuel B. Strachan's eyes darted from side to side. He had never felt more threatened in his life. Was he safe walking along Sherbrooke Street? At any moment, some lunatic lurking about could pounce on him. He absolutely had to exercise caution. Normally, he liked the walk from the Ritz to McGill, especially as he loathed hailing a cab for such a short distance. Besides, he needed the air. This morning's news in *The Gazette* had shaken him. Exactly what impact it would have on the psychiatric world remained to be seen. And if that wasn't enough, he now had the CIA and Marcus Maloney asking questions. How the hell was he going to get out of this one?

As he entered the wrought-iron gates of McGill, Strachan glanced suspiciously around the campus. Students absorbed in conversations, carting satchels of books under their arms, took little notice of another greying middle-aged man. *I blend in harmoniously with the throng of aging professors*, he thought. But when he approached the door of the limestone building housing the Department of Psychiatry, he heard his name.

"Dr. Strachan … Dr. Strachan. Is it true that you knowingly administered LSD to your patients? Is it true that your funding came from the CIA?" a reporter from CJAD radio station shouted over the cacophony of the campus.

Strachan froze. It seemed like everywhere he went, he was being watched, observed … dissected.

"No comment." He brushed the microphone away and rushed into the building, slamming the door behind him. He didn't have to answer to anyone, let alone some reporter.

Securely inside, he strode down the long northeast corridor to Conference Room B and pushed open the heavy oak doors. He was only a few minutes late. When he entered the foyer, his heart was pounding. The noise level in the large room decreased abruptly with the sound of the doors shutting behind him. Clusters of psychiatrists interrupted their conversations to turn and look at him. He felt like he was in a Shakespearean play—curtain up, stage set with characters milling about chatting. Enter the king. Suddenly, all action ceases, voices trail off. Had they seen the morning paper? His lips quivered as he cleared his throat and smiled feebly. There was a nodding of heads.

"Good to see you, Samuel." Boris Bilinsky, the Montreal psychiatrist who organized the conference, walked across the room and offered his hand.

"Likewise. It's good to be back in Montreal." Strachan clasped his hand.

"We're honoured that you could make it. How are things back in Virginia?"

Strachan's sharp look searched Bilinsky's face for clues. "Pardon me?"

"CIA headquarters. It must be an inspiring place to be."

"It is, indeed." Strachan examined the faces of the other doctors surrounding him.

"Welcome back." A buzz of salutations ensued. But at least as to them, there was not a word or other reference made to the shattering morning news. Strachan felt a surge of relief.

Marvellous. They've probably seen the paper, but do they believe a word of it? Of course not. They know they are dealing with an honourable professional.

"Gentlemen, shall we proceed to the conference room? We have an exciting agenda ahead of us. After you, Samuel." Boris Bilinsky motioned to him.

"Thanks, Boris." Strachan took a deep breath and loosened his tie slightly. He felt like he was choking. But everything was going to be okay. He was sure it would be.

****

"Max, I honestly can't believe the response. It's overwhelming." Arms overflowing with papers and phone messages, Tanya stood in front of his cluttered desk. "Where do you think we should go from here?"

"I think we have enough to nail the bastard." Max looked up from his desk, butting his cigarette in a metal ashtray.

"I'm sure we do. I've just heard from Clarissa Schmedeck. She and Sheldon are more than willing to testify if we can bring this thing to court."

"We will. Oh, yes, indeedy we will." The look in Max's eyes was wild. "I'm on a roll and nothing can stop me now."

"I'm impressed."

"And you should be." Max grinned at her.

"So, what's next on our agenda?"

"We'll have to tread lightly for awhile. But Strachan is probably feeling the pressure and just might do something stupid. Now, *that* would definitely be to our advantage."

"Like what?" Tanya reached for a cigarette.

"He's got one hell of a lot to sell to the CIA. He'll probably try to convince them that it was a setup. No doubt the CIA is freaking out about the scandal."

"But how can he? There's all the evidence—the charts, the ex-patients, the relatives."

"We'll see. I really think he's a bully who's used to getting his way. Right now he's running scared and will do anything to get out of this mess. That's what cowards do when the pressure's on."

"You're right. The man thought he was infallible, a god-like creature put on the earth to save mankind. I'd like to go for the jugular." Tanya smiled.

"My thoughts completely."

"Do you think we can nail him on criminal charges? That is providing noxious and illegal substances like LSD to patients?"

"I'm ever hopeful it'll be criminal. I've checked it out. Even though the crimes were committed a decade ago, the statute of limitations hasn't run because he deliberately concealed what he did, and his victims didn't discover it until now."

"Well, that's good news." Tanya brushed back her hair.

"I'll confirm it with my brother, Daniel. He's one hell of a criminal lawyer."

"Good idea."

"What do you say I give Daniel a call and see what advice he can give us?" Max fiddled with his pen.

"Okay. We'll need all the help we can get. Strachan is such a powerful man. I'm sure he's capable of destroying anything or anyone who gets in his way. I've seen him in action, and he's ruthless."

"Quite frankly, I don't know how he can get out of this one. We have the cold, hard facts. We just have to know how to proceed. I'm sure Daniel will be more than willing to help. Besides, he owes me a favour." Max took a drag on his cigarette.

"Dare I ask what?"

"That's strictly between the two of us. You know, that brotherly love/hate stuff that families struggle with," he told her, neatly evading the question.

"Well, whatever it takes, I'm all for it if we get Strachan." Tanya leaned back in her chair. "But now I'm exhausted. It was just too much excitement for me in one day."

Max rolled back his cuff to look at his watch. "How about some supper? I think we've sung for it, don't you?"

"Certainly."

"What are you in the mood for?"

"I wouldn't mind some Italian at Luigi's. How about you?" Tanya asked.

"Okay—Luigi's it is."

After their productive day at *The Gazette*, Tanya's spirits were soaring. She laughed at Max's witticisms. He was acting silly, and she loved it. As he recalled his earlier episodes with the Montreal underworld, he joked and looked furtively around Luigi's restaurant, spying on possible members of the Mafia. He whispered and looked over his shoulder, double-checking that Carlo Pasquali wasn't at the next table eavesdropping, then telling her there could easily be a conspiracy going on. At any moment, the door could be flung open and pistols pointed at them. After all, Max had attempted to expose them and their crimes. Tanya laughed uncontrollably.

When the cheque arrived, Max rested his chin on his right hand and grinned at Tanya.

"How about a nightcap at my apartment?"

After a moment's hesitation, she looked directly at him. "I'd like that."

Ever since Larry had moved out the previous month, Tanya had devoted most of her time working on the Strachan exposé at *The Gazette* office. Usually Max was there, and quite often after a lengthy day's work they would go out and continue their discussion. It was becoming increasingly difficult to separate business and pleasure—the two things Max had sworn he didn't like to mix. He referred to it as a Molotov cocktail. They had both honestly tried. But with the long hours they were spending together, it was almost impossible. A little drink here, a little dinner there. It all added up.

And especially tonight, Tanya thought. Blame it on the nightcap. Just an extra glass of wine, but it had lowered her defences. Not that she was too concerned about it. As it turned out, it was pretty difficult *not* to stay over at Max's apartment. With Ella Fitzgerald crooning in the background, a log burning in the fireplace and an inviting sheepskin rug in front of it, the temptation was too much. They danced slowly, leaning their bodies closer together. She smelled his faint musk and felt his warm breath on her ear. When he kissed her lips and slowly removed her blouse, she didn't resist.

"Hmmm … " She began unbuckling his belt.

They made love on the sheepskin with the logs crackling and the golden flames soaring. She'd never enjoyed a man so much. When he reached his climax, the shadows of the flames engulfed his glistening body. She gripped his shoulders, as her body shuddered with her orgasm. *Oh, Prometheus. My god of fire.*

They lay on the sheepskin, Tanya's head resting on his shoulder, watching the fire subsiding. "You know what?" Max leaned over and stroked Tanya's moist brow.

"What?"

"To hell with not mixing business and pleasure. There's a lot to be said for it."

"You've got that right." Tanya laughed.

"What do you say we go to bed? We've got a big day coming up."

"I didn't bring my toothbrush."

"If you're good, you can use mine."

"What do you mean if I'm good?"

"You'll see." Max kissed her gently.

"*Bonsoir*," Tanya murmured.

"*Bonsoir. Au matin.*"

****

Reva hung up the phone and put her right hand on her chest. Palpitations. She thought she might be having a heart attack. She broke out in a sweat as soon as she recognized the cold, resolute voice of Dr. Strachan at the other end. In his controlled manner, he had asked her what exactly was going on. Did she know anything about this? Had she been in touch with Tanya? Where did this information come from?

Her worst fear was to be exposed as the informant. She tried to act surprised. How could this possibly happen? And then she attempted to pacify him, reassuring him that he'd taken all his files. She reminded him that his secretary had moved on to another job just as he was leaving the institute. But to the best of her knowledge, the secretary had packed and shipped the rest of the files as he had instructed. If he'd failed to take his personal and confidential files, it was not Reva's fault.

"I'm a nurse, *not* a secretary," she said coldly.

The big question was, did he believe her? Her only way out was to deny everything. She had a lot at stake— her job, her 20-year reputation in psychiatry. Hadn't Tanya and Max promised her that she would be protected? Perhaps Dr. Strachan was simply digging for information, not actually pointing an accusatory finger at her. That's what it was. He couldn't possibly know she had found those two files. Even though she was ready to collapse, she thought she'd handled it quite well.

It was almost three o'clock. One hour and she'd be finished for the day. She wanted nothing more than to go home, pour herself a stiff gin and tonic and put her feet up. God, she needed to calm down to think things through. And to phone Tanya. She wondered if Dr. Strachan had called *The Gazette*. She'd soon find out. Four o'clock couldn't come soon enough.

****

Doctor Samuel B. Strachan not only phoned Tanya and Max, but the publisher of *The Gazette*, demanding a retraction and apology in the newspaper. "Answers—I want answers to my questions," he barked over the phone to Tanya. "Just what right do you have to slander my reputation?"

"Dr. Strachan, we have proof that you knowingly administered LSD to your patients in the Sleep Room." Tanya tried to speak calmly.

"That's not true," Strachan shouted.

"And we have further proof that your doing so was funded by the CIA."

"Lies. All lies."

Tanya stood up, holding the receiver away from her ear and peered around the partition, signalling for Max to come over to her desk. As he approached, he reached over and scribbled on a pad in front of her, *Stay calm. Don't let him bully you.*

"And you call yourself a *professional*? I've never known anyone to sink so low." Strachan slammed down the phone.

****

Within minutes, he had gotten through to the publisher, Frederick Morton, and continued his rant, threatening to sue if there wasn't an apology and correction published in the next day's paper.

"It's absolutely appalling. What kind of people do you employ?" Strachan hissed.

"I'm sorry, doctor, but we stand by our reporters. We would never publish anything that hasn't been well researched. Tanya Kowalski and Max Callaghan have spent months getting the facts, and they've proven to me and our lawyers that their report is accurate."

"You dare to speak to me like that? Do you know what powerful entities you're dealing with?" Strachan bellowed.

"I don't know what powerful entities you're referring to. But I do know I'm dealing with facts," Morton said.

"Well, be prepared. You'll rue the day that you published this." Strachan hung up.

****

"Close the door behind you, Samuel," Marcus Maloney directed as Dr. Strachan entered his large oak-panelled office in the CIA building in Langley, Virginia. "I want this to be as private as possible."

In the 15 years Marcus had known Samuel Strachan, he had never seen him look worse. The usually dapper, fit man, dressed in an immaculately pressed suit appeared drawn and pale with squinting eyes peering through his metal-framed spectacles. His motions were unsteady as he shut the door and walked slowly toward the desk. Marcus leaned back in his oak swivel chair watching him.

"Look, Marcus, I just don't know how it could've happened. I'm sure I took all my personal and confidential files and documents when I left Montreal. I honestly don't know." Strachan's voice quavered.

"Well, we'll have to find out, won't we?" Marcus said coolly. The tension in the room was perceptible.

"Of course, but whose goddamn idea was it in the first place?" Strachan gripped the arms of his chair.

"The CIA's. But we were all sworn to secrecy, weren't we?"

Strachan put his handkerchief to his brow and shifted in his seat. "I've threatened to sue the whole lot of them at *The Montreal Gazette*."

"And what good will that do?"

"It's our reputations—the CIA's, yours, mine. We've got to deny every last word."

"What proof do they have? Do they have the documents in hand?" Marcus asked.

"Some rat has leaked the info. We've got to find out who it is. I'm sure I took all those files—all the evidence. I don't know how this could've happened." Strachan repeated. "We covered our tracks. Who on earth could be the mole?"

"How is this going to play out up there?" Marcus tapped the back of his pen on a pad of paper on his desk.

"In Canada? I don't know—I just don't know." Strachan shook his head.

"If the files go to the RCMP, I think we can handle it. We do a lot of business with them, and they owe us some favours. But, if the politicians get hold of it, I don't know where it'll go." Marcus's eyes locked with Strachan's.

"Good God, are you referring to a public inquiry?".

"That's exactly what I mean. And that's exactly what we can't afford," Marcus told him.

****

"I'm sure that won't happen." Strachan felt his cheeks flush. He was silent for a moment as he thought about it.

But what if that did happen? The last thing he needed was a public inquiry with those pesky politicians nosing around. Who knew what they would find? God, he'd covered his tracks, hadn't he? He was sure he'd taken every precaution possible. Right now, the situation was bad enough, without anything else coming to light. He was still fuming about his phone calls to that turncoat Tanya Kowalski and smug reporter Max Callaghan. And if that wasn't enough, their pompous publisher had added the finishing touches. For sure, he'd sue every last one of them and put them out of business. That's what he'd do.

But where did he start? He knew he wasn't thinking straight. He was losing control, something he rarely did. But there was no doubt, someone was out to get him. It was a conspiracy. One that must be stopped at all costs. He had to think fast.

"Look, Marcus, don't worry," he finally murmured. "I'll clear this up. It may just take a little time, but it'll be done. Hopefully in a week or so, it'll all be forgotten."

"I certainly hope so, Samuel, not only for your sake but for mine. We've got to think of the CIA."

"Yes. Of course."

"Let's talk next week," Marcus said, dismissing him.

****

As Strachan shut the door behind him, Marcus Maloney reached for the phone.

"Charles, Strachan's just left. It's imperative that this problem with the Canadians be resolved as soon as possible."

"Yes, sir."

****

"We've got all the evidence we need right here." Max leafed through the documents on his cluttered desk. "And now that Daniel's given us the go-ahead, what's to stop us?"

Tanya pulled a chair up to his desk. "That's the best news we've had all week."

"Right." Max looked at her and nodded. What a relief it had been when Daniel had confirmed the statute of limitations hadn't run. After the fiasco of his Montreal underworld investigative piece, Max was determined to make the Strachan exposé a success. It was painful to think his mob case had failed simply because a key witness had refused to testify. With the Strachan disclosure, he'd do everything possible to ensure that everyone was on the right side and faithful to the cause.

"As far as I can see, there's nothing to stop us from nailing Strachan," Tanya said excitedly.

"Nothing … but … I don't know what to make of it." Max tapped his pen on the desk.

"What?"

"I can't understand why the guys at the RCMP are dragging their feet. I've sent copies of all the documents, but don't seem to be getting much of a response." He inhaled deeply and blew a cloud of smoke out the right side of his mouth.

"What about calling them?"

"I've called a number of times, but still nothing."

"I guess we have to put more pressure on them. There's no doubt whatsoever that Strachan committed a criminal

148

offence. And it's the RCMP we should be dealing with," Tanya reminded him.

"You know, Daniel didn't even hesitate when he saw our evidence. He was pretty impressed with the report on LSD. Everything points to Strachan knowingly administering an illegal substance." Max leaned back in his chair and ran his fingers through his hair.

"That's fantastic." Tanya smiled.

Max returned her smile. He had noticed quite a change in Tanya. Especially after the night they'd spent together. By some miracle, it hadn't altered their working relationship. They were both focussed on bringing Strachan to trial. Tanya was becoming more self-assured and absorbed in the disclosure. He was certain she wouldn't back out now, as she was too committed. Ever since she'd separated from her pompous husband, she had an aura of confidence which he found increasingly attractive. Strong women were like an aphrodisiac to him. But after the failure of two marriages and too many relationships to count, he was treading cautiously, simply hoping this one would be different.

Besides, he needed Tanya as his mediator to calm things down. Ever since the newspaper article and Strachan's call, Reva Rothwell had become quite agitated. The documents she provided were crucial to the exposé, and the last thing he needed was for her to be having anxiety attacks. But when you looked at it, who could blame her? If Strachan went after her, which he was certainly capable of doing, her career could be in jeopardy. Strachan was fighting to save his reputation and no doubt felt the forces moving in on him, so he could do anything.

"What are you thinking about?" Tanya asked.

Max looked up abruptly. "Wait a minute. Why didn't I think of it before?" He pounded his desk. "It's the CIA. That's what it's all about. The CIA has somehow gotten to its Canadian counterpart."

"What do you mean?"

"I think the CIA and the RCMP are both involved in the stonewalling of a criminal charge. We've got to think fast, Tanya."

****

Daniel Callaghan stood at his spacious office window in the Sun Life Building overlooking leafy Dominion Square. The large hand of the clock on Windsor Station inched its way toward nine o'clock. Small figures filed out of the station and hurriedly crossed the square to their respective offices. He glanced admiringly at the view from his 18th-floor office. To the south stood the grand Cathedral Marie-Reine-du-Monde, modelled after St. Peter's Basilica in Rome. Nearby, the handsome Queen Elizabeth Hotel, Montreal's largest, cast a great shadow over the cathedral. Caleches were already lining up on rue Dorchester around the park.

Daniel had been at his neatly organized mahogany desk for more than two hours. It was during these early hours that his best ideas came to him. He treasured the silence of the office before his secretary arrived. All it took was a little discipline, of which Daniel had plenty.

Each morning he rose at 5:15 and headed for the gym at the Montreal Athletic Association. After a vigorous run on the treadmill followed by 100 push-ups and weights, he showered and dressed in his well-tailored suit with a monogrammed silk shirt and tie. Breakfast usually consisted of yoghurt, fruit and coffee in the casual dining area, after which he had a brisk five-minute walk to the office.

Daniel lowered his tall, lean frame into his swivel chair. Surrounding his desk were his gold-framed degrees and certificates: Honours B.A., McGill University; Washington University Law School, St. Louis, Missouri and Member, Quebec Bar Association. After graduating summa cum laude from the U.S. law school, he'd returned to Canada to immerse himself in studying for the Quebec bar exams. Over the next five years he'd built up a prosperous criminal law practice. Unlike his brother Max, he'd always known what he wanted out of life—success, health and justice—but not necessarily in that order.

He'd worked on some of the biggest criminal trials, but his greatest claim to fame was defending the handyman accused of killing Carmen Paganini's lover, who had been employed as a horse trainer on their estate in the Montreal suburb of Laval. It was a notorious case which had the Montreal Italian community mesmerized, as it played out like a soap opera. Most of the evidence had pointed toward the handyman, but Daniel was convinced that Carmen's husband, Giovanni, had framed him. When Giovanni was convicted and sent to prison for life, he wept openly, denying his guilt and screaming at Daniel that he would get him in the end. Much to Daniel's surprise, despite his victory, it was one of the most emotional trials in which he'd been involved, and he suffered nightmares about Giovanni coming after him.

The ringing of his private line interrupted his thoughts. It was Max.

"Morning, Daniel. How are things going?"

"You mean with the Strachan case?"

"The very one."

"Progressing slowly. You know the bureaucracy in Ottawa … but I'm optimistic."

"Well, I was wondering about that. Could the RCMP be stalling because of their pals at the CIA?" Max asked.

"In the intelligence community, anything's possible. If Strachan's charged, the CIA is in deep shit."

"That's what I thought. I've booked our meeting with the ex-patients on July 17th. Is that date still okay with you?"

"Yes. I'm sure everything will be in order by then. What time and where?"

"Three-thirty. In *The Gazette* conference room."

Daniel checked his calendar. "That's fine with me."

"Let me know if you need anything before then, will you?" Max said.

"Will do." Daniel replaced the receiver and looked at the notes he'd made on the case. He was looking forward to the challenge of representing the victims and bringing Strachan to trial. Max had filled him in on the details— how this god-like psychiatrist had destroyed so many lives with his arrogance and quest for recognition. He thought of the ruin left behind and what a pleasure it would be to humble the egomaniac.

But now, with the RCMP stalling, he had to think of the well-connected people he knew in Ottawa who might provide a helping hand. He leafed through his federal government index. His index finger stabbed at a familiar name. There she was: Madeleine Carmichael, a young lawyer who had assisted on the Carmen Paganini case, was now a political affairs officer in the External Affairs department. Hopefully, she knew someone influential in the Justice Department. Daniel knew how unrelenting she had been on the case. And being a female in a male-dominated field rendered her even more aggressive. If she could go after Giovanni the way she did, she just might help him pursue Strachan with the same fervour. All Daniel had to do was convince her that Strachan was the villain, someone totally abhorrent. With all the evidence piling up, it shouldn't be too difficult. And he was pretty certain that Madeleine would prove to be one hell of a justice seeker.

When he placed the call, her secretary informed him that she was out of the office for the day. However, he was able to reach her the next morning.

****

Madeleine Carmichael didn't need much convincing. When she'd first read about Dr. Strachan's experiments in *The Gazette*, she'd been shocked, particularly when she came to the section about Sarah Conway. She remembered the nausea she felt as she read on. What kind of psychiatrist would administer such a convoluted therapy? He'd have to be some kind of psychopath.

But most importantly, was it the same Sarah Conway she knew? Back in the mid-fifties, both Madeleine and Sarah had attended the local Pointe Claire high school on the West Island of Montreal. When Madeleine had last seen Sarah at their 10th reunion, she was surprised at how much Sarah had changed. Gone was the carefree, willing-to-try-anything person. Sarah appeared distracted and fragile, almost child-like. So *that* was it. Years of Dr. Strachan's worldly psychiatry had done this to her—his drugs, shock treatment and sleep therapy. And all because she'd suffered postpartum depression. It was disgusting, absolutely intolerable.

Madeleine's deep voice resonated over the phone. "I'm absolutely seething about what that son-of-a-bitch has done to these people."

"I was hoping you'd feel that way."

"And what the hell. The CIA was actually funding this thing in Canada?"

"Hard to believe, isn't it?"

"Damn right."

"You know, Madeleine, I'll never forget how you went after that Giovanni Paganini. You were unrelenting," Daniel laughed.

"Well, he got what he deserved," she said.

"Any thoughts on how this case can move forward?"

"First, tell me how I can help."

"Well, I'm baffled. We've sent copies of the documents to the commissioner of the RCMP and left phone messages, but there's been no response. It's been over a month now."

After a slight hesitation, she replied abruptly, "Just leave it to me. I'll get back to you. It shouldn't take long."

Within minutes of hanging up the phone, Madeleine phoned her counterpart, Harold Hastings, at the Canadian Embassy in Washington, demanding answers as to how the CIA could possibly have funded Strachan's experiments without informing the Canadian government. It was, once again, a classic case of American arrogance in showing no respect whatsoever for Canadian sovereignty. Madeleine was furious and railed on. What about the CIA's connection or liaison with the RCMP? Was the RCMP informed? Did he know why the RCMP was shuffling about instead of doing anything?

She finished up, "In other words, Harold, we desperately need answers so we can bring Strachan to trial pronto."

"I'll see what I can do." Harold hung up the phone. She knew he realized this wasn't going to be easy, as he'd had dealings with her before and knew her tenacity.

****

Scott Beauford felt the pressure building in his head as the Air Canada DC 9 approached Montreal's Dorval airport. So many bad memories. As much as he'd tried, Scott couldn't get rid of his demons. Fifteen years ago, in desperation, he'd driven north through the night non-stop from Georgia. Dr. Strachan was supposed to make him better, erase all the sinful memories. Everyone had told him so. After all, Strachan was known for his ability to perform miracles, wasn't he?

Opening his carry-on case, Scott checked to see that he had all his medication. His hands were shaking. His thinking about Strachan meant the anxiety was becoming unbearable.

A stewardess approached. "Sir, would you please put your seat in an upright position."

"What … what did y-you say?"

She helped him put his seat upright. "Are you okay, sir?"

What's wrong with me? Could she see how shaky I am? "Y-y-yeah, I'm f-fine," he stammered, hoping to get rid of her. Lately whenever he was upset, his stutter came back. The horrible, embarrassing stutter from his childhood. But he'd be okay—he knew he would. He had a mission. *Stick with the plan,* he told himself, *and everything will be okay. Just stick to the plan.*

When the story had broken in Montreal and been picked up by *The Washington Post* in early June, he'd read Tanya and Max's account, his body going rigid. Ever since their meeting in Georgetown, he'd known they would be writing the Dr. Strachan exposé, but actually reading about it in the newspaper made it real. It was a scathing report, accusing the good doctor of criminal acts. There was no turning back now. Strachan was exposed for the world to see him as he truly was: an evil man who preyed upon his patients, experimenting with their delicate psyches for his own gratification and glory. From the doctor's point of view, who cared about these patients anyway? They were all nuts, weren't they?

As he'd read on about himself, Christy Amherst, Sarah Conway and the others who came forward, Scott felt a twisting in his gut. The bastard had done it to each and every one of them. And now, apparently, he was denying everything; trying to save his rotten skin. Well, he had another thing coming—no matter how powerful he was, Strachan would never get away with this one. It really came down to good and evil, and Strachan was evil. He had to be punished.

Scott reached into his briefcase and checked his Day-Timer once again to make certain he had the correct date: July 17, 1976, 3:30 P.M., *The Montreal Gazette,* conference room, second floor. They'd all be there. He wasn't quite sure about this Max guy, but Tanya had said that he'd be fine. Scott was actually looking forward to this reunion with his fellow patients. And Tanya always made sure that things ran smoothly—or, given the situation, at least as peacefully as possible.

He thought about taking another tranquilizer, just to make sure he could cope with everything. Yes, that's what he'd do—his little yellow calming pill, and maybe just a small bourbon once he arrived at the hotel. He had an hour before the meeting. One little drink wouldn't hurt him, would it? It would make him better able to cope. After all, he was on a mission. They were going to get the bastard, weren't they?

****

Tanya and Max arrived at *The Gazette's* conference room an hour before the meeting. It was crucial that the gathering went as smoothly as possible, but with the group attending, anything could go awry. Tanya rearranged the chairs around the rectangular oak table and placed two water pitchers and glasses at either end. To avoid confusion, she and Max had organized the seating arrangements ahead of time. She would sit between Scott and Christy, with Max beside Sarah. Sitting at the head of the table would be Daniel Callaghan.

Clarissa Schmedeck had called Tanya to reschedule her mother's meeting with them, saying Mrs. Smythe wasn't feeling up to it. However, Tanya ordered taxis to pick up the rest of the ex-patients wherever they might be living or staying in the city and deliver them to *The Gazette's* main entrance.

"I think I should be at the entrance to greet them," Tanya told Max.

"You're sure? I could get one of the newsroom assistants to be there."

"No. Given how nervous they'll be, I think it's best that someone they know is there."

"Okay. We'll have the attendant ring up when they arrive."

"Max, I have to admit, I'm feeling a little shaky myself."

"Is there anything I can do to calm you?" Max touched her left wrist.

Tanya laughed. "Right here?"

"Not a bad idea. Not bad at all." Max raised her chin and kissed her lips. "Why don't I lock the door?"

****

The meeting began harmoniously with great salutations and a coming together of harmed brethren, seeking justice. "H-how're you doin'?" Scott smiled at Christy.

Christy swept her hair behind her right ear and held out her hand. "It's so darn good to see you, Scott. It's been too long. I missed seeing you."

Scott's face flushed. "M-me too."

Sarah hugged Tanya. "God, it's good to be here."

"You're looking well, Sarah," Tanya said softly.

"It's been a long haul."

Daniel Callaghan cleared his throat. "Shall we take our seats? I think we're ready to begin."

Scott looked around the room with drooping eyelids. "Y-yeah, we're r-ready."

"First, I'd like to welcome all of you to this meeting." Daniel glanced around the conference table at the three ex-patients. "I admire your courage. I'm sure this isn't easy for any of you."

"N-no, it's not." Scott leaned forward. His eyes were glazed, but seemed to be trying to focus on Daniel.

"Aw, it's not that bad. We've been through lots of group meetings at the hospital before," Christy reminded them.

"Yeah. But this is different," Sarah responded. "I'd say it's a lot more serious than a hospital meeting, wouldn't you?"

Christy shrugged and narrowed her eyes. "Guess so."

Max and Tanya exchanged looks across the table. She felt her cheeks flush as she thought about their passionate encounter a mere hour ago. Admittedly, she did feel calmer.

Before the meeting, they'd agreed to sit back and observe the proceedings while letting Daniel take charge. Max had laughed. "He'll enjoy that. He likes to be in control at all times."

And there Daniel sat at the head of the table—the handsome and successful criminal lawyer in his navy pin-striped suit, azure silk shirt and navy tie. His wavy, silver-streaked hair fell slightly over his forehead, accentuating his hazel eyes. Tanya thought if she weren't involved with Max, she might be interested.

Daniel cleared his throat and spoke calmly, his deep voice resonating throughout the room. "I'm pleased to hear that you're all willing to testify against Dr. Strachan."

There was a general mumbling of assent as they watched him carefully.

"I've been going over the documents and we have a lot of evidence here. I just want to make sure you're aware of what is involved."

The room was silent. Daniel walked around the table as he continued, "Even though you've agreed to testify, it may be difficult to answer all the questions Dr. Strachan's lawyer asks you."

"What should we do if we can't answer them?" Christy asked.

"Just say you don't know. I'll be there to support you."

"I think we'll need it," Sarah said. "I've heard it can get pretty tense during cross-examination."

"Sometimes it can, but if Strachan's lawyer is being too hard on you, I'll intervene by lodging an objection."

"Will t-that stop them from yelling at us?" Scott asked.

"I don't think there'll be any yelling. But it can get pretty heated in a courtroom."

"It's making me kinda nervous thinking about it," Christy said.

"That's understandable, but just remember—I'm there. Now are there any other concerns?"

Sarah pulled her chair closer to the table. "Yeah, what's it actually like in the courtroom? I've never been in one before."

"That's a good question. All of you should be familiar with the surroundings. If you're interested, I'll take you to the courthouse ahead of time to show you where you'll sit and what will be involved in the trial."

"I'd like that," Christy said. Other heads nodded.

****

Max sat quietly observing the interplay between his brother and the ex-patients. He thought about how persuasive Daniel had been in his cross-examination during the final days of the Paganini murder case. Mickey Shaw, who reported on the case for *The Gazette,* had recounted the courtroom theatrics over drinks one night at the Montreal Press Club.

"I tell you, Max. You wouldn't want to be cross-examined by that brother of yours. He's a terrier if I ever saw one," Mickey had chortled. "Remember the sweat running down Giovanni Paganini's face as he sat in the courtroom?"

Daniel might appear calm to most people, but he was one of the most intense persons Max had ever met—someone who always wanted to win. And it had paid off: accomplished criminal lawyer, devoted family man and fitness fanatic. Sometimes, he was too perfect for Max. But lately, there seemed to be something upsetting Daniel. Max couldn't understand why Daniel's moods changed so rapidly. At times he appeared distracted, mumbling some vague remark when Max inquired about his practice. Not like Daniel at all.

Like a courtroom scene, all eyes followed Daniel as he returned to the head of the table. He hesitated and spoke slowly. "I've been working on trying Strachan in criminal court … but it may not be as easy as I first thought."

"What do you mean?" Max asked sharply.

"It'll take a lot of pressure in Ottawa to get a charge laid," Daniel said.

"But everyone knows he's committed a criminal offence," Max countered.

"Yes, we all know that. But the RCMP would have to step in and interview everyone who's involved. And you know they're stalling."

"Well, what about your connections in Ottawa?"

"They can only put so much pressure on." The muscles in Daniel's jaw tightened.

Tanya interrupted. "Daniel's right. You know how hard we've been working on the RCMP, Max."

****

Scott's eyelids drooped as he tried to concentrate. *For god's sake, stay focussed*, he thought. But it wasn't easy, as the shots of bourbon he'd had earlier had taken effect.

Christy opened her compact, studied her scarlet lipstick, and wiped a smudge from her left cheek.

Sarah clasped her hands together under the table. "Wait a minute. What about us? Isn't this what it's supposed to be about—how Strachan ruined our lives?"

Everyone turned to look at her.

"I've gone through hell. Christy and Scott have gone through hell. The big question is: are we bringing Strachan to trial?"

"Please … let's try to be calm. This isn't getting us anywhere," Tanya said.

"And just what is anywhere?" Christy pouted her full red lips.

"Listen, everyone. We're trying to help you. The reason we came together was to see Dr. Strachan brought to justice. We know what he's put you through," Max said.

****

Tanya felt a throbbing in her head. What if they lost these former patients? Even though the documented evidence discovered by Reva Rothwell was damning, the patients' testimony would strengthen their case immensely. They needed them. Especially after all the time Tanya had spent on the disclosure, collecting evidence, getting everyone on their side. And if she really wanted to think about it, losing a marriage. No, she had given too much of herself to let this exposé die and Strachan escape.

****

Christy had reverted to the demanding attention seeker. "Well, then, for Christ's sake let's stop the bickering. I saw enough of it in my family. It brings back horrible memories."

"Y-yeah. Let's get along," Scott stammered. "Or … we'll all have to leave the room."

Max was horrified. There was absolutely no way this was going to turn out like his Montreal gangster fiasco with the main source reneging on testifying. When Tanya had approached him with the Strachan story idea, he knew it could be one of the biggest. And there was something else he'd noticed: he was becoming quite fond of the ex-patients and their childish innocence. It was heartbreaking. By putting Strachan behind bars, he'd at least help them obtain justice.

All he had to deal with now was that domineering brother of his. Most of his life Max had been in the background, and some things never change. But he had to forget the sibling rivalry; move on. He lit a cigarette and inhaled deeply. As the nicotine entered his brain, he felt light-headed.

"Scott's right. Let's stay focussed and go after our criminal," Max said calmly. Christy smiled and winked at him.

****

Nothing was going right. Absolutely nothing. Daniel grimaced as he hung up the phone. Madeleine Carmichael was backtracking. She was having difficulties with her counterpart, Harold Hastings, at the Canadian Embassy in Washington. He wasn't cooperating; no doubt, he was stalling due to pressure from the CIA. It wasn't difficult to figure out. Why on earth would the CIA want any further leaks? It had to protect itself, and this included Strachan who was now a part of the organization. Strachan was denying everything. When the story broke about his involvement with the CIA, he'd gone on the defence, verbally attacking Reva, Max, Tanya and *The Gazette.* An ominous silence followed his threats to bring lawsuits.

Now, Max was calling daily asking, "How are things, Daniel? Any new developments on bringing our case to criminal court?"

****

When things were not going exactly as Daniel wanted, it put him in a bad humour. What the hell was he to do? No one was cooperating. Maybe they were afraid to. He leafed through the Strachan file to a copy of a letter he'd sent to the Prime Minister's Office in Ottawa:

Daniel Callaghan,
Callaghan & Forrester, Barristers,
Sun Life Building,
1155 Metcalfe Street, Suite 1903,
Montreal, Quebec. H3B 2V6
Phone: (514) 486-7009

July 30, 1976

The Right Honourable Darcy Donnelly,
Office of the Prime Minister,
80 Wellington Street,
Ottawa, Ontario.
K1A 0A2

Dear Prime Minister:

I am writing to express grave concern about Dr. Samuel Strachan's treatment of his patients at the Montreal Psychiatric Institute during the period April 1958 through September 1969. Our research and documentation (per attached letter and dossier) provides complete evidence that Dr. Strachan knowingly administered toxic drugs including LSD to his patients. His treatment of these patients as experimental guinea pigs involved massive dosages of drugs, electro-shock treatment and sleep-induced therapy, all funded by the CIA.

Four of these former patients have come forward and are willing to testify in criminal court. I have contacted the RCMP, but have had no response to date regarding an investigation.

Would you please contact me regarding this matter as soon as possible?

Sincerely,
Daniel Callaghan

Two weeks later, the prime minister replied with a carefully worded promise to look into the allegations. However, since then nothing had transpired.

Daniel picked up *The Gazette* on his desk and smirked as he looked at the front page photograph of Prime Minister Donnelly smiling with his hand clasped on U.S. President Louis Talbot's right shoulder. They were enjoying a game of golf at the posh Seigneury Club on the Ottawa River. It was difficult not to be cynical. Donnelly was nothing but a puppet of the U.S. Republican government. Nothing had been the same since JFK's assassination. *Really*, Daniel thought, *the country was going to ruin*. It was big money that counted, and Talbot was backed by the powerful business elite.

To add to Daniel's woes, Reva had informed him that Donnelly's father-in-law was a psychiatrist at the Montreal Psychiatric Institute and had been there during Dr. Strachan's reign. No, things were not going very well. Quite an upset when he was so accustomed to winning.

Nevertheless, he was determined to see Strachan brought to trial. If criminal court was an impossibility, it'd have to be a civil case. He reached in the bottom drawer of his desk and pulled out his silver flask. The first sip of scotch burned as it made its way down his throat. No more time could be wasted. After Scott, Christy and Sarah had agreed to testify, he'd heard that Clarissa and Sheldon Schmedeck also wanted to go to court on behalf of Clarissa's mother, Mrs. Smythe, but she was very fragile. Daniel knew that he had to act promptly. He couldn't take the chance on losing the patients' testimonies.

As he felt the effects of the scotch, he had an idea: he'd bring the goddamn thing to civil court but fight it like a criminal lawyer. Be damned. He slowly opened the drawer again and reached in.

****

When she answered her phone in *The Gazette* office, Tanya was surprised to hear Larry's voice. It had been six months since their separation. She'd heard from Sheldon Schmedeck that Larry had taken a flat on Pine Avenue near the hospital.

"What the hell are you trying to do?" Larry demanded. "Everyone's talking about it at the hospital. Have you gone completely mad?

"You know exactly what I'm doing, Larry. Bringing that monster Strachan to trial."

"You *have* gone mad … Tanya, you don't have a chance in hell of winning."

"I'm not so sure about that. You'll see." Tanya gripped the receiver tightly.

"I can't believe it. You've become one of those raging feminists. What's next, burning your bra?"

"Is that why you phoned me? To berate me?"

"I thought you might've come to your senses. But I see it's hopeless."

"I don't have to listen to this." Tanya hung up the phone. She thought about the collapse of her marriage. She couldn't blame it on the exposé. The fault lay in an accumulation of events and the inevitable scenario of two people searching for different things in life. Larry was right: she was a feminist, and maybe it wasn't such a bad idea to burn her bra. He simply couldn't cope with her independence and determination. Chances of a reconciliation, which she had thought about over the past few months, was now impossible. However painful, she was convinced that she'd made the right decision. Their separation was like a death, although Larry was still around and probably would be for some time. It saddened her to think of how their relationship had deteriorated from one of love to hostility.

Max looked up from his desk. "More domestic bliss?"

"Oh, Max—I can't stand it. Nothing's changed since my last conversation with him."

"Maybe a drink at the Berkeley would cheer you up. Besides, I've got something interesting I'd like to tell you."

****

Tanya sipped her wine and leaned her head back against the banquette. Berkeley's was reasonably quiet. There was at least half an hour before the noisy after-five crowd arrived. Playing softly in the background was a recording of Lena Horne's "Autumn in New York." The waiter returned with napkins and a small dish of peanuts, which he placed on the table in front of them. Max lit Tanya's cigarette and gently stroked her cheek with his fingertips.

"I feel better already," she said.

"You're looking better too."

"Now what's this interesting thing you have to tell me?"

Max told her that he'd been doing some research at the McGill library on brainwashing. "I was astounded to read that Josef Mengele, who conducted gruesome experiments on concentration camp victims at Auschwitz, secretly entered Canada under the auspices of the CIA in the early 1960s. The techniques developed in Nazi camps to control human behaviour—radiation, electro-shock and hallucinogenic drugs—were used on psychiatric guinea pigs. This, of course, was done under the pretense of national security."

"What! Are you serious?" Tanya put her hand over her mouth.

"Absolutely. And this 'Angel of Death' Dr. Mengele was involved with our dear Dr. Strachan's experiments at the Psychiatric Institute."

"That's bloody unbelievable."

Max continued to tell her how Strachan and Mengele had met in Bavaria in 1945. At the time, Mengele was in hiding while Strachan was at the Nuremberg Trials. Then back in Montreal in the early 1950s, Strachan exposed links between schizophrenia and eye colour.

"You know, Mengele's obsession was eye colour," Max said.

"I didn't know that."

"It's well documented. So it all ties in."

"Perfectly." Tanya sipped her wine.

"Although much of this has been denied, the evidence is there. Strachan and Mengele had a connection."

"You know Max, this is dynamite. What more could we ask for?"

"We'll have to double-check all our facts before we present this to Daniel."

"I'll start work on it tomorrow," Tanya promised.

"In the meantime, how about some dinner and a little R&R at my apartment?"

"I'd like that." Tanya placed her hand on his.

****

Max quickly stubbed out his cigarette and rose from his seat as Clarissa and her mother walked arm-in-arm into the small, informal meeting room on the fifth floor of *The Gazette.* Even though Tanya had forewarned him about Mrs. Smythe's frailty, Max wasn't prepared for such a bird-like creature. He estimated she couldn't weigh more than 85 pounds.

Mrs. Smythe's white hair was tied back in a chignon with a few wisps circling her ears. As she glanced from Max to Tanya, her thin, quivering lips curled up at the corners. A touch of rouge and lip gloss camouflaged her ghost-like appearance. Draped around her shoulders was a pale yellow shawl which she clutched with her bony fingers. Underneath the shawl, a paisley dress reached well below her knees, almost touching her matching yellow pumps. Clarissa told Tanya that although her mother required a walking cane, she'd insisted on wearing the heels. Since Tanya had last visited her at Atwater, her sad grey eyes hadn't changed. The most heartening thing was how much more alert she appeared.

When Clarissa phoned Tanya, she'd confirmed that her mother wished to meet at *The Gazette* rather than at the nursing home. Apparently, lately, Mrs. Smythe wanted outings. This was quite a contrast from when she lay weeping and barely speaking in the dingy Atwater ward. Since her discharge from the institution into Clarissa and Sheldon's care, there had been a marked improvement in her state of mind. Clarissa had reported that one of the nursing home's psychiatrists saw her on a regular basis and adjusted her medication accordingly.

Max helped Mrs. Smythe into a cozy leather armchair as Clarissa adjusted her mother's dress and shawl. "Comfortable, Mom?"

"Quite." Mrs. Smythe's tapped her silver-handled cane on the floor for emphasis.

Tanya pulled up a chair next to hers. "I see you've made quite an improvement since the last time we met at the hospital."

"It's good to be out of *that place*."

Tanya noticed Clarissa staring at her mother. Although glamorous and impeccably dressed as always, Clarissa appeared more distant and on edge. Perhaps she was regretting her decision to expose her frail mother to this investigation. But Mrs. Smythe was lucid enough to understand what was going on and had insisted she be part of it. Now that she was out of the institution, she wanted to tell her story.

Max raised his eyebrows, as his eyes met Tanya's. Clearly he was also wondering whether they were making a mistake asking this little old lady to testify.

Abruptly, Mrs. Smythe pounded her tiny fist on her armchair. "Why is everyone pussyfooting around me? Do you think I don't know what's going on?"

Clarissa rushed over and put an arm around her shoulder. "Mom, please—don't upset yourself. It's not good for your heart."

Mrs. Smythe shook her arm off. "I'll be the judge of what's good for my heart." She eased herself out of the armchair and walked gingerly over to the window, leaning on the sill for support.

"Look, I've had enough of being dictated to. All the psychiatrists telling me what to do, trying to force all those drugs on me. I'm sick and tired of it," she said.

Everyone froze. Max cleared his throat. Tanya watched Clarissa carefully.

"It must be the new medication. I've never seen her like this," Clarissa told them.

"What do you mean you've never seen me like this? When do I ever get a chance to speak out? You all think you know what's best for me, don't you?"

"Please, Mom."

Max lit a cigarette and inhaled deeply. "Wait a minute—let her speak. I think there's one hell of a lot that wants to come out."

"You're darn right there is. For years I've been treated like a guinea pig —Dr. Strachan's drugs, electro-shock treatment and his disgusting brainwashing. Well, it's not working now, I can tell you that. You know those little pink pills that make people stupid? I flushed them down the toilet." She turned around from the window and looked at the shocked faces.

"Now are you ready to hear my story?"

****

When *The Gazette* published Mrs. Smythe's story on September 5, 1976, no one was more surprised at the overwhelming response than Tanya and Max. They'd expected the phones would ring nonstop as occurred after the initial story with Scott Beauford, Christy Amherst and Sarah Conroy. That, of course, did happen. But, in addition, angry demonstrators set up stations with placards outside *The Gazette* and the Montreal Psychiatric

Institution, demanding justice. Many of the participants were former psychiatric patients and outraged relatives. What triggered the outcry was the front page headline:

A Trip to Hell at the Montreal Psychiatric Institute

Seventy-five-year-old woman tells her story

By Max Callaghan and Tanya Kowalski

It was followed by a photograph of Mrs. Smythe in her wheelchair looking frail and drawn. Her arthritic fingers clutched her shawl as she stared directly into the camera with her forlorn grey eyes. It would grip any reader's heart. The explosive lead read:

Sally Smythe, a former psychiatric patient of the world-renowned Dr. Strachan of the Montreal Psychiatric Institute, is struggling to get her life together after her devastating experience in the Sleep Room where she underwent massive drug therapy, electro-shock and brainwashing.

"Dr. Strachan tried to erase all my memories of anything that happened in the past. He said it was the only way to cure my depression. I believed in him," said Mrs. Smythe.

For almost five years, Mrs. Smythe was in and out of the Montreal Psychiatric Institute. She became completely dependent on Dr. Strachan, who reduced her to an infantile state where she slept for days and had to have her diapers changed. Tape recordings under her pillow repeated over and over how she should behave if she wanted to be loved. She was helpless to care for herself and remembers little of the weeks she was in the Sleep Room.

Mrs. Smythe vaguely recalled being wheeled on a stretcher to the basement laboratory where electrodes were attached to her head. After a tremendous jolt, she remembered nothing until waking in a daze in an unfamiliar room. She later discovered that it was the Sleep Room. Piercing shouts and whimpers from somewhere in the distance filled the room. She'd awake only long enough to receive more medication and hear Dr. Strachan's voice reassuring her that she would get better.

"I lost track of all time," said Mrs. Smythe. "It could have been months later when I realized that I was in another hospital. How could I possibly have gotten there?"

The hospital in question was the long-term Atwater Psychiatric Hospital where patients diagnosed as incurables were sent. Mrs. Smythe's daughter, Clarissa and her physician husband diligently fought to have her released into their care.

"Never have I seen such a helpless creature," Clarissa declared. "She was on a downhill spiral. All she'd repeat to me was 'I want to walk. I want to walk'. I couldn't hide the tears whenever I visited her. Obviously, there was something inside her head telling her that she had to get out, no matter what."

The article went on to reinforce that Dr. Strachan had knowingly administered LSD to his unsuspecting patients:

Criminal lawyer Daniel Callaghan, who has been retained by the former psychiatric patients and their relatives, has been attempting to have Dr. Strachan tried in criminal court, but has run into many obstacles. When he sent a letter to Prime Minister Donnelly expressing his concerns about Dr. Strachan's experiments and the CIA involvement, the terse response was, "I'll look into the matter." Since the letter, there has been no action on the part of the Prime Minister. In addition, the CIA, RCMP and the Department of Justice have been stalling.

Upon further research, Daniel Callaghan has discovered that one of the prominent psychiatrists at the Montreal Psychiatric Institute is related to the Prime Minister through marriage.

Legal fees have escalated and a concerned group has been diligently fundraising in the Montreal community in hopes of bringing this case to trial as soon as possible.

"It is almost impossible to get any answers from the CIA or the RCMP," said Daniel Callaghan. "It looks like the only course we can now pursue is to enter an action re Dr. Strachan in a civil law court. That's certainly better than nothing. But it's a sad day for justice in Canada when the Crown won't bring a charge."

In response, Dr. Strachan has threatened to sue *The Montreal Gazette* and journalists Max

Callaghan and Tanya Kowalski for slander. He denies all allegations, citing it was in the name of psychiatry, that he had attempted to treat these patients to the best of his abilities.

Repeated phone calls to the CIA headquarters in Washington have not been returned.

"Whatever is going on, no matter what kind of cover up we are confronted with, we'll get to the bottom of it," Daniel Callaghan said adamantly.

Meanwhile, Mrs. Smythe has started walking again, something she and her daughter thought would never happen.

"I may be old and frail, but I'm going to walk. Just watch me and see for yourselves," she says as she pushes herself out of her wheelchair.

****

In Washington, Scott Beauford had been following the *Gazette* articles faithfully. Whenever he read about the psychiatric ward, he felt the fury festering like an old wound, its poison seeping into his bloodstream. He slapped down the September 5th *Gazette* on the coffee table, looking at tiny Mrs. Smythe staring up at him. *What the hell. What right did anyone have to prey upon this fragile, white-haired lady? Just what had she done to deserve it?* It all came back to Dr. Strachan. He had done it to each and every one of them. Blindly, they had all gone to him in the belief he would cure them. They were to be transformed into better people.

But Scott wasn't that much better off than before he'd started seeing Strachan. Although he was back at Georgetown assisting his sister with the administrative work, he kept forgetting things. Simple things, like where he'd put his keys, or if he'd locked the door when he went out. It had to be that bastard Strachan who'd bent his mind in the Sleep Room. Although some of those LSD trips weren't so bad after all. The drug had given him a real high, much more than the booze did. It was the electro-shocks that fried his brain, making him forget not only the bad things but the good.

As far as he could see, there was only one good thing that had come out of this horrific experience: Christy Amherst. He could feel himself getting excited at the thought of her, and those full red lips and sexy eyes flashing at him whenever they met. Oh, she was a cagey one, for sure. But so enticing. When she'd slipped him her phone number at the last *Gazette* meeting, he was pretty certain that he'd follow up. He walked over to his oak writing desk and pulled out his telephone index.

The phone rang four times before she picked up the receiver. "Scott, great to hear from you. What's up?"

"I was wondering if you'd seen *The Gazette*."

"You mean the story on Mrs. Smythe? I read it yesterday, and I've been fuming ever since," Christy said.

"Yeah. It makes me furious to think of what he did to all of us," Scott said.

There was a moment's silence. "Are you there, Christy?"

Christy's voice cracked. "I'm here all right. But I just feel so awful every time that man's name comes up."

"I know. So do I … Christy, how'd you like to meet me in Montreal this weekend?"

"I'd like to, but I honestly can't afford another trip right now."

"How about if I pay for your airfare? It'll be my treat."

"I don't know. It's kinda expensive. I hate to put you out."

"You don't have to worry about that. Just say you'll come. I think it'll be good for both of us," Scott said.

Barely three days later he was on an Air Canada DC 9 flying to Montreal. He leaned his head against the back of his seat and closed his eyes, thinking about their weekend ahead. As the plane approached Montreal's Dorval airport, he felt the sweat on the back of his neck. Maybe it was the medication, but somehow he doubted it. He knew it was Christy. He'd noticed the strong attraction between them the first time at one of the Friday afternoon dances at the Psychiatric Institute. He'd felt a little uncomfortable when Christy had rested her head on his shoulder and swayed to the music with him. But he felt the excitement—the smell of her hair and her jasmine perfume.

And here he was, some ten years later, smelling the same jasmine scent as Christy rounded the corner at L'hotel de la Montagne's lobby bar. She was wearing a lime green angora sweater buttoned up the back. Her blonde hair was pulled back and held in place with a matching scarf. A few wisps of hair fell playfully around her ears. She had on her black leather miniskirt that she had worn to the meeting at *The Gazette.* He felt light-headed.

"Hi there," she said as she slipped onto the bar stool beside him.

"Great to see you, Christy."

Scott blew a smoke ring in the air and sipped his bourbon on the rocks. Christy leaned against his arm as she reached for one of his Winston cigarettes.

"May I?" She smiled at him.

"By all means." Scott slipped the package closer to her and flicked his lighter.

"How're you doing?" she asked.

"Not too bad. It's … really good to see you." Although her perfume was intoxicating, it made him slightly uneasy. The scent was similar to what his mother had worn. But now with her death, surely he could get on with his life. As long as he took his daily medications, he could control his anger.

He ordered a rye and ginger for Christy and another bourbon for himself. In the past, a couple of bourbons helped to calm him as long as he didn't have too much. He was pretty sure he could discipline himself this evening. It was important that he do so. Strangely, it was almost as if Christy and he had come together because of a common bond. Incest. Could anyone ever get over it? Probably not.

They had talked at length about it the last time they'd met for a drink after *The Gazette* meeting. Each had empathized with the other's hurt, betrayal and disappointment. It was all part of their healing process. And now that they'd openly discussed it, they could move forward.

Over the years, both had been in and out of unsatisfactory relationships. Christy had married briefly and divorced. Scott also couldn't make a long-term commitment.

He lit another cigarette and turned to look at Christy. "I was wondering … what do you say we go up to the suite and order room service for dinner?"

"Sounds good to me," Christy said.

He finished his drink and called for the chit.

During dinner the discussion turned to Dr. Strachan. Even though both attempted to avoid it, it was inevitable.

"What do you think about the court case?" Christy asked.

"Things aren't moving quickly enough." Scott put his knife and fork on his plate.

"Well, I guess these things always take longer than you think they will."

"Yeah. But what I'd like to know is why that monster isn't in criminal court like Tanya and Max said he would be," Scott said.

"I think they're still trying, but … "

"Not hard enough," Scott cut in angrily. "Now they and that lawyer brother of Max's are talking about just a civil action. That makes me really mad."

"What are you saying?"

"I'm saying a civil court case isn't enough. The guy has to be tried as a criminal for what he's done to us." Scott pushed his plate away.

"At least we get to try him in court," Christy commented.

"So what? All that'll come out of it is they'll try to pay us off, so we go away. Goddamn money. No amount of money could ever be enough compensation," Scott said loudly.

"Look, Scott, I'm growing kinda fond of you. Just don't go and do anything stupid. It's not worth it."

"Like what?"

"I don't know. But you scare me when you talk like that. You get a kind of wild look in your eyes. I just don't want you to go off the deep end."

"Okay, let's forget it. There are more important things to talk about than that old bastard." Scott put his arms around her back, kissed her lips and slowly started unbuttoning her sweater.

****

When Reva Rothwell handed in her resignation at the Montreal Psychiatric Institute, there was an outcry from both staff and patients alike. After 25 years, she'd established such a reputation that her expertise was sought by psychiatric hospitals throughout Canada. Frequently she was the guest speaker at the psychiatric nurses' convention.

Reva thought about the accumulation of events that had led to her decision. It had been a laborious journey since she had agreed to cooperate with Tanya and Max on the Strachan exposé. The pressure was mounting at both the institution and at home. Reva's edginess was putting a strain on her relationship with Lydia. The final denouement was the harassing phone calls from Strachan. She knew he was extremely agitated, but then, so was she.

It was also becoming increasingly difficult to keep her involvement a secret from Lydia. Although Lydia had seen *The Gazette* articles, she was unaware of the extent of Reva's participation in the disclosure. Then one evening, Lydia had arrived home unexpectedly after a nurses' conference when Reva was slumped in the sofa chair weeping.

"Reva, what's wrong?" Lydia had rushed to her.

"I can't take the pressure any more," Reva had cried.

"You mean the hospital?"

"Yeah. It's getting to me."

"You've been acting so strange lately, I knew it must be serious. Tell me what's happened." Lydia spoke softly.

After much agonizing, Reva told Lydia about how she had discovered the files in the basement vault and gone to Tanya with the documentation, and that now Dr. Strachan was making harassing phone calls to her.

"You've got to get the hell out of there before you have a breakdown," Lydia advised her.

"I know I do."

So in the final analysis, Reva agreed to resign from the hospital. It just wasn't worth the stress it was putting on their relationship. Lydia was the one person in Reva's life whom she loved and was strongly connected to. Lydia was her stability. She provided a modicum of sanity in their insane lives. And Reva knew how tempting the tranquillizers and booze could become after a stressful day at the institute.

Now two weeks after their conversation, Reva was alone again. Lydia was out of town at another conference in Sault Ste. Marie. But it was good to be alone. What Reva needed was time to think this whole thing through. Tanya and Max had promised to protect her from any harassment from her employer. But now, with her resignation, she was *free* to go public like everyone else who was involved. With the thought of that freedom, the pressure was dissipating.

She reached over and turned up the volume on the stereo beside the sofa. The Beatles were singing "Love Me Do"— one of her favourites. She poured a glass of red wine from the scarlet pitcher and took a sip. God, was it good. She could feel it immediately warming her body. Her cheeks felt flushed as she sang along with the Beatles. "Love, love me … " Putting her glass down on the coffee table, she turned up the volume one more notch and started dancing around the small room.

"Love, love me …" she belted out, laughing and swirling around, arms flailing in the air. *I'm as crazy as the rest of them*, she tittered, almost falling over the pine rocking chair. *But I'll play on, that's what I'll do. No one can get me here, not even Strachan. We'll see him in court in no time. I honestly can't wait.* She picked up her wineglass and took a big gulp as the music played on.

****

Tanya reached over and tapped a cigarette out of the Old Winston packet on the bedside table. She lit it, took a long drag and slowly exhaled. A wispy cloud of smoke swirled up over the bed circling toward the ceiling. Resting her head on a pillow propped up against the headboard, she closed her eyes and savoured that first jolt of nicotine. *God, it felt good— especially after sex.*

Max was as skilled in his lovemaking as he was at journalism. Inquisitive, cerebral, gently probing and playful. It was great to be with this craggy man who wanted to know how she felt and what pleased her in bed. How things had changed in a couple of generations. Tanya thought about what her mother had told her about Grandma Kowalski. A timid woman, Granny was reluctant to undress in front of her husband. One evening, burly Grandpa Kowalski had snarled at her, "Who wants to see your shaggy *pyrih*, anyway?" Tanya had laughed at the Ukrainian name *pyrih*, a playful reference to the intimate part of the female anatomy. Much like the French *fleur intime*.

It was difficult to imagine how this older generation of women coped with their sexual duties after a long day of cooking, cleaning and child rearing. It was almost ritualistic. After the kids were put to bed, no matter how tired a woman was, she was expected to meet her husband's demands. Working the farmland from morning to dusk seemed to increase men's sexual appetites.

Max rounded the corner from the bathroom with an aquamarine bath towel wrapped around his waist. His hair was more dishevelled than usual, and without his glasses, his eyes looked mischievous. Even though he was rumpled, he really was a sexy man.

"You look at peace with the world. A glass of wine to celebrate?" he asked, lighting a cigarette.

"Please."

"You know I'm glad I scrapped that ridiculous policy of mine."

"What's that?"

"No mixing business and pleasure." Max grinned.

"It's called pillow talk. I think it works well for us, don't you?" Tanya asked.

"I do." Max leaned over and kissed her lips.

"Speaking of that, I think we should get out another piece as soon as possible. Keep the public interested," he said.

"A piece?" Tanya teased.

Max's raspy laughter filled the room. "I think we should follow up with the Mengele connection. It could be just what we need for another public outcry."

"Well, all your research checks out. Mengele and Strachan did meet and share ideas on brainwashing."

"Right. We have all the facts, so what's to stop us?" Max asked.

"Nothing as far as I can see."

"Hopefully it'll jolt the government into taking action."

"Hopefully." Tanya sipped her wine.

As they lay on the bed, Tanya and Max discussed the response from the previous *Gazette* articles. Public pressure was building. From all the phone calls they'd received, it seemed the public was indignant and rightfully so, particularly regarding Mrs. Smythe. No one liked to see an elderly lady being taken advantage of. The front page photograph of her and the story were scooped up by newspapers across Canada and the United States. One of the first American newspapers to publish the article was *The Washington Post*. Scott Beauford had eagerly called expressing his gratitude to Tanya and his outrage at Strachan's tactics.

Phone calls to *The Gazette* came from every direction. One of great interest was from the Leader of the Opposition in Ottawa, who was demanding answers from Prime Minister Donnelly. Once again, Donnelly was denying any knowledge of Dr. Strachan except from what he'd read in the *Gazette*. He also tried to cover up the fact that his father-in-law was a psychiatrist at the Montreal Psychiatric Institute. Television coverage of the parliamentary proceedings reached one of its largest audiences since JFK's assassination.

"From all that's happened, I'd say we're a good team," Max said.

"Couldn't agree more." Tanya reached over and butted her cigarette in the bedside ashtray.

"Well, there's nothing that makes people more indignant than someone taking advantage of an elderly lady. But who said anything about taking advantage of a young one?" Max laughed as he pulled the sheet off Tanya.

****

The Montreal Gazette
May 10, 1977

Montreal Psychiatrist Conferred with Nazi Angel of Death
An exclusive report
By Max Callaghan and Tanya Kowalski

In the early 1960s Dr. Josef Mengele secretly entered Canada under the auspices of the CIA. Mengele, who had conducted gruesome experiments on concentration camp victims at Auschwitz, is well known as the "Angel of Death." Under the guise of national security, the techniques developed in Nazi camps to control human behaviour were used on psychiatric "guinea pigs." Mengele conferred with Dr. Samuel Strachan of the Montreal Psychiatric Institute who was at this time conducting his own experiments of electro-shock and drug therapy, including LSD, on his Sleep Room patients. The psychiatric treatment involved erasing patients' memories and reprogramming them with controlled human behaviour.

After the meetings, the CIA secretly deported Mengele from Montreal to Brazil where he remains in hiding. Mengele is one of the top targets of Nazi hunter Simon Wiesenthal who is credited with bringing Nazi war criminals to justice after the genocide of the Jews in World War II. Wiesenthal helped track down Adolph Eichmann in Argentina in the 1950s.

Mengele and Strachan's history dates back to when they first met in Bavaria in 1945. At the time, Strachan was at the Nuremberg Trials while Mengele was in hiding, protected by the CIA. When Strachan returned to Montreal, he exposed links between schizophrenia and eye colour. Mengele had done extensive research in this area.

Max put the paper down and looked over his spectacles at Tanya. "It's all there. Just as we reported."

"Did you know the switchboard had fifty calls today?" Tanya asked.

"That's great. Now all we have to do is wait to hear from the government. Strachan consorting with a war criminal should jolt them, if anything will," Max said.

"You'd think so."

"There's only one thing that concerns me." Max lit another cigarette.

"What's that?"

"They could stonewall it until Parliament adjourns for summer break, hoping it doesn't come back in the fall."

"Oh, damn—I hadn't thought about that."

"Right now I think the government of Canada is up to its neck with the CIA, hoping it will go away. But I'll tell you something: it won't. We'll sue in civil court just as Daniel has advised."

One of the first phone calls Max received that morning was from Daniel, who had been counselling them carefully on the legal implications of the story. Satisfied with the thorough research of factual material, he too was convinced of the importance of the Mengele/Strachan connection. It would strengthen their case, be it criminal or civil. Most likely the way events were going, Strachan would be tried in a civil courtroom. However, the important thing was that he was tried. Daniel was anxious to bring the case to trial before the public lost interest.

When Max hung up the phone, he jotted down some notes and turned to Tanya. "Looks like Daniel is as anxious to bring Strachan to trial as we are."

"Any new developments on his side?"

"Not really. He's exasperated that the government has been able to stonewall this as long as it has."

"I don't blame him one bit."

Max sighed. "I thought we had a bombshell, but it seems the CIA has more clout in Ottawa than we do."

"Well, I think some of the best news to date is Reva's support now that she's free of the institute." Tanya reported that Reva was considerably calmer since she'd handed in her resignation. The threatening phone calls from Dr. Strachan had ceased. And now that she had told Lydia about her involvement, the tension at home had eased up. During their last phone call, Reva had said emphatically, "I'm ready to testify at any time."

All was moving along smoothly with the ex-patients as well, although Scott was still expressing significant anger. However, this could be a good thing, as long as it was channelled in the right direction: Strachan's court case.

Tanya glanced out the lead-paned window at the sun dancing on the budding willow trees. She loved this time of year approaching June. It was always a new beginning, new growth. And with this June, there were new challenges. Not only the Strachan trial, but her entering into a formal separation agreement with Larry, in which he appeared to be as anxious to settle issues as she was. Although it was a lot to deal with, the renewal of spring and her relationship with Max seemed to give her strength and fortitude to draw on.

Max looked at her affectionately. "It's been a real challenge getting everyone on our side. But as they say in horse racing, 'They're at the post.'"

****

When Samuel B. Strachan received the subpoena, he gripped the left side of his chest. His heart pounded so rapidly he could hear it thumping. Good God, was he having a heart attack? Never in his life had he felt such pressure. Everyone had let him down, including the traitors at the CIA and RCMP who were probably trying to make some out-of-court settlement.

He reached for the phone and dialled the familiar number.

"Good afternoon. Mr. Maloney's office."

"Is he there?" Strachan asked.

"I'm sorry, Dr. Strachan—he's in a meeting."

God damn it. Lately, he'd noticed a strained atmosphere at the CIA headquarters in Langley. Whenever he attempted to contact Maloney, his secretary too quickly said that he was busy or out of town. All this after Maloney had reassured him that they were doing everything they could to protect him and crush the accusations against him. But the evidence was damning. The allegation of administering LSD and brainwashing unsuspecting psychiatric patients was supported with documentation and the former patients' testimonies.

It was an insuperable mission. Strachan felt trapped. What was he to do? After the last two decades of being revered around the world as a god-like figure, he couldn't figure out his next move. He'd never been questioned before. On the contrary, everyone listened to him, carried out his orders promptly. Now it was he who had received orders to appear in Canadian court on September 13, 1977.

It had been a difficult 10 months. No matter where he turned, he felt abandoned. Even some of his colleagues were looking at him strangely. His worst fears were becoming true—he was becoming paranoid like so many of his patients. Everywhere he went, he noticed people staring at him, and if he looked back, they would abruptly avert their eyes, or so he thought.

But he'd fight it out. What he needed was a top-notch lawyer, then he could beat this thing. Beat the rotten journalists and publisher at *The Gazette* who were defaming his character in their scathing articles. And to think how low they had stooped to get that pathetic old Mrs. Smythe out of her psychiatric bed to come forward. But they were all out there—Scott Beauford,

Christy Amherst, Sarah Conway—ready to testify, go after the kill. Traitors. All of them traitors after all he had done for them. Just where would they be if it hadn't been for him? He loathed to think about it.

And they'd all still believe in him if it hadn't been for that Tanya and Max at *The Gazette* interfering. He thought back to the night on Ward Five when that insolent nurse had dared to question him, Dr. Strachan. A paltry psychiatric nurse. Who did she think she was, anyway? He'd get those two if his life depended on it. He just had to stay calm and figure out how.

****

Daniel Callaghan was becoming impatient. After six months, there was still no response from Prime Minister Donnelly's office. Whenever he phoned, the curt response "We're looking into it" infuriated him. He'd tried calling Madeline Carmichael in External Affairs again, but she'd told him, "Look, Daniel. I've done all I can. It's a dead end. The boys in Ottawa and Langley are simply not cooperating."

Apparently her Washington counterpart Harold Hastings who'd promised to look into it had now reneged, saying he couldn't get any answers. Madeleine had also attempted to contact Maxwell Maloney at the CIA, but with no luck. Maloney had made himself scarce—either out of the office or out of town. It didn't really matter which because he was obviously not collaborating. At least not with her or Hastings. Maybe the RCMP was having better luck.

"But we've got all the documents," Daniel said once again.

"I'm well aware of it. What else can I do short of putting a stick of dynamite up their asses?"

"Really, Madeleine."

After he hung up the phone, Daniel called Max and asked to meet him alone at the Berkeley.

The bar was dimly lit as Max made his way through the haze of cigarette smoke. Sammy, the pianist, looked up and nodded. Daniel was at his regular table at the back of the room sipping his scotch and soda. He'd taken off his navy suit jacket and loosened his red silk tie. The first thing Max noticed was Daniel's bleary eyes and the grey-flecked stubble on his chin. *Quite unusual for impeccable Daniel. Something must be up.*

"Thanks for coming, Max." Daniel motioned to the seat beside him. "What'll you have?"

Max turned to the young waitress who had approached their table. "*Vin rouge, s'il vous plait.*"

"*A bientôt.* Our house wine is Côte du Rhone or would you prefer a Bordeaux?"

"*Vin de la maison, merci.*" Max lit a cigarette.

As soon as the waitress left their table, an awkward silence followed. There was always tension when the brothers first met. Usually it took a drink to ease them into conversation. Max watched Daniel as he stirred the ice in his glass with a plastic swizzle stick. Sammy was playing one of his signatures: "Satin Doll." Max hummed along.

Within minutes the waitress returned with Max's glass of wine. Taking a sip, Max looked at Daniel. "What's up?"

"You and Tanya did a great job on the Mengele article."

"Thanks." Max raised his glass. "Here's hoping it'll strengthen our case."

"Can't do anything but." Daniel cleared his throat. "I'm getting a little frustrated—no response from the Department of Justice, the PMO ... or the RCMP ... or the CIA."

"Pretty pathetic, isn't it?"

"You'd think at least with the uproar in the House of Commons and all the publicity that something would have happened."

"All I know is that Tanya and I've had tremendous response to our articles, and then absolutely no follow-up by the government. It's all very strange."

"I can only reach one conclusion. *Somehow* the Canadian government is involved in this whole mess."

"Why do you figure that?" Max asked.

"Look at the facts—no cooperation whatsoever on the part of either government, and no indication that this stonewalling will ever cease. If our government wasn't involved, why won't it lay a criminal charge against Strachan? It would be the easiest thing to do."

"So what you're saying is that we've no alternative but to proceed on our own in civil court?"

"Right."

As they talked, Max carefully observed his brother. Generally, Daniel exuded confidence, but on this particular evening he appeared vulnerable. He constantly fiddled with the swizzle stick in his glass, at one point snapping it in half and saying, "That's what I'd like to do to each and every one of those fuckers."

Usually it took a lot to shock Max but he had to admit that Daniel's last comment had succeeded. No, not like Daniel at all. But then Daniel had always liked to win.

"Pretty strong sentiments."

"Well, I'm so pissed off."

Daniel excused himself to go to the bathroom. As he walked across the room, Max noticed his unsteady gait. The tall erect body and muscular shoulders were still there, although he'd gained a few pounds over the last year or so.

Max remembered all the years of competition he had endured growing up in Notre-Dame-de-Grace, a leafy, middle-class Montreal suburb. As early as he could recollect, Daniel had excelled in school and sports. Academically, Max did fairly well, but in sports, he was inept. He'd tried out for volleyball and basketball but never made the teams. While Daniel revelled in his status as a football quarterback, Max withdrew from all team sports and focussed on his love of history and English literature. Shakespearean heroes and villains figured prominently. Where else could one escape so magnificently with someone throwing a cloak and dagger on the ground or imagining washing one's hands in blood? Or travel along with the brave legendary Roman commander Coriolanus, who was fearless in battle in the fifth century BC? Max thought about the parallels of famed men: their strong sense of honour and pride, their desire for power and control and their eventual paranoia and tragic downfall.

Strachan, no doubt, saw himself as an honourable doctor, a great healer of the mind—someone who was morally doing the right thing. In his mind, all his experiments were done for the *good* of the psychiatric patients. During the l950s and early '60s he'd been hailed as one of the great modern psychiatrists. But it was his huge ego and obsessive nature that led him to believe he was a god-like figure, saving mankind. He revelled in his power and control until his experiments and brainwashing techniques became a merciless masquerade as the tragedy unfolded.

Max's thoughts were interrupted by the reappearance of the waitress who inquired if they wanted refills. She also asked whether he was a professor at McGill, as she thought she'd recognized him. When Dan returned to the table, Max was deeply engaged in conversation with her. "But Mengele of all people—my god, I can't believe it," she said, and then excused herself to retrieve the drinks.

"What was that all about?" Daniel asked.

"She's in third-year Jewish Studies at McGill and was shocked to read about the Strachan/Mengele connection."

"But how did it come up?"

"She asked if I taught journalism at McGill and made the association. She'd seen me around the campus."

"What's the response from the Jewish community?"

"Outrage. As a matter of fact, I had a call from Mrs. Smythe's son-in-law, Dr. Sheldon Schmedeck. He and his wife, Clarissa are pushing to get this thing moving faster," Max told him.

"I'm glad to hear that."

"It gets even better. Dr. Schmedeck is very involved with the Canadian Jewish Congress in Montreal. Mengele is bringing back all the horrors of the Holocaust. Schmedeck hears time and again from the Jews lamenting the persecution of a relative or loved one by the Nazis."

"God damn it. Even though we have the documents, the witnesses, the victims and the public opinion on our side, particularly the Jewish community, we can't budge the government." Daniel pounded the table.

"Wait a minute." Max reached for a cigarette. "Do you think our government is stonewalling because it's involved in the funding as well?"

"Absolutely. There couldn't be any other reason."

"I'd just like to know how on earth Strachan ever thought he could get away with this."

"Well, he can't. I think it's time to close in on him," Daniel said.

"Agreed." They looked at each other and shook hands. Max noticed the ice slowly melting in Daniel's glass.

****

When Tanya entered Clarissa's Sherbrooke Street art gallery, she was impressed with the scenic array of Québécois paintings. To the right of the entrance was an attractive 1855 Cornelius Krieghoff oil on canvas titled *Winter Scene with Horse and Sleigh.* A father stood holding the reins while mother and child huddled together in a fire-engine red sleigh with a horse galloping toward a bridge. The contrast of the white snow and red sleigh was striking. Tanya inched her way closer to admire the painting.

It had been almost three years since she'd bought the bold, colourful Arthur Schilling *Lady with Cloak* painting from Clarissa's exhibition. She and Larry had hung it over the mantelpiece above the fireplace in the living room. Over the years the Ojibwa lady with her spiritual soul and watchful dark eyes had been witness to many passions

196

and conflicts in their marriage. So much had changed: Larry was gone. The house was up for sale, and the Schilling painting would soon be in storage until Tanya found somewhere to live. Lately, she had been staying at Max's after a long day at *The Gazette* rather than return to the lonely house. A sense of sadness and failure overcame her any time she went back there. Things would be better once she moved out, away from the old memories. The separation agreement had been formalized and they were both ready to move on to their new lives.

"What do you think of it?" Clarissa approached so quietly that Tanya was startled.

Tanya turned to greet her. As usual, Clarissa was immaculately dressed in a scarlet suit with gold-brushed buttons and matching pumps. Her dark hair swooped up in a French twist accentuated her high cheekbones and long slender neck.

"Oh, hi. Clarissa. I love it. But now is definitely not the time for me to buy any new painting."

"Perhaps when you are a little more settled."

"Perhaps." Tanya wondered what she had heard from Sheldon about the separation.

"Why don't we go into my office where we can be more comfortable?" Clarissa suggested.

Clarissa's office, like its occupant, was tastefully put together and as glamorous as ever. It exuded the richness of mahogany and leather. On the windowsill stood a large cut-crystal vase overflowing with violet lilacs, their delightful smell permeating the room. Tanya inhaled the scent, remembering the lilac trees surrounding her childhood home.

Once they were seated comfortably, Tanya looked at the youthful photograph of Mrs. Smythe on Clarissa's desk. "How's your mother?"

"Much better thank you ... now that she's had her meds cut in half."

"And she still wants to go to court to testify?"

"Not a particle of doubt in her mind. She wants to go for Strachan's throat."

Tanya laughed, encouraged that Clarissa was more relaxed about her mother testifying. "I guess we don't have to worry about her holding her own. She'll probably fare better than the others."

"Since the article on Mom was published, she's become more confident, and is really enjoying the attention. It's so heart-warming after all her years of confinement at the Psychiatric Institute and Atwater."

Tanya nodded in agreement, noting the intensity of Clarissa's eyes as she spoke.

"What Mom hated most of all was not being in control of her life. Dr. Strachan had taken that away from her, and she was angry. She felt cheated that she'd wasted too much time in a state of confusion. And as if the drugs and shock treatments weren't enough, Strachan had to brainwash her into thinking she was incapable of surviving on her own in the outside world." Clarissa tapped her long red fingernails on the desk and stared at Tanya.

"I'll never forget how depressed she was when I first met her at the Atwater," Tanya said.

"The Atwater was a nightmare but, by some miracle, Mom escaped. And she's proven Dr. Strachan wrong—he can't get to her now."

"No he can't."

"I'm a little worried that the defence lawyers might be too demanding for Mom to deal with. Even though she appears more assertive, she is still fragile." Tanya thought about Mrs. Smythe's frailty—her diminutive frame, heavily lined face, and white hair. "But I can assure you she's a force to be reckoned with," Clarissa added as she looked at the photograph again.

"We have about a month to prepare for the trial. As I told you before, it'll be a civil action. Does she want to see the Palais de Justice beforehand?"

"Definitely. I really appreciate Daniel Callaghan's kind offer to take the patients to the courthouse."

"Hopefully it'll make it a little easier for them when they have to testify. I spoke to him the other day, and he's anxious to get the case moving along."

Clarissa leaned back in her chair. "I was thinking … by the time Strachan's case is heard, more than a decade will have elapsed. Ten long years of grieving and hoping for a cure."

"But we're getting there, slowly but surely." Tanya smiled.

"It's the injustice. How does anyone ever get over it?" Clarissa asked.

"By bringing Strachan to trial we're demanding that justice be served. It's the only way."

Clarissa lit a cigarette, then offered Tanya one. "But it's just so damn painful when it's your own mother."

"Is Sheldon as supportive as ever?"

"I don't know how I'd have survived this without him."

Clarissa told her about Sheldon's involvement with the Jewish Congress and the Jewish community's outrage when the Mengele article was published. Sheldon was more determined than ever to pursue the case. Consequently, a rift had unfolded between him and Larry, who refused to support Sheldon.

"I never thought I'd see this happen," Tanya said.

"Larry is being impossible. After all the evidence, he still refuses to believe that Strachan is an evil man. It's the old doctors' network."

"Some things never change. Maybe now you can see why Larry and I parted ways."

"Totally. Tanya, you have Sheldon's and my support … 100 per cent."

"I appreciate it. I know it's difficult to choose sides when a couple splits."

"Well, circumstances have made the decision a lot easier."

"Thanks. How about I take you out for a little celebration?"

****

"Look Max, we've got all our facts. Things are moving along just like we wanted. So what's your problem?" Tanya cleared a space on the cluttered kitchen table and set down two mugs of coffee. Lately they'd been working into the evening, trying to get all the documents ready for Daniel before the court date, so she often ended up staying at his flat on rue Saint Denis. Like his office at *The Gazette*, it was overflowing with newspapers, books and ashtrays.

"I don't know. It's that sixth sense. I feel there's going to be a snag." He sipped his black coffee.

"But Daniel has all the documents. He's filed the lawsuit with the civil court identifying all of us. Everyone's ready to testify … even Reva."

"Well, I'm relieved to hear that."

Up until her resignation, Reva had been hesitant in her commitment to testify. She had phoned Tanya at least three times a week expressing her concerns about being discovered as the "mole" and losing her job. Once she resigned, her paranoia seemed to subside and Tanya found her more rational about the case.

"I'd say *everything's* in place," Tanya said.

"Hmm … there's only one thing. Strachan is such a crafty bastard. You know he's hired that defence lawyer Irving Hershbaum, and Daniel says he's one hell of a tough guy."

"Isn't Daniel also when he goes after his target? You told me so yourself."

"Usually. I've only seen him shaken once … a long time ago … when he was up against that gruelling criminal lawyer, Gamborini. Apparently they savaged each other."

"But who won?" Tanya poured him another cup of coffee.

"Daniel. But it really took its toll on him. Said he never wanted to go through it again."

"Well, let's hope he doesn't have to." Tanya looked at her watch. "Good lord, it's nine o'clock. Better get ready. Do you want to shower together?" She reached over and playfully took his hand.

"I just don't want Hershbaum to bully our witnesses. They're fragile enough as it is." Max followed her to the bathroom.

****

September 13, 1977

THE TRIAL

Samuel B. Strachan awoke groggily after an extremely restless night in his Ritz Carlton hotel suite. The nightmares had been overwhelming. They were coming after him. Everywhere he looked, another angry face was shouting at him. The long, dark tunnel he ran along led nowhere. There were no escape routes.

He'd gone to bed around midnight, but wakened every hour sweating profusely. The bed covers were in a heap on the floor where he had thrown them. It must have been around three o'clock when he thought a tranquilizer might help him get some sleep. After gulping down two pills with the remainder of his vodka and tonic left on the bedside table, he waited. But nothing seemed to be working. Nothing could relieve his anxiety of what he would have to cope with shortly.

And of all things, it happened to be September 13th. Thirteen had always been his unlucky number. For most of his life, he'd avoided anything with the number in it, including hotel rooms and airplane seats, and absolutely refused to travel on the 13th. Now it again seemed like a bad omen. He cursed Tanya Kowalski and Max Callaghan for initiating the worst nightmare of his life.

Leaning over, he looked at the bedside clock and moaned: five-thirty. God, he'd barely slept. Might as well get up and try to gain some composure before his ten o'clock court appearance. He had four hours before he had to set out for the rue Notre-Dame Palais de Justice—four hours to think about how he and his lawyer were going to defend his reputation. The only good thing that had come out of this wretched ordeal was that he was spared criminal court. At least the traitors at the CIA had unknowingly done him this favour when they abandoned him, as had the RCMP by stonewalling the investigation. But the civil lawsuit named each and every one of them: Strachan, the Psychiatric Institute, the CIA and the Government of Canada. Well, he'd show all of them that he could fend for himself.

Besides, he'd hired Irving Hershbaum, one of Montreal's best defence lawyers, and had managed to get through the preliminary inquiries and examinations for discovery. Hershbaum, who was balding and rotund, had a husky voice and a reputation of peering over his large-framed glasses to intimidate the plaintiffs. Strachan was convinced he had the ability to outwit Daniel Callaghan, that arrogant brother of pinko journalist Max. In all his years of defending some of the most difficult cases, Hershbaum had lost only one. In that case, his client was declared guilty in the murder of his wife. He had lied to Hershbaum about his whereabouts on the night of the brutal slaying and the prosecutor had shredded his arguments. Hershbaum was furious and vowed publicly it would never happen again.

Strachan knew Hershbaum was determined to win this case by portraying him as the honourable and noble saviour of the psychiatric patients. His logic revolved around whose testimony the court would believe: a brilliant doctor, or the unstable ex-patients. He had spent months preparing his case, knowing that he could cleverly intimidate the susceptible plaintiffs. His strategy was carefully thought out—see who was the most vulnerable, and then like a laser beam, penetrate the most delicate organ of a human being: the brain. If Strachan was capable of doing so, Hershbaum could easily do the same. He had all the necessary characteristics: a commanding presence, clarity and perseverance. He lacked only the drugs. And Hershbaum was well aware that he would have to deal with the damning LSD evidence documented in the files that Reva had intercepted. He'd told Strachan he had lain awake many nights planning his next move.

When Strachan thought about Hershbaum's tenacity, he relaxed a little. Surely he would win the case and restore Strachan's impeccable reputation. But why was he having the self-doubts and nightmares? He'd done the best he could in the name of psychiatry. It was a complete misconception that he'd harmed the patients. Absolute rubbish. They were lost souls without him. The brainwashing had erased all the horrid memories of their childhoods so that they could be taught how to function in the world. There was no doubt about it: he'd helped heal their minds, and they should all be grateful. What more could he have done?

It was six o'clock. He picked up the phone and called room service for an early breakfast.

****

Reva ran her fingers through her greying, wiry hair and slowly unfastened the bolt on her apartment door. Pushing the door open, she bent down and picked up *The Montreal Gazette,* tossed carelessly on the wrought-iron staircase. God, she felt awful. She hadn't felt this bad in a long time—not since she had handed in her resignation to the Psychiatric Institute. She was wearing her old, lime green velour dressing gown and fleecy slippers, which she found comforting on a day like today. The sky was slightly overcast, and there was a morning chill in the autumn air. Reva breathed deeply through her nostrils, hoping the fresh air would permeate her cloudy cerebrum.

Lydia was out of town, and for some unexplainable reason, when this happened, Reva found solace in her red wine. If Lydia had been there to supervise, it would have been different. She would never have opened that second bottle—the one that was now throbbing in her temples, telling her that one was enough.

Ever since she had resigned, Reva felt a void in her life. She was a person who had to be needed. Wasn't that why she'd chosen psychiatric nursing as a vocation in the first place? The helpless psychiatric patients needed her, always told her so. But she'd survive this ordeal, wouldn't she? She lit a cigarette and took a sip of her black coffee as she glanced at the front page of the newspaper:

Prominent Psychiatrist Dr. Strachan to Appear in Court Today

Take a look at that. Old Strachan going to court. Not a criminal one, but at least a court where he'd be tried and hopefully convicted of ruining so many innocent lives. Now that she had no commitments to the Psychiatric Institute, she felt it was her duty to testify. No matter how much Strachan had tried to bully Reva with his threatening phone calls prior to the filing of the lawsuit, she hadn't backed off. But it had profoundly affected her psyche. She was anxiety-ridden and wished she'd never agreed in the first place.

But Tanya had been so convincing and cunning at the same time. Now that they had arrived at this point, she knew Tanya was delighted. Not that Reva gave a shit. She'd been trying to please people all her life. Now, all she wanted was to see that bastard in court. Reva reached for the phone and waited patiently for three long rings.

"Hello." Tanya's upbeat voice resonated over the line.

"Hi, Tanya. Are you sure everything's in order?"

"Every last thing."

"I just feel so awful," Reva told her.

"You've got nothing to worry about. Daniel's got everything organized."

"But what if that Hershbaum lawyer tries to attack one of us? I don't know if I can take any more."

"If you could get through Strachan's calls, I think you can get through anything."

"I just don't know anymore."

"Look, Reva—would you like Max and me to pick you up?"

"No … I'll be okay. I'll see you at the courthouse." Reva hung up the phone and put her head in her hands. She felt ghastly.

****

Clarissa carefully combed back her mother's thinning, white hair into a chignon and added a touch of rouge to her pale cheeks. She had calmly helped her mother dress in her favourite navy silk frock with an ivory, fringed shawl draped around her shoulders. Mrs. Smythe had insisted on wearing her matching navy and white pumps, to which Clarissa had agreed, as long as they could take her wheelchair. There was a ramp leading to the courthouse and inside were long corridors that would require some manoeuvring.

As always, Mrs. Smythe looked very fragile as she sat in the wing chair in her room and repeatedly smoothed her dress over her knees with unsteady hands. Her spirits seemed better since they'd moved her into the Sherbooke nursing home, which was about halfway between Clarissa's gallery and home. Most days Clarissa would drop in for a short visit. Occasionally when she was working late, Sheldon took over on his return from the hospital. Clarissa and Sheldon had worried about her mother testifying, but she'd insisted.

"Mom, I just want to ask you this last time: are you okay to go through with this?"

"How many times do I have to tell you? Are you deaf?"

"Just asking, that's all. You know I love you."

"I know. That's what got me out of Atwater. But I want you to stop treating me like a child."

"Okay. But tell me what you'll say."

"This is the last time I'll say it. I'm going to tell them how Dr. Strachan gave me all those drugs and shock treatments. Then I'm going to tell them how he tried to brainwash me. And if that's not enough, I'm going to tell them how he said I should behave if I wanted to be loved."

Clarissa stood silently at the window overlooking the courtyard. "You are loved, Mom," she repeated.

"We've been over all that before." Mrs. Smythe sat upright in her chair. "I just want to say, old lady or not, I'm ready to testify. I've waited long enough."

****

Christy Amherst stepped into her turquoise sheath and zipped it up the back. Her blonde tresses were tied back in a ponytail with a matching diaphanous scarf that brushed her slender shoulders. Daniel had advised her to dress more conservatively for the court appearance, so she'd chosen her black ballerina slippers rather than her scarlet high heels. When she leaned closer to the mirror to apply a touch of bronzed blush and pale lipstick, she felt a hand on her shoulder.

Scott Beauford kissed the back of her neck and gently ran his fingertips down her right arm. "You smell wonderful. Hmmm—I love jasmine."

She turned, and as she pressed her lips to his, felt his tongue enter her mouth. "Not now. We don't have time, you naughty boy."

"Just thought it would relax us for what we've got coming up."

"I guess, as Tanya keeps telling us, we just have to stay calm."

"Yeah." Scott put his arms around her shoulders and hugged her.

"You okay, Scott?"

Scott was silent. A couple of weeks ago, when they had talked to Tanya, she told them how old Saul Rosenfeld had committed suicide. Apparently, the night nurse at Atwater Psychiatric Hospital was making her rounds when she heard a gurgling sound. Saul had somehow found a cord large enough to put around his neck. The autopsy revealed he'd died of strangulation with a large amount of drugs in his body. Having shared a hospital room with Saul at the Psychiatric Institute almost ten years ago, she knew Scott was shaken by the news.

"I asked you, Scott—are you okay?"

"I … I think I need one of my tranquilizers. It's just last-minute jitters."

"As long as you don't take too many. You know what happens to you."

"How about you, Christy? How are you feeling about bringing everything up again?"

"I think I can handle it. I mean, I've been over it so many times before with Daniel when we were preparing the case."

"But it might be different once we are in the courtroom, don't you think?"

"Maybe." Christy walked over to the sofa chair beside the king-sized bed in their hotel suite. The bed sheets were in disarray from their night of lovemaking. They had woken during the night, reached out for one another, and fallen asleep exhausted. From the first time they made love, the sex was always great.

"Come and sit with me, Scott. We have a few minutes before we have to leave."

Scott pulled up a chair next to hers and held her hand. "I love you, Christy. I want us to stay like this forever."

"Me too." She stroked his flushed cheek. "Just remember why we're going through with this."

"Yeah. Don't worry, Christy—I won't crack."

"Just keep telling yourself, we're going to bring that evil man to justice."

They sat there hand in hand silently until the receptionist called to say their taxi had arrived.

****

Sarah Conroy knew that today could be extremely difficult if she were called to testify. It was imperative that she had all her facts. In preparation, she had read everything she possibly could about postpartum depression. She opened her file folder to a page she'd highlighted with a bright yellow marker:

Depression is one of the most common complications during and after pregnancy. Hormonal changes in a woman's body may trigger symptoms of depression. During pregnancy, the amount of two female hormones, estrogen and progesterone, in a woman's body increases greatly. In the first 24 hours after childbirth, the amount of these hormones rapidly drops back down to their normal non-pregnancy levels. Researchers think the fast change in hormone levels may lead to depression.

That was precisely what had happened to her. She was feeling tired and overwhelmed after the birth of her daughter. As Calley was her first child, she doubted her ability to be a good mother. Recalling this guilt, she thought about her own mother who had shown signs of depression when she was raising Sarah's sister, who was a decade younger. There was a family history of depression dating back to her great-grandparents, who had struggled as new Canadian immigrants. Rumour had it that one had committed suicide, but when Sarah asked questions, the story had always been hushed up. Depression then was something shameful, something that should be hidden in the attic.

"What's for breakfast?" Calley said with a yawn as she came into the kitchen.

Sarah looked up from her notes. "Freshly squeezed orange juice, cream of wheat with banana and blueberries, toast … "

"Think I'll skip the OJ. Do we have any more bagels and cream cheese?"

"Are you sure you don't want any … " Sarah hesitated.

Calley shook her head.

Lately, anything Sarah suggested, Calley vetoed. Maybe she was just going through a minor contrary stage, and if Sarah didn't force her, it would pass. It was when they recently celebrated Calley's 13th birthday that Sarah had noticed a major change in her attitude—and not for the better. Although Calley's earlier behavioural problems in school seemed to be easing up, she was still prone to wide-ranging mood swings—giggling one moment, followed by a sullen withdrawal.

Sarah had always felt guilty about her hospitalization at the Psychiatric Institute shortly after Calley's birth. When Calley needed her mother the most, Sarah was not there for her. Sarah blamed Dr. Strachan. It was he who had taken her away from her child and sent her to that wretched Sleep Room when all she had was postpartum depression that probably would have passed in a couple of weeks if she hadn't sought Dr. Strachan's help. It was an arduous journey, but she was feeling more in control now than she ever had.

"You going to court today?" Calley asked.

"Yes. It's the first day of the trial."

"What are you going to tell them?"

"How unnecessary it was for Dr. Strachan to put me in the Sleep Room. I was just feeling a little blue after you were born."

"It was my fault, wasn't it?" Calley smeared peanut butter on her toast.

"Absolutely not." Sarah reached over and put her hand on her daughter's shoulder. "Don't you ever blame yourself."

"But if I wasn't born … "

"Stop that. Right now. It was Dr. Strachan who did it to me and that's why I'm going to testify."

Calley's eyes remained downcast, staring at the food on her plate.

Sarah thought about the mood changes and sleep problems that Calley was experiencing lately. *God, please don't let it be. My own daughter suffering guilt about her birth.* Maybe this was something to be concerned about and they should be seeing a therapist before it got out of control. Sarah walked over to Calley, bent down and hugged her. "Come on, sweetheart. I'll drive you to school."

****

It was shortly before nine o'clock in the morning. The sky was slightly overcast as Tanya and Max set out from his rue Saint-Denis flat for the Palais de Justice on Notre-Dame Est. As they walked south past narrow shops and three-story duplexes with wrought-iron stairways, Tanya noticed a group of young men and women loitering around an abandoned building at the junction of rue de la Gauchetiere. A gaunt girl, about 16, approached them with a crooked smile and extended her dirty palm. "Monsieur.

Spare change for some food?" Max pulled a five-dollar bill out of his trouser pocket and dropped it in her hand. "Make *sure* you get something to eat," he said.

He turned to Tanya as they walked away. "We've got to figure out a way to get these kids off the street and back in school. It seems to be getting worse." Recently, the area had become infiltrated with young people seeking highs from marijuana, cocaine, and booze.

"I'll speak to Sarah Conroy about it. She's on the board of Street Kids International."

"I didn't know that."

"Sarah's been involved with the organization for about two years now. She's so grateful that it didn't happen to her own daughter after the turmoil they've been through."

"Will they both be here today?"

She said she didn't know about Calley, as she and Max crossed the street and continued along Saint-Denis until they reached rue Notre-Dame. The leafy, grand Old Montreal street housed three courthouses. On the north side stood the Vieux Palais de Justice, inaugurated in 1856 in the neoclassic tradition of the first half of the 19th century. Across the street a 1925 courthouse of classic simplicity with an impressive colonnade housed the Court of Appeal. From 1925 to the 1970s the old courthouse handled civil cases while the new one dealt with criminal matters. A block west of the Vieux Palais de Justice was the spacious contemporary courthouse at 1 Notre-Dame Est where Dr. Strachan's civil case was scheduled for 10 o'clock. Since the early 1970s the new courthouse handled both criminal and civil trials. The older courthouse now functioned as an administrative building.

As Max and Tanya approached 1 Notre-Dame Est, they noticed a crowd milling around the main entrance of the courthouse and the adjacent park.

"Look at that." Max took Tanya's arm and guided her through the masses.

"Never in my wildest dreams did I think we'd get such a turnout," Tanya said.

They were all there: the ex-psychiatric patients, chatting nervously to each other while family and friends waved placards and boldly called out. "We want justice" and "Justice must be served." Tanya recognized Scott's sister, Gloria Beauford, with a placard saying, "Let's try Dr. Strachan. Just like he condemned our loved ones." Throngs of reporters and photographers from the *Washington Post, Langley Leader* and *Ottawa Citizen*, as well as *The Montreal Gazette* and the French language daily *La Presse*, were stationed in strategic positions. Some were rapidly taking notes as they chatted to patients and relatives.

Near the steps leading to the courthouse, Tanya noticed Christy clinging to Scott's arm as a reporter attempted to interview them. Tanya laughed and turned to Max. "Well, I guess she did take Daniel's advice about dressing more conservatively. At least she's not wearing her black leather miniskirt and red stiletto heels."

"Yeah. But dig that turquoise dress and those ballerina slippers."

Clarissa arrived with Mrs. Smythe in her wheelchair and waved at Tanya through the crowd. Mrs. Smythe clasped at her shawl, appearing bewildered by the activity. Just behind them, Daniel Callaghan in his natty pin-striped suit escorted Reva, who looked like she was about to faint.

"My god. It's a mob scene," Tanya said.

"Let's get the patients into the courthouse. Away from those reporters."

Tanya felt someone grab her arm. Sarah Conroy, looking older than Tanya recalled, smiled feebly as she embraced her. "I'm so nervous."

"We still have half an hour before the trial starts. Why don't we go in and try to relax?"

Tanya suggested.

"Good idea. I'll round up the rest of them," Max said.

In the midst of the commotion, a taxi arrived around the west corner on rue Saint-Jacque and Dr. Strachan stepped out. Apparently he was hoping to avoid the press. He looked as dapper as ever in a tan-coloured Burberry trench coat and black fedora. After shutting the taxi door, he glanced stealthily around and tugged at his fedora to cover his face. His lawyer, Irving Hershbaum, eased his big belly out of the back seat of the taxi and grabbed his black briefcase. Reporters and photographers raced to the taxi.

Max and Tanya ushered the ex-patients through the main revolving door of the Palais de Justice. The wide entranceway leading to the reception desk was tiled in grey granite with two large planters of green foliage rising toward the top of the atrium, giving the main floor an airy effect. The time was 9:45. An elevator took them to the 16th floor. After walking down a long corridor, they reached courtroom 1610 where Dr. Strachan's trial was scheduled to begin shortly. Some weeks ago, they had rehearsed the seating arrangements. Daniel Callaghan would be on the left-hand side of Judge Jacques Boudreau, while Dr. Strachan and Irving Hershbaum would be to the right. Behind the plaintiff and defence desks were six rows of pine benches where the media, observers and relatives could comfortably sit.

Daniel, who had previously encountered Judge Boudreau in court, had warned Max and Tanya that he was not often acquiescent. His previous judgments reflected a conservative bias. In particular, he seemed to have a bias against plaintiffs in civil cases. Daniel was well aware that to win the court case, he had to convince Judge Boudreau of the damage Dr. Strachan had inflicted on his patients. He had the evidence, the documentation and the witnesses well rehearsed. As he had done in past trials, gentle persuasion would be his chiselling tool.

Judge Boudreau had granted Irving Hershbaum's request for the exclusion of witnesses in the courtroom. They would sit in the hallway until called to testify. No one knew how the patients might react to probing questions about their psychiatric backgrounds. They were well aware of Hershbaum's reputation, as Daniel had informed everyone how thorough he was in his examinations for discovery. And now, with the exclusion granted, it was evident that he was hoping to find inconsistency in the patients' testimonies.

There was a low buzz of voices as the procession slowly filed into the courtroom and took their seats. Shortly after, a door on the back wall opened and Judge Boudreau entered majestically with his flowing black gown, white shirt and scarlet sash.

"Order. All rise."

There was a shuffling of feet and whispers as everyone stood up. Judge Boudreau sat on the dais, peered over his spectacles at the courtroom and nodded. "Good morning."

"Court is now in session. Please be seated," the court registrar said.

Judge Boudreau's broad face showed signs of crankiness with his furrowed brow and deep lines around his mouth. Thirty-five years of Cuban cigar smoking had given his skin a greyish tone, except for his nose which was patterned with tiny bluish red veins. A streak of yellow nicotine highlighted the part of his white hair. He was known as a nasty old conservative judge, demanding and difficult. What could have rendered him so, was the tragic loss of his wife in a ski accident.

Tanya had read about it while conducting her research. Years ago, there had been a tribute to him with a thoughtful magazine profile. In it, he'd spoken about how he thought about his late wife every day, remembering her lifeless body after she hit a tree on a narrow trail in Vermont. Perhaps if he'd taken her on a less challenging run, she would still be alive. He was quoted as describing the pain as "a festering sore that never seemed to heal."

Judge Boudreau removed his spectacles, wiped them with a tissue and cleared his throat. He turned to Daniel. "Mr. Callaghan, I'd like to have you outline your case."

"Thank you, Milord." Daniel approached the lectern and carefully adjusted his papers. "During the 1950s to the mid 1960s, Dr. Samuel B. Strachan knowingly administered a noxious and illegal substance to his patients without their knowledge or consent, and without the knowledge or consent of their loved ones. Some of the victims will testify for you about this illegal therapy and how their lives have been seriously damaged by Dr. Strachan's psychiatric experiments. These patients went to Dr. Strachan in the belief that he would cure their mental distress. Instead, they became guinea pigs on which Dr. Strachan experimented. They were rendered unable to function and transferred to the Sleep Room where his treatments continued with large dosages of drugs, including LSD, electro-shock and brainwashing. Dr. Strachan attempted to reprogram these patients without their knowledge or consent. Each one is willing to testify as to the devastating effect it has had on each and every one's life." For the next 15 minutes, Daniel continued his case with a careful analysis of Dr. Strachan's program and the patients' suffering.

"Thank you, Mr. Callaghan. Does Mr. Hershbaum have an opening statement?"

Irving Hershbaum rose. "Indeed we do, Milord."

"Please proceed."

"Dr. Strachan is an exemplary world-renowned physician and psychiatrist who has devoted his life to healing the minds, bodies and souls of the mentally ill. His research papers and advice are sought the world over. He is published in learned medical journals and is frequently the guest speaker at psychiatric conferences. We have before us a noble man who has sworn his allegiance to the medical field and has in every endeavour honoured those principles. He is a most honourable doctor and has done his best to heal the ex-patients in this courtroom who now stand to accuse him of this heinous act. You will hear the patients' testimony. But I ask you—if they were not so mentally ill, would they have sought his help? They needed him and he did his best to cure them." Hershbaum paused and looked directly at the judge. "Milord, either the patients' testimonies are questionable because they are mentally ill, or if they can be believed, then Dr. Strachan must have cured them."

There was a murmuring across the courtroom. "But that's a lie," Gloria Beauford hissed.

"Order." Judge Boudreau banged his gavel on his desk. "Please continue."

Hershbaum concluded by referring to the fact that he would be calling expert doctors from the psychiatric field who would be testifying as to Dr. Strachan's competence and his therapy.

"Are you finished, Mr. Hershbaum?" Judge Boudreau asked.

"I am, Milord."

"Let's call the first witness for the plaintiffs."

A moment later, Reva Rothwell was ushered into the courtroom and seated in the witness box.

"Do you swear to tell the truth and nothing but the truth, so help you God?"

Reva put her unsteady hand on the Bible. "I do."

"Can you tell me what your position is at the Psychiatric Institute?" Daniel asked.

"I'm retired now, but I was the Head Nurse on Ward Five for sixteen years."

"When exactly was that?"

"From 1959 to 1975."

"Was Dr. Strachan the psychiatrist on Ward Five during those years?"

"He was there from 1959 until he left for Washington."

Judge Boudreau interrupted. "Just answer the questions, Miss Rothwell. Was he there the entire time you were?"

"No. He left in 1970."

"Tell me about Ward Five," Daniel continued.

"When I was there, Ward Five generally had 15 patients—manic depressives, schizophrenics and suicidals, five of whom were in the Sleep Room."

"So these were patients who had serious mental illnesses?"

"They required constant medical care."

"What was the Sleep Room?"

"It was a separate room at the end of Ward Five where the most serious patients were sent."

"When you say serious, what do you mean?"

"Unable to function in daily activities on the ward or if Dr. Strachan felt they were out of control."

"What happened in the Sleep Room?"

"The patients were given large dosages of drugs and were subjected to electro-shock treatment to erase their bad memories."

"What were the drugs?"

"The anti-psychotic Largactil–chlorpromazine—and Seconal, a barbiturate which is highly addictive. The result was to put them into a chemically-induced sleep."

"How did the patients respond?"

"They slept most of the time with tape recorders under their pillows telling them how to behave. They had to be fed and have their diapers changed. It was all part of Dr. Strachan's brainwashing techniques. He was reprogramming the patients."

"Objection," Hershbaum shouted. "This is Dr. Strachan's sleep therapy you are referring to, is it not?"

"Sustained," said Judge Boudreau.

"I'm sorry," Reva said. "I meant the sleep therapy."

"What happened after Dr. Strachan left the Psychiatric Institute in 1970?" Daniel continued.

"I found a file marked 'personal and confidential' he had left behind in the basement vault."

Daniel held up the file. "Is this what you found?"

"Yes." Reva's voice was barely audible.

"Speak up," Judge Boudreau bellowed.

"Yes, Milord."

"And what did you find in this file?" Daniel asked.

"I found Dr. Strachan's application to the CIA requesting funding for his sleep therapy program." Reva wiped her forehead with a handkerchief.

"And what did that application contain?"

"Well, it was quite long with a detailed description of his therapy, including drugs such as sodium pentothal and LSD that were required."

"Hearsay," Hershbaum objected.

"Overruled."

"Milord," Daniel said. "I have before you Exhibit A—the documentation of Dr. Strachan's experiments on these unsuspecting patients. It is clear evidence of his illegal intention."

"Objection. Lack of foundation." Irving Hershbaum stood up suddenly.

"Objection overruled. Does your witness have anything further to say, Mr. Callaghan?"

"No, Milord," Daniel said.

"We'll take a fifteen-minute break and hear from Mr. Hershbaum when we reconvene. Miss Rothwell, make sure you have no communication with the others during this period." Judge Boudreau stood up and walked out of the courtroom.

****

Max lit a cigarette and blew a ring of smoke skyward. Billowy clouds moving in from the St. Lawrence River cast shadows on the east side of the Palais de Justice. They had gathered for the courtroom break in the park adjoining the courthouse. Tanya could feel the tension. The patients felt cheated that Judge Boudreau had ordered them excluded from the courtroom until it was their time to testify. When they had first rehearsed, Daniel had shown them where they would be sitting. It was comforting to know that they would be together to support one another. But later, Daniel informed them of the ruling to exclude the witnesses. Not knowing what was going on inside increased their mental strain. Tanya knew that much like at the Psychiatric Institute, they had the feeling of not being included in the decision-making process; the feeling of being out of control.

"What do you think that man Hershbaum is going to ask Reva?" Christy asked. She grasped Scott's arm and shaded her eyes from the sunlight with her right hand.

"I … I think he's gonna be tough on her," stammered Scott. "Just like he's g-gonna be on all of us."

Tanya felt a sense of malaise, seeing Scott's discomfort and hearing the return of his stutter. She and Max had briefed the patients as best they could. *Damn. Things would've been a hell of a lot easier if they'd been allowed*

223

to sit in the courtroom giving each other moral support. All Tanya could do was reassure them that Daniel would be there and would do everything he possibly could to support them during Hershbaum's cross-examinations.

Tanya looked at Max, who had his hand on Mrs. Smythe's wheelchair. She overheard him telling Clarissa that they didn't have to attend court until her mother was called to testify.

"I won't hear of it," said Mrs. Smythe. "Do you think I want to miss any of this trial?"

Clarissa raised her eyes to the sky. "Of course you don't, Mom."

"Well, when are they going to call me in to testify?"

"It may not be for a couple of days," Max said. "They have to hear the rest from Reva Rothwell, and then the pathologist."

"What pathologist?" Mrs. Smythe asked.

"The one who did the autopsy on Saul Rosenberg."

"I forgot about that poor man." Mrs. Smythe shook her head.

"Well, I didn't," Scott faltered. "I could never forget. The poor guy never had a chance."

Christy put her arm around Scott's shoulder. "Oh, honey. I feel so badly every time Saul's name is mentioned."

"Yeah, brings back the nightmares." Scott turned his face to kiss her hand. "The goddamn nightmares of the Sleep Room."

A sudden cool breeze gave way to light rain. "We'd better go back inside," Tanya said. "If any of you want to leave, you can. I don't think you'll be called to testify today." She turned to Max. "What do you think? It's probably time for Reva's cross-examination. Even though we're not in the courtroom, I'd like her to know that we are here to support her."

****

Reva was wearing a pale grey pantsuit, which matched her hair and complexion. A gold cross on a chain stood out against her black turtleneck sweater under the jacket. Whenever Irving Hershbaum posed a question, her right hand automatically reached for the cross and caressed it. Last week she had gone to mass every day and prayed that the trial would go as smoothly as possible, especially that Hershbaum would spare her a vicious attack. She took a deep breath and mumbled a Hail Mary. She was feeling more fragile than ever.

Reva glanced around the courtroom, avoiding Dr. Strachan's glare. When their eyes had met earlier, he'd scowled at her. She thought about how much she loathed him as he sat there defiantly. Not only had he destroyed the lives of the patients, he had almost destroyed hers. His vicious phone calls had been brutal. When she saw him sitting there so smugly, she had the urge to walk over and slap his face. The man who thought he was a god was nothing but a criminal.

She crossed her legs and uncrossed them a few seconds later. Reva was having trouble focussing. She stared at her shoes, wondering why she had chosen this particular pair of dull loafers. Surely, a stylish pump would have made her feel more confident. But when she'd dressed that morning, all Reva could think about was the trial and how much she didn't want to attend. Her hangover was raging, and the black coffee only made her more jittery. Reva heard a drone in the background.

"Answer the question," Judge Boudreau said.

"I'm sorry. Would you please repeat it?" Reva asked.

"You say you worked closely with Dr. Strachan from 1959 to 1970?" Irving Hershbaum stared at Reva over his glasses.

"Yes."

"And in that time, did Dr. Strachan not work diligently to help his patients?"

"Yes, but … not the patients in the Sleep Room."

"Did he not cure many of his very sick patients?"

"Yes, he did."

"I see. Can you describe a typical day on Ward Five?"

"Typical?"

"Like what happened when you first arrived in the morning on Ward Five?"

"After receiving the report from the night nurse, I would assign each nurse her patients for the day."

"How many patients?"

"Usually five."

"And one nurse could competently look after five, as I understand, very sick patients?"

"Depending on the circumstances, it could sometimes become too much."

"What do you mean by *too much*?"

"If one of the patients had a crisis and was out of control, it took more time than one nurse could handle."

"And what would you do if a patient, as you say, was out of control?"

"Put in an emergency call to Dr. Strachan."

"And how long would it take for Dr. Strachan to respond?"

Reva hesitated. "He usually phoned back within five or ten minutes."

"Within five or ten minutes." Hershbaum shuffled some notes. "If he responded that quickly, would you not agree that showed he cared about his patients?"

"Well … yes."

Irving Hershbaum walked over to Exhibit A. "Would you tell the court how you came across this file?"

Reva recounted the events of Dr. Strachan's move to the United States and the sudden resignation of his secretary who had found other work. This, in turn, left Reva to clean up the files, resulting in the discovery in the basement vault.

"Are you usually in the habit of taking other people's files distinctly marked 'Private and Confidential'?"

"Objection," Daniel shouted. "Counsel is harassing the witness. Miss Rothwell has explained how she came across the file."

"Objection overruled," Judge Boudreau said.

Hershbaum held up the file. "Are you referring to this document, Exhibit A?"

"Yes, sir."

Hershbaum continued. "I asked you. Do you usually look at files marked 'Private and Confidential'?"

"No, sir. But I figured if Dr. Strachan didn't take it, he didn't want it."

"Is that not presumptive on your part, Miss Rothwell?"

"I thought I was doing the right thing." Reva clasped her hands together.

"Thank you, Miss Rothwell. That's all for now." Hershbaum pushed his spectacles up on his nose and returned to his seat next to Dr. Strachan.

****

Shortly after noon, the overcast sky cleared giving way to a warm autumn sun. Tanya and Max left the courthouse and led their entourage of ex-patients along rue Saint-Jacques to Place Jacques-Cartier. The square was overflowing with sidewalk cafés and restaurants, street artists and entertainers. The view of the Old Port was superb. They strolled through the square to rue Saint-Paul, a cobblestone street lined with old grey stone buildings of shops, galleries and restaurants. Clarissa gingerly guided Mrs. Smythe's wheelchair along the narrow street until they reached Chez Antoine, a courtyard bistro decorated with lively Québécois paintings and pottery.

After being seated, Max ordered a carafe of red wine and checked out the specials on the chalkboard. "My favourite, *steak bavette et frites*," he exclaimed.

"I think I'll have the same. *Avec salade*." Tanya winked at him.

At the far end of the pine table, Christy sat beside Scott, apparently immersed in the menu. Scott stroked her hand as she turned the page. Sarah Conroy, Clarissa and Mrs. Smythe discussed the pros and cons of what was being offered. Many of the French dishes would be too heavily laden with sauces for Mrs. Smythe's delicate appetite. After a thorough dissection of the menu, Max signalled the waiter, and Monsieur Antoine appeared to welcome them to his bistro.

The luncheon conversation revolved around the excitement of the court case. Questions abounded. When would they be called to testify? Would Daniel help them get through the questions? Would Dr. Strachan and Irving Hershbaum try to intimidate them?

Tanya shook her head. "We'll just have to take this a day at a time … you won't be called today … yes, Daniel will do his best to help you through the proceedings." How many times had she tried to reassure them? She couldn't count. But she did feel better about getting them together in a more relaxed setting, as they all seemed to be coping. But the courtroom could be another story.

****

The trial was now into its third day. Montrealers were talking about it at their offices, in restaurants and on the streets. *The Gazette* reported how both lawyers Daniel Callaghan and Irving Hershbaum were unrelenting in their examinations. Accompanying the story was a photograph of the ex-patients in the adjoining park during the court recess. The camera had focussed on Mrs. Smythe in her wheelchair, summoning up memories as the previous newspaper article had when she boldly spoke out about her plight at the Psychiatric Institute.

In the courtroom things were turning nasty. When the pathologist Sydney Mann testified that there was evidence of cerebral swelling and large dosages of drugs in Saul Rosenfeld's liver, Hershbaum responded, "Saul Rosenfeld was an extremely disturbed paranoid schizophrenic who would have harmed himself without medication. He could not function without it."

"But he did harm himself," Dr. Mann said calmly. "He committed suicide."

"It happened at the Atwater, not the Psychiatric Institute. Mr. Rosenfeld was no longer a patient of Dr. Strachan's."

"We have clear evidence that there was an accumulation of drugs over a long period of time. We also found traces of LSD in Mr. Rosenfeld's liver tissue." Dr. Mann pointed to a photograph and circled the area.

"Do you have any evidence that it was Dr. Strachan who administered this drug?" Hershbaum asked.

"No. I'm simply reporting what I found in Mr. Rosenfeld's autopsy. And I might add: in my 20-year association with Atwater, I have never known a case where LSD has been prescribed to a patient." To illustrate his point, he stuck his index finger in the air. Dr. Mann's soft voice enunciated each word. He was a small man with a gaunt face that gave him a rat-like appearance. His right cheek had a slight twitch to it, which made him appear to be winking at the judge and Hershbaum.

For the next half hour, the arguments continued, interspersed with objections, most of which were overruled by Judge Boudreau. Finally, Daniel Callaghan stood up and walked over to Exhibit A. "We have all the evidence here. Dr. Mann, would you agree this file provides complete documentation of the application and approval for funding by the CIA for Dr. Strachan's psychiatric experiments which included electro-shock, the Sleep Room and LSD?"

"Objection. Lack of foundation."

"Objection sustained."

"Dr. Mann, does this file not indicate that Dr. Strachan's therapy included the Sleep Room and LSD?"

"Yes."

"And was Saul Rosenfeld not part of this proposed therapy?"

"Yes."

"You said that you found LSD in the liver tissue?"

"That is correct. When we examined him there was a substantial residue of LSD in his liver. This was administered to him before he was sent to the Atwater Psychiatric Hospital."

Hershbaum leapt out of his seat. "Objection. There is *no* proof it was given before Atwater."

Judge Boudreau banged his gavel. "Order. Is there anything further you would like to add, Mr. Callaghan?"

"No, Milord."

"Mr. Hershbaum, would you like to cross-examine."

"No, Milord. I've stated my case."

"This witness is excused." Judge Boudreau nodded to Dr. Mann. "Court will now adjourn until ten tomorrow morning."

****

The taxi drive back to the Ritz Carlton was tense. Dr. Strachan's jaw was firmly set as he stared out the window. His coat collar was pulled up around his ears meeting his fedora and making him look like a private detective. Strachan was furious. He'd become accustomed to succeeding in his life, and it was important to him. Recognition propelled him, and he loathed failure. Strachan thought about his mother who had deserted the family when he was five. He could almost visualize the note she'd left, saying that she was going back to her family in Scotland, that it was the best thing for all of them. How could anyone ever get over it—the betrayal and abandonment? Well, *he* couldn't. And that was precisely why he had vowed that he'd make something of himself and nothing would get in his way.

But lately, very little seemed to be going his way. And today's court scene, with that supercilious rat Dr. Mann, did nothing to lighten his mood. He turned to Irving Hershbaum who was sitting beside him in the back seat.

"Look Irving, I didn't cause Saul Rosenfeld's death. I did everything possible to help him. And now those bastards want to blame me."

Hershbaum was sweating. "Of course you didn't. You know I've been working diligently to get medical experts to testify that you are a competent, well-respected doctor."

"Make sure they don't back down," Strachan ordered.

"I'll make damn sure. The testimonies will be glowing. You *are* a psychiatrist with stellar credentials— recognized throughout the world as a caring and loving doctor whose advice is widely sought, as well as the author of brilliant articles in psychiatric journals. Your reputation is well known in the medical field."

"But what about that autopsy and that damn file?"

"We'll deal with it." Hershbaum took a deep breath as the taxi pulled up to the Ritz.

****

"That son-of-a-bitch Hershbaum. I don't trust him." Max was standing at the stove in his flat, frying hamburgers and onions in a cast-iron skillet. "I think he's determined to parade all of Dr. Strachan's old cronies across that courtroom."

Sitting at the pine kitchen table, Tanya skilfully chopped red peppers and tomatoes for their salad. "But can't Daniel somehow convince them of what Strachan's done? For god's sake, they've seen the documentation."

"Some things never change. Politics or medicine— they both reek of cronyism."

"Proof yet again of the old boys' club." Tanya poured two glasses of red wine. "To us, as we prepare this wonderful gourmet feast."

"We've got to make our case stronger." Max said. "Seems like even though it's all there in black and white, the file is not enough."

"I think Reva did as well as she could under the circumstances, don't you?"

"Yeah. But Hershbaum can be so intimidating. Reva was clutching that holy cross of hers."

Max reached for his cigarette in the ashtray and took a drag.

"I think Reva is sorry she ever agreed to be part of this," Tanya said.

They discussed the ex-patients' upcoming testimonies and how they could better prepare them for Hershbaum's cross-examinations. If he could intimidate Reva, what was to await them in the courtroom?

Mrs. Smythe was the most anxious to testify. After years of being locked up in Atwater, she was anxious to make up for lost time. She asked Tanya daily when she would be called to the stand. Clarissa continued to fret about her mother's frailty, but to no avail. Mrs. Smythe now had a mission in life and was determined no one would stop her this time. She'd told Tanya she had a strong sense of good and evil, and in her mind, Dr. Strachan was evil. He had preyed upon them for his own gratification and recognition, much like a stalker of children. Not that they were children, but like children, they had been under the guidance of someone they trusted, but had been betrayed. And that, Mrs. Smythe believed, constituted the act of evil. Now, after seven decades on earth, she was calling on God's help to seek justice in condemning Dr. Strachan.

****

On day four of the trial, when Mrs. Smythe was called to testify, she looked calm and confident. Clarissa pushed her wheelchair into the courtroom for the morning session. Although she seemed fragile, Mrs. Smythe had an aura about her. She smiled, nodding her head toward Judge Boudreau as he sat on the dais. He responded with a quick nod and brought his eyes back to her face. It was almost as if there was a connection between them, whether it was simply advanced age or having endured a tragedy in both their lives.

Judge Boudreau turned to Daniel. "Mr. Callaghan, would you like to call your next witness to the stand?"

"Thank you, Milord."

Daniel pushed Mrs. Smythe's wheelchair to the lectern, angling it so that she was facing both him and Judge Boudreau. She pulled her white shawl tightly around her shoulders. As she glanced from Clarissa to

Daniel to Judge Boudreau, she smiled and shakily pushed back a wisp of silver hair from her forehead.

"Mrs. Smythe, can you tell us why you went to Dr. Strachan," Daniel asked.

"I had been suffering from depression and my doctor recommended him."

"How long had you been depressed?"

"On and off for years. It got worse after my husband died."

Daniel looked at his notes. "Your husband died when you were quite young ... you were only 45. Is that correct?"

"Yes."

"And your daughter, Clarissa, was away at college at the time?"

Mrs. Smythe wiped her eyes with her handkerchief. "Yes."

"Can you tell us how you were feeling at this time?" Daniel gently asked.

"I've never felt more abandoned in my life. It was like I had no one in the world."

"But Clarissa came home from college to be with you, didn't she?"

"Clarissa is a good daughter. She's a beautiful person."

"And she loves you, doesn't she?"

"Very much." Mrs. Smythe looked across the courtroom at Clarissa.

"Objection," said Irving Hershbaum. "What does this have to do with Mrs. Smythe as a patient of Dr. Strachan's?"

"Overruled." Judge Boudreau motioned for Daniel Callaghan to continue.

"When Dr. Strachan was recommended to you, did your doctor not tell you that he would be the best one to help your depression?" Daniel inquired.

"I was told he was a great world-renowned psychiatrist." Mrs. Smythe hesitated. "I was hurting so much that I needed to believe that he could help cure my depression."

"Can you tell us what happened?"

"Dr. Strachan said it would be best if I was admitted to the Montreal Psychiatric Institute where he could keep a closer watch on me."

"And you and Clarissa agreed?"

"Yes. Anything to get better." Mrs. Smythe's eyes met Dr. Strachan's and she quickly turned away.

"Mrs. Smythe, I know how difficult this is for you, but can you tell us what happened once you were admitted to the Montreal Psychiatric Institute?" Daniel asked.

"I was admitted to Ward ... Five, I think it was. The first morning after breakfast Dr. Strachan came to see me and asked how I was feeling. I cried and told him how lonely I was. He put his hand on mine and said he'd give me something to make me feel better."

"And did he?"

"You know, it's all a little hazy ... I remember taking some little pink pills.... And I remember being strapped down and wheeled on a stretcher downstairs somewhere. They told me they were putting these things on my head and I would feel a little jolt, that it would help to get rid of my depression."

The courtroom was silent, as Daniel paused. "What happened then, Mrs. Smythe?

"I don't know. The next thing I knew I was in a room where all I did was sleep. Whenever I woke up, I'd hear a recording telling me how to behave so I'd be loved."

Mrs. Smythe put her head in her hands. "Please, I need some water."

Daniel held the glass to her lips. "Are you sure you want to continue?" he whispered to her.

"I'll be okay. Just need some water."

Daniel put his hand on Mrs. Smythe's shoulder to calm her. She took another sip of water. "I'm okay. Let's go on," she said.

"Mrs. Smythe, you spent months in the Sleep Room, didn't you?"

"Yes."

"And then you were transferred to the Atwater Psychiatric Hospital for long-term care patients?"

"I was. I felt like I had been dumped there."

"What happened at Atwater?" Daniel asked.

"It was a downward spiral into hell—the Atwater Psychiatric Hospital. Yes, it was … like living in hell. All I can remember was how much I wanted to die. My life was hopeless."

Judge Boudreau listened attentively, the deep creases in his face slowly receding. He combed his fingers through his white hair and shuffled in his seat.

"Mrs. Smythe, do you have anything further you would like to say?" Daniel said.

"I do. I never thought I'd live to see that evil man in this courtroom. Look at how my hands are trembling. He brings back all the awful memories of how helpless I was. I trusted him to heal my mind, but he made me worse." She stood up from her wheelchair and gripped the lectern. "I beg you." Mrs. Smythe turned to address the judge. "I only ask that justice be done in the name of our Lord."

"Thank you, Mrs. Smythe." Judge Boudreau's voice faltered. "Court will now be adjourned for fifteen minutes."

****

The editorial in *The Gazette* was beautifully written and emotionally charged. It portrayed Mrs. Smythe as a charming elderly lady whom Dr. Strachan had clearly taken advantage of with his experimental psychiatric treatments. She was quoted as saying how she had trusted him to heal her mind and instead she became worse.

The article went on to refer to how Judge Boudreau had responded to Mrs. Smythe's testimony. His face showed compassion as he smiled and nodded at her. And during Irving Hershbaum's aggressive cross-examination, Daniel Callaghan objected, accusing him of showing no consideration for her advanced years. Judge Boudreau cautioned Hershbaum to desist.

Back at their apartment hotel suite, Scott read the report to Christy as they cuddled on a love seat.

"Do you think we have a chance?" Christy asked.

"I hope so," Scott responded. "Just gotta stay calm like Tanya keeps telling us."

"Yeah. And Scott … not overdoing it with the tranquilizers. Promise me?"

"I promise." He kissed her. "For you I'd promise anything."

"Are you okay about testifying tomorrow?"

"I'll be okay as long as I get a good night's sleep. Lately the nightmares have been awful."

"Yeah, we'll have to make sure you do. I have the best sleeping pill in the whole wide world." She reached over and put her hand on his inner thigh.

****

Things were not going well for Dr. Samuel B. Strachan. No matter how much his lawyer tried to reassure him that they would win the case, with all the medical experts testifying on his behalf, Strachan's fears were mounting. *If* Reva hadn't discovered that damn file and old Saul Rosenfeld hadn't committed suicide, he might have been able to dismiss the damning accusations. But now, with the ex-patients testifying, the foreboding was consuming him.

He dropped some ice cubes into a crystal tumbler and added two ounces of Ballantyne's. It was his second scotch since he'd returned to his Ritz Carlton suite after the frustrating day in court. Hershbaum was doing his best, but could he really trust the man? Lately, it was difficult to trust anyone. Look at what had happened to him at the hands of the traitorous nurses and patients after all his dedicated years at the Montreal Psychiatric Institute. And the boys at CIA headquarters were even worse, deserting him when he needed them most.

Strachan took a sip of his drink and closed his eyes. He was spent. It was humiliating listening to Reva Rothwell and Dr. Mann testify against him. Even worse, it was downright degrading to hear Mrs. Smythe, whom he had done his utmost to help, say how he had almost ruined her life with his psychiatric therapy. Could any of this be true?

Lord knows, he had done his best, but maybe the drugs and electro-shock had been too much for the old lady. Maybe the LSD had pushed some of the patients over the edge. They were unstable to begin with. But what was he to do? He was well aware that the CIA's funding was contingent on the effectiveness of his brainwashing techniques. And to achieve the ideal results of de-patterning, he had no alternative but to administer the drugs and increase the number of electro-shock treatments. It was the best way to erase the patients' memories so that he could reprogram their minds with his carefully devised psychic driving. That was what the CIA had requested. The CIA believed it had happened during the Korean War with the Chinese communists brainwashing American prisoners of war to force confessions. And with the threat of communism insidiously permeating America, the CIA wanted more experiments to perfect the technique. *Damn it, I hope I did the right thing.* He took another sip of his drink.

But there was something else bothering him. What was most disturbing about the courtroom was the change in Judge Boudreau. The judge looked at Mrs. Smythe with an expression bordering on awe, his craggy face and jaw hanging like a bulldog's, as she spoke about Dr. Strachan's assault. There seemed to be some strange bond developing between them. He reached for the bottle. *Maybe one more scotch will help me sleep.*

****

When Sarah Conroy took the stand the following day, she wept as she related how she had suffered from postpartum depression and the guilt of abandoning her baby daughter. Dressed in a crisp white blouse, navy blazer and grey flannel skirt, she looked like a frightened schoolgirl. She removed her metal-framed glasses and dabbed her eyes with a tissue. Her dark hair fell around her shoulders. Daniel Callaghan hesitated and waited for her to compose herself before he cautiously asked about her experience in the Sleep Room.

Sarah cleared her throat and was silent for a moment. When she spoke, her voice faltered. "I had nightmares. All these frightening images and monsters coming after me. They were trying to grab my baby … I clutched my baby and ran away screaming, but they wouldn't go away. They just kept coming after us. It was such a vivid hallucination that I'll never forget the horror."

Daniel Callaghan spoke quietly before the hushed courtroom. "Sarah, I know how difficult this is for you. Are you okay to go on?"

"I've got to. You have to know what it was like. After they gave me drugs, I remember flashes of vibrant colours—bright reds, yellow and blues, like a spectacular rainbow in the sky after a violent storm. Then I had this incredible out-of-body experience where I was looking down at a frail body on the hospital bed. I realized it was my body. I was so drugged that I couldn't think clearly. But the one thing I *distinctly* remember is crying out for my baby. I wanted to see her; to smell her; feel her soft skin against mine."

"What happened then?" Daniel asked.

"I'll tell you what happened then," Sarah said angrily. "I was given an injection to ease my 'anxiety.' Yeah, that's what they called it—*anxiety*. The shot made me feel so listless and tired, I'd fall sleep. That's all I did: was sleep,

sleep, sleep. I guess that's why it was called the Sleep Room."

Irving Hershbaum's cross-examinations were brutal. As with the others, he questioned whether Sarah or any one of them was capable of remembering the events accurately if they were —as they said—so full of drugs and electro-shock therapy.

"And furthermore, Mrs. Conroy," Hershbaum asked. "If all you did was sleep, what could you possibly remember about Dr. Strachan's therapy?"

"I told you … I remember the flashes, the shocks to my head. It was agony. And I wasn't allowed to even visit my daughter," Sarah cried out. "*He* … Dr. Strachan wouldn't allow it." She glared across the courtroom at Dr. Strachan who was busily writing on a pad of paper.

"Do you think you were fit to see your daughter? Weren't you too sick?"

"I wanted to see my baby … to hold her." Sarah folded her arms on the lectern and put her head down.

Judge Boudreau spoke, "Mr. Hershbaum, if you have no further questions, we'll adjourn for the day."

****

Tomorrow would be more of the same with Scott Beauford testifying, followed by Irving Hershbaum's cross-examination. After that, Daniel Callaghan would summon Christy Amherst as the last ex-patient to testify. Dr. Strachan had advised Irving Hershbaum about the patients' vulnerability: Mrs. Smythe's depression and loneliness, Sarah's guilt over abandoning her baby, Scott's remorse regarding his sexual relationship with his mother and Christy's abhorrence of having sex with her father.

"Make sure you put a lot of pressure on all of them, Irving. It's imperative that you authenticate, without a doubt, that it is I who is being judged unfairly; that I am an honourable and esteemed psychiatrist with impeccable credentials who devoted his life to the healing of his patients."

Irving Hershbaum quietly nodded.

****

Scott was shaking. He popped a "calming yellow pill" in his mouth and washed it down with the remainder of his morning coffee. It was nine forty-five and he was having what he referred to as the jitters. All he had to do was think about Christy and how important this was for both of them. They had promised that once the trial was over, they would start talking about marriage plans and their new beginning. Maybe even move to New York City where he had a cousin who could help them find work.

Every time Scott thought about Christy, he felt a stirring in his groin. She was so beautiful and eager to make love. He'd never felt so strongly about a woman. Scott wanted Christy to be proud of him, and if he could get through his testimony without an angry outburst, he wouldn't disappoint her.

Yet when Daniel Callaghan called him to the stand, he felt like he was in a daze. Scott was having trouble focussing on the questions. *God, I've gotta get through this, for Christy's sake*, he thought. When Daniel asked him how he was feeling, Scott replied, "I feel a little funny being in this courtroom and all."

As Daniel slowly took him through the motions, Scott began to relax and relate his experiences with Dr.

Strachan. Like the other ex-patients, he testified how the therapy had made him worse. Made him forget things.

Upon cross-examination, Hershbaum demanded, "If Dr. Strachan's therapy made you worse, then why were you discharged from the Psychiatric Institute, and how are you able to testify in this courtroom?"

"I finally got out of the Sleep Room and off all the drugs. I could finally start thinking again, even though I sometimes have trouble remembering things."

"Remembering things—like how Dr. Strachan tried to cure your mental illness?" Hershbaum asked.

"N-no. Like how he tried to brainwash me and the others."

"So you don't remember Dr. Strachan trying to brainwash you?"

"No. But I know he did."

"How do you know?"

"I know he tried to wipe out all the bad memories, and then he told me how to act if I wanted to be loved and accepted."

"This seems contradictory to me," Hershbaum said. "Either you remember … or you don't."

"All I remember is that it was one hell of a trip on that LSD," Scott snorted. "Sometimes the lights were so bright I'd see flashes like flames leaping through the air."

"So you're saying that you enjoyed the drugs?"

"Objection." Daniel Callaghan jumped up. "Mr. Beauford took only what Dr. Strachan prescribed for him."

"Overruled. Answer the question, Mr. Beauford," Judge Boudreau said.

"I took what the doc gave me, and sometimes it made me feel high."

"High?"

"Yeah. High as a kite in the sky." Scott raised his hands upward.

As the cross-examination continued, Scott Beauford glanced over and smiled at Judge Boudreau, who was listening attentively. At that moment, Scott knew he had a goal. He had been a failure in most things in his life, but he wasn't going to fail Christy. Scott realized everything he said or did was for her. He loved her and was going to marry her. That was the driving force. No matter how craftily Hershbaum had tried to destroy his testimony, he couldn't penetrate Scott. The bond Scott had with Christy was spiritual. It couldn't be destroyed—not by Dr. Strachan, not by Hershbaum, not by anyone. Scott looked up toward the ceiling. He thought he saw an angel smiling down on him.

****

Tanya slipped into the banquette beside Max and Daniel Callaghan. An overflowing ashtray and empty glasses littered the table in front of them. The brothers were obviously in heavy planning strategy. Dr. Strachan's trial had been the centre of all their lives for a week now. Although the ex-patients seemed to be enduring Hershbaum's cross-examinations, there was still a tremendous amount of tension and emotions. The mood could vary from moment to moment like a changing tide.

"What'll you have, sweetheart?" Max kissed Tanya's cheek.

"A martini with an olive and lots of ice on the side."

"Wow. Must be some sort of celebration," Daniel said.

"Every day is a celebration—we're surviving Hershbaum's attacks, aren't we? I'm so proud of our patients." Tanya grabbed some peanuts from the wooden bowl in the midst of the debris on the table.

"We're still not out of the woods," Max said. "Our biggest challenge is going to be the doctors testifying on Strachan's behalf."

"On cross-examination I intend to ask each one of them if they have ever used an illegal substance in their therapy. And when they say no, I will isolate Dr. Strachan from the rest of his profession," Daniel said.

"That's brilliant, Daniel," Tanya said.

"Yeah. So the only other hurdle we have to get over is Christy testifying tomorrow," Max responded. "I hope she's okay with that intimidating interrogator. I think Hershbaum will try his best to bully her. He's getting pretty anxious."

"I worry about Christy because she's so vulnerable," Tanya said. "Thank goodness she has Scott. Did you know that they're an item?"

"An item? You mean, as in having an affair?" Daniel asked.

"They seem to be pretty serious. I think it's great how they support each other."

"Scott managed quite well with Hershbaum, although I was a little concerned about his joking about the LSD trip," Daniel said.

Tanya laughed. "Scott does have a quirky sense of humour. That's what makes him so endearing."

Max lit a cigarette and leaned toward Tanya. "Just like you."

Daniel looked at his watch. "Better run. Said I'd be home at seven. We'll see you at the courthouse tomorrow."

****

Irving Hershbaum's large frame and hefty voice created a formidable presence in the courtroom. And as promised, his cross-examination of Christy Amherst was merciless. Peering over his glasses, he asked about her family relationships. When he made reference to the incest with her father and brother, Christy was shaken, stammering as she attempted to answer his questions. The ugly memories seared her brain. She remembered the smell of tobacco on her father's breath, his rough hands stroking her shoulders. Hershbaum methodically related the build-up of events which led to her admission at the Montreal Psychiatric Institute.

"Didn't you have sex with your own father?" Hershbaum asked.

Christy covered her ears with her hands. "Please, just leave me alone."

"Objection." Daniel Callaghan shouted. "It's not necessary to go into all the details of Christy's family life. It's Dr. Strachan who is on trial."

"Objection sustained," Judge Boudreau ordered. "Mr. Hershbaum would you kindly restrict your questions to Miss Amherst's relationship with Dr. Strachan and the Montreal Psychiatric Institute."

"Yes, Milord." Irving Hershbaum lowered his eyes. "Miss Amherst, why did you seek Dr. Strachan's help?"

"I was depressed … I just had to get away."

"Away from where? Your home? Your family?"

"From everything."

"So things were not that good at your home, is that correct?"

"N-no."

"Could you tell me what was so upsetting?"

"I can't. I've been over it so many times. I just can't talk about it anymore."

Judge Boudreau intervened: "Mr. Hershbaum, please stay focussed on Miss Amherst's relationship with Dr. Strachan."

"Miss Amherst, could you tell me what happened when you were admitted to the Montreal Psychiatric Institute?" Hershbaum asked.

"Dr. Strachan talked to me and said he would give me something to make me feel better. I was feeling awful."

"And what did he give you?"

"Some pills that made me feel kinda stupid."

"Didn't the pills help your depression?"

"Sometimes I'd feel better, but then I'd get these anxiety attacks."

"What happened then?"

"He started giving me more pills and putting those awful things on my head."

"Go on." Hershbaum spoke quietly.

"I felt like I was flying, like my body was flying away from me. I was soaring in the sky like an eagle through the clouds and the sun and the moon."

"And how did you come back?"

"I don't know ... all I can remember is that I was in a haze, sleeping like a baby. I couldn't even get up to go to the bathroom. Whenever I woke up, there'd be recordings in my ears and the room would be swirling around me."

Irving Hershbaum stared at Christy. "So you were having trouble remembering things?"

"Yeah. But I do remember being out of control. I couldn't stop the voices in my head constantly talking to me. I couldn't hear my own voice in the crowd. It was scary."

"Is that why Dr. Strachan put you in the Sleep Room … to protect you?"

"He put me in the Sleep Room because he needed a guinea pig. We were all guinea pigs: me, Scott, Sarah, Mrs. Smythe, Saul. I could see how every one was getting worse, not better."

"What do you mean by 'every one was getting worse?' Did Dr. Strachan not try to make you better?"

"No, he didn't. And don't try to say he did. That's an outright lie."

The tension in the courtroom was palpable. Christy's blood red lipstick and black eyeliner emphasized her ashen face. She looked so small and helpless, her slim fingers gripping the lectern. Gone was the coquetry that she so frequently exhibited. In its place was the young, vulnerable girl on the Nova Scotia farm. She put her face in her hands and wept.

"I have no further questions of this witness at this time, Milord. But I do reserve the right to recall her," Hershbaum said.

"Miss Amherst," Judge Boudreau nodded to her. "You are excused for now."

Holding a handkerchief to her face, Christy tottered out of the courtroom.

****

"Aw, Christy, honey. I'm so sorry." Scott put his arm around her shoulder. They were back at their apartment hotel suite and instead of making love, Christy had recoiled when he started to unbutton her sweater.

"Look, Scott. I'm just not in the mood. I feel nauseated with that pig bringing up all the old stuff."

"You're right. He's nothing but a swine. He'd do anything to get Dr. Strachan off the hook."

"There's nothing we can do about it now. It's too late. I just feel awful." Christy wept.

"But Christy, think about our marriage. Everything's gonna work out okay."

"I don't know. I just don't know."

"What do you mean? Are you having doubts?"

"Why would anyone want to marry someone like me? I'm not a good person. I had sex with my father. If you could've seen the way that bastard Hershbaum looked at me when he asked me that question ... and that smug look on Dr. Strachan's face. It was horrible."

"He was trying to get to you, Christy. That's all. He means nothing to us. Besides, the sex with your dad wasn't your idea. We both know that."

"Oh, Scott. I wanted so much for us to run away together; leave all this shit behind."

"We will. I promise ... we will."

"I just feel so goddamn awful," Christy said. "I feel dirty."

Scott held her in his arms and rocked her gently. He kissed her cheek, smoothing back her hair, wet from her tears. "I love you, baby. More than anything in the world. Everything's gonna be okay."

****

The weekend was to be one of celebration for Tanya and Max who were both exhausted after the week-long trial. In the midst of everything, Tanya had heard from her divorce lawyer that a settlement had finally been reached with Larry. Their assets had been divided up with the sale of the house. Surprisingly, they had remained fairly civil over the division of the furnishings. The Schilling Ojibwa painting, *Lady with the Cloak,* now hung over the fireplace mantel in the St. Denis flat that she shared with Max. The dark eyes looked at Tanya knowingly. Tanya thought she could detect the Lady's approval, as the domicile was definitely more harmonious than the Westmount house where she'd previously resided. Max was easy to love with his great satirical wit even though he could become quite tense when working on a deadline.

They had moved from his cluttered apartment to a larger one which encompassed the expansive third floor of an Old Montreal walk-up. Even though there was more space, the clutter seemed to follow Max around. Tanya had removed all the ashtrays when Max announced his determination to quit smoking. But the trial had been too stressful and he had started again, so the ashtrays had to be retrieved.

Max tapped a cigarette out of the packet. "What do you say we go out to Carmen's tonight?"

"Love to." Tanya sipped her wine.

"What are you thinking about? You seem quieter than usual."

"I'm just relieved that my divorce has finally been settled. You know how difficult Larry can be. Apparently, he still believes that Strachan is a great man and we are the wrongdoers. Sheldon saw him at a conference a couple of weeks ago."

"It would appear there's nothing anyone can do to change his mind once it's made up."

"You've got that right," Tanya said.

"What do you hear about Reva?"

"I was a little concerned about her drinking. When I last spoke to her, she and Lydia were thinking of moving to the Laurentians. Lydia took an early retirement and wants to be closer to her remaining family. I think it'll be a good change for Reva. Living so close to the Psychiatric Institute was getting to her."

"I don't think she ever recovered from the wrath of our dear Dr. Strachan," Max said.

"No. And I suppose we should prepare ourselves for this Monday when Strachan takes the stand."

"I can't wait to see him sweat," Max said.

"All we can hope for is that Daniel will be as ruthless as that Irving Hershbaum."

"Oh, he will be. I know that brother of mine." Max grinned. "Daniel just told me today that on reviewing the defendant's witness list, he couldn't find one former patient who they can bring forth to testify that Strachan's wretched Sleep Room therapy cured them."

****

Samuel B. Strachan poured himself a generous scotch and picked up the phone. After eight rings, he cursed and hung up. *Where the hell is that Hershbaum when I need him?* He checked his address book again and found another number scrawled under his name. On the third ring, Irving Hershbaum picked up the phone.

"Irving, I need to talk to you."

"What is it, Samuel?"

"Can you meet me here at the Ritz for dinner tonight?"

"Unfortunately, I can't. We've got company arriving in about half an hour and it's something I can't get out of."

"Damn. I told you I need to talk. Things aren't going as well as they should. I don't know if you came down as hard on those patients as you could have."

"Samuel, please, we discussed all of that in the taxi on the way to your hotel. I thought we had resolved it."

"Nothing's resolved until my name is cleared of any wrongdoing." Strachan added more whiskey to his glass.

"That's what we'll be working on this Monday at the courthouse. We've done all our homework, and things should go quite smoothly," Hershbaum said.

"But what about that bleeding heart, Daniel Callaghan? I know we've discussed it before, but what kind of questions do you think he's going to spring on me? I don't trust the guy."

"Look, Samuel, I can handle him. I've been up against tougher litigators than him."

"I'm asking … what kind of questions will I have to deal with?"

"What I've told you before: your psychiatric therapy and how it benefited the patients."

"I did everything I could to help them. You know that, Irving."

"Yes, Samuel, I know that."

"Are you sure you can't get away for a quick dinner?"

"I'm sorry. That's impossible tonight."

Dr. Strachan hesitated. "Well … I guess I'll see you Monday morning." He hung up the phone and replenished his glass. After he called room service to order his dinner, Strachan sat on the sofa and reminisced. He was feeling tipsy, knowing it was the only way to get through this evening. Or, for that matter, most evenings lately.

Where the hell was anyone when he really needed them? All his life had been one abandonment after another, starting with his own mother. He tried to do his best and all he got were traitors—the Psychiatric Institute, the nurses, the patients, the CIA—all traitors. And now that Hershbaum. *Can he be trusted, or is he like all the rest?*

His thoughts were interrupted with the arrival of his dinner. The waiter lifted the silver lid to show Strachan the lobster and melted garlic butter for his approval. Strachan nodded and signed the chit. When he returned to the table, he removed the lid. As the aroma of garlic permeated his nostrils, he stared at the red lobster. It had been chopped in decorative pieces with the pincer-like claws and tail arranged artistically on a bed of lettuce. He stabbed his fork in the lobster tail and gouged out the succulent flesh of the crustacean. After a few mouthfuls he felt a sharp pain in his chest. God, was he having a cardiac arrest? He threw his fork down and went back to the sofa. He'd never felt so abandoned in his life. They had all deserted him, and the enemy was coming after him. He had to escape.

****

October 10, 1977

THE VERDICT

The sky looked threatening as the crowds started gathering around the Palais du Justice. In the distance, the sun was attempting to eclipse a grey-laden cloud. Sirens from an ambulance and fire truck echoed in the background. Montreal was waking to the eclectic sounds and smells of a bustling metropolis. Curious people, rushing to work, paused for a moment to catch a glimpse of what was going on.

For almost a month now, Montrealers had been consumed with the *The Gazette's* daily front page coverage of Dr. Strachan's trial. During Irving Hershbaum's two-week defence arguments, he paraded a stellar cast of professionals from the psychiatric field into the courtroom. Daniel Callaghan had cross-examined each one so thoroughly that Tanya and Max were feeling quite optimistic about the trial outcome. As promised, Daniel had asked if any of them had ever used an illegal substance in their therapy. The answer was an unanimous *no*. After hearing the three weeks of plaintiff and defence arguments, Judge Boudreau had deliberated for a week. Today was the day everyone anxiously awaited. Shortly, Judge Boudreau would hand down his decision.

Milling around the main entrance of the courthouse on *rue Notre-Dame Est*, the crowd had started gathering at eight-thirty that morning. By nine-thirty they were all there—the ex-psychiatric patients, family and friends with their placards, reporters, photographers, and French and English television crews.

In the midst of the commotion, a taxi pulled up to the side door on the west side of the courthouse on Boulevard Saint-Laurent. Wearing his customary Burberry raincoat and a jaunty black fedora, Dr. Strachan stepped out, followed by Irving Hershbaum.

It was nine-forty-five. The crescendo in front of the courthouse was building. As reporters shouted out questions, Hershbaum waved them off.

People began slowly filing into the courthouse. Dr. Strachan and Hershbaum entered the Palais du Justice through the revolving door and cautiously made their way to the courtroom. Two security guards stood at the entrance watching carefully over the procession. Spectators' murmurs and stares followed Strachan as he walked to his seat beside Hershbaum. Strachan looked as though he were well aware he was about to hear his fate. As he wiped away the sweat from his forehead, his hands trembled, and Tanya noticed the blood in his temples pulsating.

When Judge Boudreau entered the courtroom and preliminary greetings were made, a silence settled over the courtroom. After what seemed like an eternity to Tanya, the judge's gravelly voice interrupted the silence. "Dr. Strachan, will you please stand." Judge Boudreau looked directly at Dr. Strachan.

"The court has heard evidence that you knowingly administered an illegal noxious substance, LSD, to your patients without their knowledge or consent. I've carefully acknowledged the accolades on your behalf from your professional colleagues and have noted that not one of them has used LSD in his practice. You are the only one. As a consequence, your patients have suffered severely from your psychiatric experiments which included large dosages of drugs and electro-shock in addition to the LSD.

"The court finds for the plaintiffs and orders you and the Montreal Psychiatric Institute to pay $100,000 each to Scott Beauford, Christy Amherst, Sarah Conway and Sally Smythe."

The courtroom erupted with cheers.

"Order, please." Judge Boudreau looked up from his notes. "Do you have anything to say, Dr. Strachan?"

Dr. Strachan gasped and put his hands to his face. "I'm innocent." His voice faltered. "I did it in the name of psychiatry. This is blasphemy … why are you doing this to me?"

More cheering followed. Reporters raced for the phones. Christy wept as she and Scott hugged each other. Mrs. Smythe pushed herself out of her wheelchair and raised her hands in victory as Clarissa attempted to support her.

Judge Boudreau shouted, "Order in the courtroom."

"We'll appeal." Irving Hershbaum pounded the lectern.

After awhile Tanya whispered to Sarah Conway that she, Max, Daniel and Reva would meet them at Chez Antoine courtyard bistro around the corner from the Palais du Justice. There was a large round table tucked away in the back where they could all gather.

Shortly after they were seated, Christy, Scott, Sarah, Mrs. Smythe, Clarissa and Sheldon arrived, chatting excitedly. The mood was a victorious one.

"My god, I can't believe this has happened," Tanya said, as the group joined them at the table. "I'm so proud of every one of you."

Max lit a cigarette. "And might I add, Daniel, a trial brilliantly orchestrated."

"Thanks. But I couldn't have won this case without everyone's cooperation and, of course, Reva's documentation."

Reva pushed a strand of hair out of her eyes and smiled. "Hopefully we can all relax now. I thought for sure I'd have a nervous breakdown up against that Dr. Strachan. He's so intimidating."

"He absolutely terrified me," Sarah said. "Did you see his eyes? The way he looked at me was like I was a lunatic. I had to look away from his piercing glare."

"Yeah. I felt the same way," Scott added. "And think of all the money. Christy and I can take off to New York City now, can't we, Christy?" Scott beamed.

"I never, ever thought we'd make it." Christy reached over and took his hand.

Daniel leaned forward in his chair to address the ex-patients. "I've got more good news for you. Both the Government of Canada and the CIA are seeking a negotiated settlement and I'll be happy to represent you in these negotiations if you want."

"That's incredible … I can't believe it," the chorus echoed around the table.

"Me neither," Mrs. Smythe said. "Considering my age, I never thought I'd live to see it." Clarissa put her arm around Mrs. Smythe's shoulder and hugged her as Sheldon grinned.

"But you know the sad part is Dr. Strachan really believed he was doing an honourable thing to begin with. He saw himself as the great saviour of his patients," Max said.

"I've seen it happen to so many powerful men." Daniel shook his head. "Hubris got the better of them. No doubt, Irving Hershbaum will try to appeal, but I very much doubt he has any grounds."

Reva looked around the table. "I'm ever hopeful that it's a closed case; that all of us can leave it behind and get on with our lives."

"I was there at the Psychiatric Institute like many of you at this table were. What I witnessed was the transformation of Dr. Strachan from a god on Ward Five to a power-hungry evil man. Nothing could stop his ego," Tanya said. "Let's raise our glasses. I believe justice has been done. We now have closure."

Epilogue

Christy Amherst and Scott Beauford married in Montreal with Tanya and Max witnessing the nuptials at city hall. After their marriage, they moved to New York City where they found employment as extras in a variety of Broadway shows.

Sarah Conway, estranged from her husband, never remarried. She devoted her life to daughter Calley and charitable work including Street Kids International.

Mrs. Smythe lived with Clarissa and Sheldon Schmedeck until her death in 1984.

Reva Rothwell and Lydia moved to St. Sauveur in the Laurentians and established a successful bed and breakfast inn.

Tanya Kowalski and Max Callaghan continued to make love on the sheepskin in front of the fireplace, but Tanya gave up her birth control pills. Max Jr. has delighted them ever since. Both Tanya and Max work as freelance journalists and share in the parenting.

Dr. Samuel B. Strachan, discredited in the psychiatric field after Irving Hershbaum lost the appeal, became more despondent and took a fatal overdose of barbiturates with his scotch one night. He died September 13, 1979.

****

To treat the sick to the best of one's ability and to keep them from harm and injustice..

If I fulfill this oath and do not violate it, may it be granted to me to enjoy life and art, being honoured with fame among all men for all time to come; if I transgress it and swear falsely, may the opposite of all this be my lot.

Excerpt from the
Classical Hippocratic Oath
Translation from the Greek by
Ludwig Edelstein, Baltimore,
John Hopkins Press, 1943.

****

Author's Note

This book is a work of fiction based on historical psychiatric events that took place at Montreal's Allan Memorial Institute in the early 1960s. Names and characters are used fictitiously, and any resemblance to actual persons living or dead is entirely coincidental.

During those years, I interned at the Allan Memorial. Working as a young student nurse on the ward and in the Sleep Room left an indelible impression with me for four decades. About five years ago, a fortuitous encounter with the son of a former patient whose life was destroyed by the psychiatric therapy compelled me to write this novel.

In addition to my experience in the Sleep Room, my research includes Anne Collin's *In The Sleep Room* (Governor General's Award for Non-Fiction) and CBC's miniseries based on her excellent book.

Retired Superior Court Judge Norman Dyson's sage advice in courtroom procedure guided me in writing the trial scene.

****

Thanks to my mentors at the Humber School for Writers, my Writers' Group, Book Club and nursing colleagues with whom I've kept in touch. I would also like to thank my husband Basil and children Allison, Jennifer and Craig for their incredible support throughout the writing of my novel.

Printed in the United States
131636LV00001B/1-108/P

9 780595 515318